SLOW BURN 6

BLEED

A novel by

Bobby Adair

Website: www.bobbyadair.com

Facebook: www.facebook.com/BobbyAdairAuthor

D1527967

Cover Design and Layout

Alex Saskalidis, a.k.a. 187designz

Editing & Proofreading

Cathy Moeschet

Kat Kramer

Lindsay Heuertz

Linda Tooch

eBook and Print Formatting

Kat Kramer

Weapons Consultant

John Cummings

Previously, in Slow Burn

Book 1 – Zero Day

Zed Zane wakes up hung over one Sunday morning and begins to fortify himself with tequila before going to his mother's house for lunch – and to beg for rent. There, he finds his mother and a neighbor dead, and his stepfather in full-throttle, crazed cannibal mode. Zed, fighting for his life, kills his stepfather in a scuffle, during which he sustains a nasty bite wound.

He tries calling 911, but the line is perpetually busy. That's strange, but no stranger than the way that Zed is beginning to feel. He spends the next two days unconscious with a raging fever, and awakens as what soon becomes known as a "slow burn," a carrier of a virus that destroys higher brain function and turns people into vicious, flesh-eating monsters.

Together with Murphy, a fellow slow burn who escapes with Zed in the aftermath of a prison riot following his erroneous arrest for the murder of his parents and their neighbor, we follow Zed on his quest for shelter, resources, and a plan for living in the strange new world in which he finds himself.

Although Zed himself has not "turned" completely, as have most of the other infected, the ambiguous, not-immune-but-not-dangerous category in which he finds himself will from this point forward direct his every thought and step if he is to survive.

Book 2 – Infected

Infected finds Zed, Murphy, and their traveling companion, Jerome on the move again following what proves to be a brief respite in a university dormitory, in the company of some extremely, albeit justifiably, paranoid ROTC students and three coeds, one of whom befriends Zed. In the process of stealing a Humvee, Jerome is shot by soldiers and Zed and Murphy head on alone to find Murphy's family.

With Murphy's mother dead and his sister missing, their next stop is a house rumored to feature an underground survivalist bunker, where another surprise awaits.

Book 3 – Destroyer

Destroyer finds Zed saying goodbye to one friend and pressing forward with two new ones to whom we are introduced in Book 2 – Infected. Mandi, whom Zed and Murphy rescued from the bunker, is immune to the virus. Russell, whose home the others plundered in search of food and other supplies, is also a slow burn, but lower-functioning, childlike and docile.

After seeing the carnage at the dormitory, a raging, vengeful Zed wants only to kill Mark, his nemesis and the former leader of the ROTC squad. Since Mark has disappeared, Zed unleashes his fury on untold numbers of infected in his path as he makes his way back to the hospital, in an attempt to rescue Steph, a nurse whom he befriended while seeking help for the feverish Murphy shortly after the prison riot. But the brave medical staff, holed up on the tenth floor of the hospital, and running out of provisions, has decided to take matters in hand by exposing themselves to the virus, and shooting those who "turn." Zed is determined not to face another loss, but once again, time is running out…

Book 4 – Dead Fire

Dead Fire picks up following an infected attack on Sarah Mansfield's fortified house, during which 3 people seek shelter with Zed Zane and his fellow survivors. In the confusion, however, Murphy is gunned down, and an unthinking, emotional Zed strikes out to enact revenge. Unfortunately, the shooting and commotion have only attracted more Whites. A diversion plan emerges to rid the horde of the Smart One trying to figure a way through the gates, and lead the other infected away from the compound. Momentarily safe, the survivors turn to the matter of where to bury the dead. Zed, being now the only one available who would not attract the attentions of the infected, accompanies Freitag on this morbid mission. In short order, Zed is once more embittered and hardened against trust, when he finds himself stranded. After a series of developments that prove the Whites to be more formidable foes than he ever dreamed, he finds his way back to Sarah's house to find the compound overrun with infected and his friends mysteriously vanished without a trace, leaving Zed to rely once more solely on his wits to survive…

Book 5 – Torrent

Following his none-too-soon reunion with his friends at the safe house, Zed is hoping things can finally fall into a stable routine, but in post-virus Austin, things are far from stable. On a mission to raid the ammunition bunkers at Camp Mabry, Zed and Murphy spot a group of the newer, naked infected, who are exhibiting some sophisticated and disturbing new behaviors, such as scouting and hunting – for them.

After a narrow escape, the two pass the home of Mr. Mays on the return trip, stirring Zed's predictable rescuer impulse.

Finding Mr. Mays dead, Zed brings fellow chain gang escapee Nico along to join the group, whose numbers have grown again, thanks to their merger with the girls on the riverboat, where the group has moved, as seems to be the safest hiding place... Or is it?

Chapter 1

The sound of ten thousand wild apes was on the wind. It drifted over the terrain on an unsteady breeze. It floated over us and disappeared, only to come back. The naked horde was near. Where, we weren't sure.

At the end of the dam, Murphy looked at me and said, "Well?"

"Bon Jovi concert?"

Murphy bit back a laugh. "It's nice when you take that stick out of your ass. You're almost a funny guy."

"Sounds like envy talking, to me."

The moon was on the rise and its light gave us a view of Lake Travis' water level—well above normal. A park spread across a peninsula to our right. Picnic pavilions down near the water's edge were partially submerged. Waves lapped over their concrete benches and tables.

Pointing almost directly north, across the base of the peninsula, I said, "If we cut straight that way, we'll be in the woods that run along the shore."

Murphy had no preference on direction, though he swiveled his head, trying to find the location of the horde. "Okay."

"I don't know if you ever came out to Lake Travis much…"

"Can't swim."

"Yeah." I continued to point across the park. "The shore of Lake Travis is mostly a series of peninsulas separated by inlets that used to be canyons or creeks flowing down to the Colorado River."

"It's like I'm back in seventh-grade geography."

I ignored Murphy's comment. "And most of the inlets have marinas in them. Where there's no marina, there should be plenty of private boathouses. I'm betting we won't have to walk far to find a boat."

"Sounds good." Murphy looked off in the direction that the sound of the horde seemed to be coming from. "What about them?"

"Don't know. The way the sound bounces around the hills, I can't tell from one minute to the next where they are. What do you think? Should we go back across the dam and try the other side of the lake?"

Murphy looked back along the road across the top of the dam. "They could be over there too. Until we actually see 'em, we're not gonna know where they are for sure. I'd say let's stay close to the water on this side. If we need to escape, we just go in."

I pretended a double take. "You want to go in the water?"

Murphy said, "I can't swim, but I'm not neurotic about it. The water's calm, so if I have to wade in chest-deep to keep from getting eaten by a bunch of those skinny bastards, it won't bother me a bit."

I looked across the park. Nearly all of the dense cedars had been cut down, leaving only the big oaks. Despite the moonlight and shadows, I was able to see most of the park. I didn't see any infected moving about. I could only hope they weren't squatting in the deep shadows. "Let's cut across the park, get on the other side of that cove over there, and start following the shore. It'll take longer to get where we're going, but it's the safe play. You're right, having the water as an escape route is a good thing. Besides, we might come across a stray boat along the way."

"Rock on, brother."

Keeping a vigilant eye all around, we followed the road as it curved off the dam. We turned right onto the paved park road and descended as quietly as we could while the pavement changed from smooth asphalt to crunchy chip seal.

Murphy leaned in close and whispered, "In this light, you damn near glow."

I looked down at my arms and legs. He was right. I frowned. Anyone or anything in the shadows would easily see us.

Murphy grinned. "At least when the Whites see us, they'll think we're just like them."

I shrugged. He was probably right about that.

"Maybe they won't fuck with us."

It was a valid hope.

We followed the road down past the ranger's booth. Nobody was there to take our fee. I smiled at the thought of getting into the park for free, probably just a manifestation of my over-developed aversion to authority. Near the edge of the water, the road traced the curve of the cove on the north boundary of the park's peninsula.

The sound of the Whites seemed to fade as we followed the shore. The thing we didn't take into account, not really, as we walked along with the lake on our right, was that the hill rising to our left deflected most of the howls and cries above us, making the voices of the infected seem more distant than they actually were.

At the tip of the peninsula, as it started its curve back around to the next cove, the hill that ran the length of the peninsula was cut off, forming a cliff that grew to thirty or forty feet above the level of the water. Before starting up the hill, I asked, "If we go up there, we might find ourselves having to jump off. Are you afraid of heights?"

"I'm afraid of depths." Murphy said, as though his meaning was perfectly clear.

"Depths?"

"You know, how deep will that water be when I splash down? Seems that if it's deep enough for me to jump in without getting hurt, it'll be over my head and I'll drown."

"You need to learn to swim." I looked up the face at the highest point on the cliff. "Let's take it real slow. If we hear or see anybody, we can run back down before getting in the water."

With a nod, Murphy said, "Works for me."

The light from the moon grew brighter and whiter the further up it moved in the sky. Shadows shortened, and it became easier to see between the trees and understand the shapes we saw in the shadows around us. Out across the lake, the pale limestone walls of the old church at the peak of the hill on Monk's Island stood out prominently against the dark green and black background on the far shore.

"We'll be there soon enough," Murphy whispered, seeing that I was looking more toward the goal than watching for dangers.

As we neared the top of the hill, the sound of the naked horde grew exponentially louder, and it became apparent that they were somewhere down on the other side. I stopped, squatted, and looked back at Murphy. In a soft voice, I asked, "You hearing what I'm hearing?"

"Yup."

"Should we go back?" I asked.

"To go back is to go all the way around the lake." Murphy thought about that for a moment as his gaze followed the tall pale-colored dam standing high above the surface of the lake to where it merged with the far shore. "Or we cut through the woods and hope we don't run into them somewhere out there."

"So, what are you saying?"

Murphy nodded his head in the direction leading just over the crest of the hill. "They're over there. There's no doubt about that. But it doesn't sound to me like they're that close. Maybe they're across the water, on the next peninsula over. If that's the case, we might find a boat just down there in the water, and we're home free."

Stalling while I thought about it, I scanned the shadows through the thick cedar fronds. Usually, it was me rushing in with half a plan and my balls in my hand. Suddenly finding myself in the role of advocating the cautious path felt awkward. "Or there are a hundred of them squatting in the shadows just over the ridge and getting ready to eat us for dinner."

"Here's what I think." Murphy patted a big hand across his M4. "We've got these. We've got suppressors. We've got lots of ammunition."

"Murphy, you know as well as I do that I can't hit a damn thing I shoot at anymore." My frustration over that recent development came out in my tone.

"Don't get all bitchy on me, dude. The Murphy's got a plan. We're not going to shoot at anything far away, just Whites that happen to be coming at us. With our suppressors, that's kind of a safe thing for us. Sure, every White close by will come at us, but not every single one within a mile. Wear your gun down on your hip, like they do in the movies. Don't aim. Just point and shoot. When they get close enough, you'll hit them. You'll use up lots of bullets, but as long as you reload in a hurry, they'll never lay a hand on you."

"And you think that'll work." I wasn't sold.

Murphy grinned. "Sure it will."

Murphy held his rifle up. "Look at the way I'm supporting the barrel with my left hand right now. See how I have my index finger pointing parallel to the barrel?"

"Looks awkward," I said.

"It's a night firing technique. You don't aim. You just point your finger at what you want to shoot and you hit it. It's supposed to be a more natural mental process, I mean pointing your finger rather than aiming your gun."

It sounded like a lie, but what the fuck. I put my pistol in its holster and sheathed my machete. It took a moment to get my sling adjusted. I stood up, and feeling like a silent Rambo with both hands on my rifle, I practiced the grip and the movement.

"At least you look cool." Murphy chuckled softly.

And I felt pretty cool, too. I only hoped that I could hit something before it was close enough to bite me. "Let's go."

With slow, silent footsteps, we crested the hill. The wide mouth of the cove was visible down through the trees. Wide implied deep, and that implied a marina might be off to our left somewhere, out of sight. Taking alternate looks into the trees, down the hill along the edge of the cliff, and across the wide mouth of the inlet, I didn't see any white bodies glowing in the moonlight. The sound of the howling and hooting made it clear that the horde was close.

Halfway down the hill, a giant chunk of limestone jutted up to our left like a daredevil's motorcycle jumping ramp, its highest point just above the height of the trees that grew out of the hill at the foot of the ramp.

I turned to Murphy and pointed up the ramp.

He looked up, thought about it for a second and nodded. "Careful, though. I'll bet we'll be able to see the whole cove from up there—"

I interrupted, "But anything in the cove will be able to see us."

He nodded.

Double-checking the shadows in the trees to my right and left, I started my slow walk up the limestone ramp. At first, the soil was thick enough to support the growth of grass, but by the time I was halfway up, the soil had thinned to nothing. I sank to a crouch. The crouch became a crawl on my hands and knees, and at the top, that turned into a belly crawl. I poked my nubby-haired white head over the edge, silhouetting myself against the dark sky behind, hoping I'd go unnoticed.

Murphy scrambled up beside me.

Just below us, a dense canopy of cedars and oaks blanketed the slope all the way to the water's edge. A crooked finger of an inlet a few hundred feet wide and a half-mile long cut back between the hills. Down at the end of the cove, the trees gave way to a solid mass of naked, angry white bodies covering the shores, roofs, and docks—the horde. They howled, they jumped, and they grasped. They were frustrated about the expanse of water that separated them from a ski boat floating in water down near the end, trapped there by a shamble of floating docks. Those docks appeared to have detached from their moorings during the flooding and jammed themselves together to form a floating barrier across the width of the cove. And that barrier was covered with hundreds of bald-headed Whites.

Those people trapped in the ski boat had to be normal.

"We can't do anything to help those people." Murphy looked down at his watch before whispering, "I'll give you thirty seconds to lay your Null Spot bullshit on me before we get out of here."

Without looking at him, I said, "Fuck you, Murphy."

"Time's a wastin'."

I pointed to our right. "Look over there. I see three boats close enough to shore that we can get one. They're all probably far enough away from the infected that they won't notice."

In a tentative tone, Murphy said, "Okay."

"Okay?"

"I know that's not all."

I shook my head and flatly replied, "Maybe if we float out close to the docks, shoot a few Whites, toss a few hand grenades, we can give those people a chance to get out."

"Uh-huh."

"We'll be in the boat," I said. "We won't be in any danger."

"You know it won't work out like that, right?"

"Don't be such a pessimist," I told him.

"Fine, but if I get bit—"

"Yeah, I know," I said flatly. "You're going to punch me in the face."

Murphy grinned. "You're my favorite, Null Spot. I'd never punch you in the face."

We put our crawling skills in reverse and made our way back down the ramp.

Chapter 2

I chose the ski boat drifting closest to the mouth of the cove, the one furthest from the mob of Whites wreaking their havoc on the marina. The vessel wasn't close enough to shore to wade out to, but it was no trouble to swim. I climbed in at the stern, up the ski ladder, through deep ankle deep rainwater still standing on the deck, and took a seat at the helm. That's when the gaping hole in my plan exposed itself.

No key.

No fucking key.

Why in the hell did I have a blind spot in my brain for the necessity of boat keys?

"Dammit." I huffed and tried my best not to throw a toddler tantrum, and thought about punching the steering wheel as though it was the boat's fault for requiring the key. Well, I guess in a way, it was. But noise was bad, a lesson I'd been taught at least a dozen times already.

I calmed myself with a long, slow breath, looked over to where I'd left Murphy on the shore and signaled a thumbs-down. Murphy stepped out of his concealing shadow. I pantomimed turning a key in the ignition and shook my head. He deflated and looked around the cove. He was as disappointed as I was.

Nevertheless, I found a rope attached near the bow. Taking it in hand, I slipped silently into the water on the boat's starboard side and went to work towing the boat back near the shore. It was slow going, of course, but I only had to cover half the distance before my feet hit bottom, fifteen feet from shore. I stood up and waved Murphy over.

A few minutes later we were both squatted in the boat, the hull hiding us from view. I whispered, "This one's got no keys."

"Yeah, I got that." Murphy looked around inside the boat. "You thinking we should paddle this thing?"

Down at the end of the cove, the Whites erupted in an enthusiastic roar. I guessed that one of the people trapped in the ski boat had done something to raise their excitement and make them think their long-awaited meal was at hand.

"No paddling," I told Murphy. "I figured you were safer here in the boat than on shore. You can wait here while I swim to the other boats and see if I can find one that'll start."

Murphy looked up over the gunwale. "Boats are scattered all up and down the inlet. Can you swim that far?"

I looked up, though I didn't really need to. Whether I could swim that far or not was irrelevant. I'd already decided that I would swim that far and that was that. I ditched the rest of my equipment, save my knife and pants. I removed my boots and stood up to get a good look at the boats that were scattered around the cove. I figured I'd start with boats closer to the mouth of the cove and slowly work my way through the boats in order as they got close to the end of the marina. It was a choice of order that would mean more swimming than just going from boat to closest boat, but staying away from the Whites was my priority.

"If you can do it quietly, why don't you bail this water out while I check the other boats? That way, if we have to paddle, this one will weigh less." I slipped over the side. Before I swam away, I said, "Wish me luck."

"Luck."

It was a hundred-yard swim to a pontoon boat floating in the middle of the cove's mouth. In all the time I'd spent on our old pontoon boat down on Lake Austin, I'd developed an affinity for the cumbersome but useful watercraft. As I climbed up on the pontoon boat's deck, I was hoping pretty hard that the keys would be aboard. I spent ten minutes silently searching in compartments and under seat cushions for a hidden spare set, but had no luck. I slipped back into the water and headed for the next boat.

Working my way from boat to boat, back and forth across the narrowing cove from mouth to marina, I spent an hour searching fourteen boats, getting more and more discouraged as fatigue set in. With each boat I reached, I got closer and closer to the drifting docks and the grasping hands of frenzied Whites. And though I knew the Whites I'd encountered so far feared the water like kryptonite, I'd also come to realize they'd eventually figure out how to swim. It was bound to happen, either on purpose or by accident. Considering how many times I'd bet my life on their fear, I knew at some point that bet would stop paying off. Nevertheless, some quirk in my psyche required that I finish searching the boats, though my hope was gone and my perception of the risk was growing.

I dropped myself into the water and started swimming another lap across the cove. On the way, I silently cursed the marina manager for his diligence in seeing to it that none of the owners of boats in his marina had keys left onboard. I reached the stern of a boat as I felt my toes kicking rocks on the bottom. Looking around at the shore and the floating dock, I stood up and was just able to keep my head above the surface as I caught my breath. All the swimming was wearing me down. I needed calories. And I needed to start getting them on a more regular schedule.

I managed a noiseless entry into the boat and rolled over on my back, laying my head on the deck for a moment as I reconsidered how committed I was to searching the final few ski boats. When I got up on my knees and looked around for a spot to start my search, my curiosity piqued. Each of the boats I'd already searched—I guessed—had been docked when the world had run off its rails. In every boat nearly everything inside was stowed. At least half of them had canvas covers. But this boat had two gas cans sitting in the stern beside a dirty cooler, and lengths of rope were coiled sloppily on the deck. It was littered with plastic food wrappers, empty soda cans, and brass shell casings.

I flipped back the cooler lid and looked inside. Unopened soda cans, bottled water, and snack foods.

Bingo?

Something wasn't right.

I realized that this boat probably belonged to the scavengers trapped in the marina on the other side of the floating docks. They'd probably arrived on this boat to do their scavenging. The white horde showed up unexpectedly, and when they were running to get back to their boat, they got cut off and jumped into the first boat they could get to. Unfortunately for them, that boat was trapped in the end of the cove by the docks that were jammed across it.

A muted splash behind the boat startled me. I grabbed my knife and spun, peeking over the stern of the boat as I did so.

A head was on the surface and coming at me.

I got ready to stab as it occurred to me that the person in the water wasn't white—not Caucasian white, and certainly not virus white. One of the trapped scavengers, a black woman, must have swum under the floating docks, managed to get far enough up the cove to surface unseen, and come over.

The scavenger was nearly within arms' reach, and I extended a hand out to help her. But she looked up and gasped, making a sudden desperate effort to change her direction.

That confused me for half a second and I leaned farther out.

Duh!

I was white-skinned and still pretty close to bald. I was naked from the waist up and wielding a knife in one hand while I reached for her with the other. She saw that I was infected.

I laid my knife on the deck, raised my palms to show that I wasn't a threat, and whispered, "It's okay."

The girl came to a stop as she started to tread water, confusion on her face.

I waved her over. "C'mon. It's okay."

The girl cast a look at the Whites on the floating docks, gave me the same fearful look, and continued to tread water.

I pointed over the ski boat's port side, the side that couldn't be seen by the Whites on the floating docks. "Swim over here. They won't be able to see you."

The girl stayed where she was.

"It's okay. You can stand up over here. It's not that deep."

It took a few long moments of thought, but the girl eventually complied, swam over out of view, and stood up in water that came up to the middle of her chest. She kept herself well out of reach.

Whispering, I said, "Look, I know I look like them, but I'm a Slow Burn."

"What's that?"

"Doesn't really matter. I got the fever, but I recovered. I'm normal now. Well, except for my skin color."

"You look just like Them," she said.

"I know. It's a problem," I conceded. "Look, we're here to help you guys. You don't need to be afraid."

"We?"

"I've got a buddy in a boat, down over there." I pointed toward the mouth of the cove.

"What are you doing in our boat?"

I gestured across the other boats in the cove. "I've been trying to find a boat with keys in it."

"If you don't have a boat," she asked, "then how'd you get here?"

"We walked." I was running low on patience. "Jesus Christ, do you want to get in or not?"

The girl looked around, thought about it for a minute, and said, "You had a knife a moment ago."

"Yeah?"

"Give it to me," she told me.

"You're not going to stab me are you?" I smiled, not sure if I was serious or joking.

The girl glared back. "I just don't want you to stab me. Give me the knife and I'll come on board."

"You know you're not really in the best negotiating position, don't you?"

"The knife."

Rolling my eyes to show the pointlessness of it, I picked my knife up, took a good look into the shadows under the trees on the bank, turned it handle-out, and reached it out to her.

Not making any effort to reach up for the knife, the girl turned toward the woods and asked, "Who are you looking for?"

"Seriously?" I rolled my eyes again. "There are Whites everywhere."

"Whites?"

I pointed at the infected on the docks, hooting and jumping but still focused on the survivors trapped in the boat on the other side. "That's what we call them."

"Not exactly politically correct."

"Really?" I laughed harshly, but quietly. "Is that still a thing?"

The girl looked at me sternly.

I asked, "What do you call them?"

"Them," she said.

"Just…Them?" I asked.

The girl nodded.

"Imaginative." Sarcasm is such a handy device to communicate so much while saying so little. I asked, "Are you getting in the boat or not?"

The girl reached up and took the knife, finally allowing me to let go and drop my arm. She said, "Go up by the bow. I'll get in at the stern."

"Whatever." I duck-walked to the front of the boat to keep myself out of sight. I squatted while she climbed over the stern, dripping a whole new puddle onto the deck.

With the knife held ready for use, she crouched and moved up to the middle of the boat next to the helm.

"Can we be friends now?" I asked.

"You said you were going to help us. What did you have in mind?"

I shrugged and looked around.

The girl heaved a long, tired sigh. "You were just going to steal the boat, weren't you?"

"Yeah, well no. Not really." I pointed back up the cove. "My buddy thought we should, but I was thinking maybe we could help you guys out."

"Really." She didn't believe anything I was saying. It did sound like lies.

I said, "We were going to start up one of these boats, drive it over in the middle by the docks, and shoot a bunch of them so you guys could cross over and get out."

"You watch too many action movies." The girl looked at the mob of Whites.

"We have grenades, too."

The girl shook her head.

"Do you have a better idea?" I asked. "I mean, you obviously swam over here. What's your plan?"

The girl looked down at the deck.

I asked, "Are the others going to swim over as well?"

"I made it most of the way under water. None of the others can swim that far. If they come up for air too close to the floating dock, some of Them might jump in on top of them."

I looked over at the Whites who were howling loudly again. "It could happen. So what's your plan?"

"We have people."

"People?" I asked.

"I was going to go get help." The girl looked out at the dark lake.

"Cool, let's start this puppy up. My buddy is down there in the boat by the mouth of the cove. We can pick him up on the way out, and if you could drop us off somewhere up the lake, that'd be great."

The girl cast a worried look toward the mouth of the cove.

"Trust me," I said. "You'll like him. He never stops smiling except when he's talking, which is a lot. You'll love him."

The girl wasn't convinced.

"Look, I don't want to steal your boat," I said. "Just take us around the bend and let us out. That'll get us past these Whites and we can go about our business. You can go get your people and we'll all be cool."

"What business do you have in the middle of the night?"

I looked back at the Whites and into the shadows. "Probably the same business you have, okay? Looking for food. Trying to find our friends. Trying to stay alive long enough to see the sun come up."

"You're looking for lost friends?"

I was getting a little perturbed. "You've got lots of questions for somebody who doesn't seem to want our help. Can we just get going and get out of here? We'll leave you to help your friends or whatever." I pointed at the boat up the cove that Murphy was in. "Can you at least drop me off at that boat? We'll just paddle it across the cove and be on our way."

The girl looked at me without giving away anything with her expression. I waited for a few moments for a response then said, "Whatever the fuck. Look, I'll just swim back down and you can do whatever. But I want my knife back."

The girl looked at my knife still in her hand.

"It was my grandpa's knife." Sure, it was a lie, but the next part wasn't. "It has sentimental value. Will you at least hand it to me when I get back in the water? You're not going to try and steal my fucking knife, are you?"

It took the girl a moment before she said anything. "Okay. I'll give you a ride down there and I'll drop you off a little north of the cove if that's what you want." She held my knife out toward me. "Sorry about your grandpa."

"Me, too."

"What was his name?"

"Mr. Mays."

"You called your grandpa Mr. Mays?"

"It's a long story."

I put the knife back in its old leather sheath. The girl started the boat's motor. A thousand white faces turned our way and a tremendous wave of jubilant screams drowned out all other sound.

As she pressed the lock button and shifted the throttle into reverse, the engine revved and the boat moved away from the shore. Still in the bow, I looked into the trees to see if any Whites were crazy enough to make the jump out of the shadows. But as soon as I put that thought together, the rope that was attached to the bow and to a tree on the shore lifted up out of the water snapped taut, and jerked the boat to a stop. Having no such rope attached to me, I kept going and fell backwards onto the deck, bouncing my skull on the fiberglass.

Through the stars, I heard the engine rev higher. I heard the rope snap and heard it whip through the air in the space where I'd just been standing. "Ouch."

The boat was moving.

My feet were still in the bow, and I was on my back on the deck, my head next to the girl where she sat behind the wheel. She looked down at me. "You okay?"

"I guess."

"Sorry about that. Can you get up?"

"Give me a sec' for my brains to stop rattling around."

The girl reversed the throttle, he sound of the engine changed, and the boat started to move away from shore. My head rolled to the side as the boat turned and I found myself looking at her feet, and especially at her ankle. She had an owl tattoo.

Chapter 3

When I started laughing, she probably thought I was nuts.

"What are you laughing at?" she asked.

I pulled myself up into a sitting position and as I maneuvered myself into the seat opposite her, I asked, "Did you go to Rice?"

She looked at me and then down at her feet. "Oh, the tattoo. I've never had anybody laugh at it before."

"Is that a popular tattoo for Rice alumni?"

"I don't know. Why?"

"Your name wouldn't be Rachel, would it?"

The girl's mouth dropped open. Then her eyes turned angry. "How do you know that?"

We'd covered half the distance to the boat where Murphy was patiently waiting. "You're never going to believe who I'm with."

Still wary, Rachel asked, "Who?"

I thought about making Rachel wait on the answer but figured that her being on the edge of suspicion wasn't good for either of us. "Murphy."

Tears flowed. "Murphy."

I nodded.

"My brother, Murphy Smalls."

"Yep."

She shook her head. "If this is some kind of trick…"

"We'll be there in a second. You'll see for yourself."

Rachel slowed the boat and cut the engine so that we could drift up to the other boat.

It was my turn to worry. Murphy's head didn't pop up to see us coming. He didn't wave. Something was wrong.

"Quiet," I whispered.

The girl was immediately tense. "What? What's wrong?"

I shook my head. "I don't know."

I stood and hurried to the bow of the boat. Out of some innate protective habit, I motioned for Rachel to stay behind. She didn't.

The bow of our boat nudged the other ski boat on the port side and I grabbed a handful of chrome rail to hold the two boats together. I leaned over to get a look inside. Murphy was lying on the deck. His head was on a cushion. He was asleep. "Motherfucker!"

"What?"

I turned to Rachel. "He's taking a nap."

Rachel squeezed past me as I sheathed my knife. With all the grace of a gymnast, she hopped into the other boat and landed on the deck beside Murphy. Tears were flowing in earnest. She knelt beside him and shook him until he woke.

I don't know what Murphy was dreaming about, but my bet was that it wasn't as good as what he saw when he woke up. It took a few moments for him to figure out that he was really awake, but once he did, both he and Rachel hugged and smiled, cried, laughed, and hugged some more.

When they settled down, Murphy started to ask questions so fast that Rachel had no chance to answer. But Rachel knew how to get down to business. "Murphy, we'll talk later. Right now, my people are trapped on a boat over there. You guys came down here to get them out. Do you have any ideas besides that John Wayne silliness your buddy told me about?"

"Hey!" I thought it was a reasonable plan, considering the circumstances.

Murphy looked at me with a question on his face, but talked to Rachel. "When did you get so bossy?"

Rachel looked at me like I'd said something. I pointed back at Murphy. "I thought you said she was nice."

Rachel turned to Murphy. "You and your friends. How can you go through life without ever growing up?"

I said, "I'm getting kinda sorry about convincing you to get in the boat."

Rachel shot me a blazing look, then turned to stare for a minute at the infected making a ruckus on the floating docks. She looked back at me, all the hardness gone. "Thank you for being patient enough to convince me to get in the boat with you."

The switch took me aback. "You're welcome."

Murphy said, "Don't be hard on him. He's a good guy. He saved my life."

"Thank you for that, too." Rachel stuck out a hand. "You know my name…"

"I'm Zed."

"Zed? Really?"

"Don't ask. It's not as interesting nor as immature as it seems."

Rachel looked back at the floating docks. "I have an idea."

Chapter 4

"He can hold his breath forever. I seen him do it." That's what Murphy had said to convince Rachel that I should be the one to go into the water with the rope. I hadn't wanted the job, but I wasn't going to argue about it. Based on little more than the fact that I had dangling genitalia, I believed I could do pretty much any physically demanding task better than Rachel.

So there I was, holding my breath beneath one of the floating docks, trying my best to tie a knot in the rope that I'd just wrapped around a metal brace before I ran out of air. If I didn't finish it, there was no room to surface beneath the dock, as it floated on giant cubes of Styrofoam. I'd have to swim away from the dock underwater, catch my breath, and come back for another try. But I'd already been under three times; I was losing my patience, and my endurance was shortening with each submersion. When I wrapped the end of the rope under and through a loop for probably the fourth time, I decided that was good enough, and I pushed myself off of the brace and swam through the black water until I ran out of air.

I surfaced a good twenty feet from the dock. Many of the infected were very interested in what I was doing, but I was too far out in the water for any of them to think about coming for me. I swam another ten or fifteen feet to the boat, and Murphy gave me a hand climbing in.

"All secure?" Rachel asked from the driver's seat.

"Good to go," I answered.

She started the boat motor and got the attention of any Whites on the dock that weren't already sizing us up. She engaged the propeller, and the boat started its slow progress forward.

"Easy," Murphy told her. There was a lot of slack in the ski rope that connected the boat to the floating dock. We didn't want it to jerk and break. "Easy."

We passed through a few more boat lengths.

"How am I doing?" Rachel asked.

Murphy was standing in the stern of the boat. I was standing there as well. The rope was attached to some ski rope thingy between us on the back of the boat. It was designed to pull skiers, and we deduced that it was the best place to attach the rope.

Murphy turned to Rachel. "All the slack is coming out. Almost there."

The rope pulled up out of the lake and drew taut. As the tension squeezed all the water out of the rope's fibers the boat stopped moving.

Murphy said, "Okay."

Rachel revved the engine higher. The propeller churned the water to white foam behind the boat. The rope hummed under the added tension. The docks groaned and lurched, but the section we'd tied onto didn't break away from the ones it was jammed against.

Rachel looked back. "Is it working?"

"More gas." Murphy told her.

More water turned white. The dock didn't move.

"C'mon," I muttered.

Rachel pushed the throttle all the way forward. The engine whined. Whites were coming up on both sides of the cove. Still, the docks didn't separate.

To Murphy, I said, "It seemed like a solid plan."

With the sound of a gunshot, the ski rope snapped. A length of it ripped the air between Murphy and me, slung through the center of the boat and out over the bow, popping again before flinging itself up above the boat to fall harmlessly down.

"God damn!" Murphy looked at me. "You all right?"

To my surprise, I was. I nodded without a word.

"Damn, Rachel," said Murphy "You almost put my eye out."

"You sound like my mom," she said. "Are you guys okay?"

"Except for the mess in my pants," joked Murphy.

"Zed, you okay?" she asked.

"I might have to change my pants, too," I answered.

Rachel rolled her eyes and huffed. "I guess we're back to the John Wayne plan."

Chapter 5

Our boat floated sideways near the center of the cove, fifty or sixty feet from the nearest of the log-jammed docks. Murphy had his M4 ready. Rachel had my M4. I had my pistol and machete ready just in case any of the Whites fell into the water and figured that they could swim after us. We didn't need any passengers besides the ones we were trying to collect.

Murphy looked at Rachel and me. "Here's the way this is going to work. I count to three and we all throw a hand grenade."

Rachel gestured toward the dock and hefted a grenade, testing its weight. "I don't know if I can throw it that far."

Murphy rolled his eyes. "Trust me. You can throw it that far."

"Can't we get a bit closer?" she asked.

"If we get closer we'll get hit by shrapnel."

I said, "I vote we don't move closer."

Murphy rolled his eyes again. "Rachel, you toss yours right over at those Whites in front of us. Zed will throw one down that way, I'll throw mine down this way. Try not to get them in the water. They'll be useless if that happens."

Rachel looked at the grenade in her hand and back up at the dock. She wasn't sure.

"The first hand grenade will be easy," Murphy explained. "Just throw it at one of them. It'll hit and drop down to the dock. When you throw the second, hopefully there will be fewer of them still standing on the docks, so it'll be harder to get the grenade to land there."

Rachel answered, "Okay."

I nodded.

Murphy continued. "This is the important part. I'll count to three and we all throw on three. Both times. As soon as you throw, drop down onto the deck. You don't want any shrapnel coming back and hitting you."

"I thought you said we were far enough out for that not to happen?" Rachel asked.

"Stay on your feet if you want to." Murphy closed one eye. "But you might put your eye out." He laughed. "After the grenades, we shoot everything that moves on the docks. Questions?"

Looking at Rachel, I asked, "And your friends will know to start swimming this way when they see most of the Whites on the docks are preoccupied with us or busy bleeding out?"

"Yes."

"Good, we don't have enough bullets to kill all of them, and we'll use them up pretty quickly."

Murphy laughed, "The bullets will last a lot longer now that you're not shooting."

Rachel didn't understand why Murphy was teasing me about my shooting. "They'll come."

"Ready?" Murphy asked.

Both Rachel and I gave him a nod.

"Pull your pins."

We did.

"One. Two. Three."

All three grenades flew at the dock and we dropped to the boat's deck. Moments later, three near-simultaneous explosions rocked across the water. Bits of shrapnel smacked the boat's hull.

The tenor of the White's screams changed dramatically. The ones close by wailed in pain. Those on shore screamed in anger over their empty bellies and the number of white bodies standing between them and the feast left in the wake of the explosions.

Murphy jumped to his feet. Rachel and I were up a half second later, each of us already pulling a pin from a grenade.

The first three grenades had found their marks and left big gaps in what was a solid wall of white flesh. Bodies were down, broken and bleeding. Some of the infected were dazed and wounded but still on their feet. Others had been knocked into the water by the blasts. Most of those were drowning. Some were keeping their heads above the surface.

"One. Two. Three!"

Three more grenades arced toward the dock and again, Murphy, Rachel, and I dropped to the deck, with a little more conviction than on the previous time. We'd all heard the shrapnel hitting the hull and zinging through the air overhead.

Explosions followed, two on the dock, one in the water.

I jumped to my feet, machete and pistol ready to work. Murphy was already firing. Rachel squeezed off her first rounds a moment later. Bodies were down across seventy or eighty feet of the dock. Plenty were still standing upright, enraged and screaming. Others were starting to feed on their fallen brethren. Bullets ripped indiscriminately through them all.

Rachel stopped firing, waved a hand, and hollered to the passengers of the trapped boat. "Swim! Now! Go! Swim!" She went back to shooting.

I waved at the three to come.

It took a moment for them to reach a decision, or maybe just to figure out what was being requested, but one of them shed his weapon and dove over the side. The other two stood up, lost their heavy gear, and followed their partner into the water.

I shouted, "They're coming!"

Whites pressed thickly together, trying to rush across the docks toward the middle. Some fell as Murphy and Rachel shot. Others were pushed into the water. Some were trampled in the mob.

The first of Rachel's trapped friends made it to the dock, ducked under, and surfaced a moment later on our side. His eyes were wide with fear. He splashed rapidly and inefficiently as panic drove him to claw his way through the water.

I waved him over to me. "C'mon."

A White howled nearby.

To my right, a White had somehow made it over to lay a hand on the stern. I hacked his wrist through with my machete and the White went under, getting a mouthful of water, leaving his hand behind.

The first swimmer reached the boat. I holstered my pistol and reached down. "I gotcha! C'mon."

The man gripped my hand and I pulled. He got another hand on the rail. I let go and reached over his back to pull on his belt. As second later, he flopped over the gunwale and rolled onto his back on the deck.

One down!

I quickly searched across the water around us. No Whites were close enough to be a danger.

Under the cover of bullets, the other two swimmers had cleared the dock. I sheathed my machete and reached out across the gap to the one in the lead. He took my hand and I pulled him up. A moment later, he was in the boat.

The last of the swimmers was a woman. These guys definitely weren't the chivalrous types.

I reached down, and the girl's small hand grasped mine. I pulled her up, and about the time she was halfway into the boat, she stopped. I looked at her face. She seemed to deflate as the word, "Shit," hissed past her lips.

I couldn't believe it.

"Fucking Freitag."

Chapter 6

I wasted zero time in getting my M4 back from Rachel, irritating her significantly, as her first priority once the other three were in the boat was getting her butt planted in the seat at the helm. As each of the three caught their breaths and realized just how completely virus-white Murphy and I each were, the tension shot up rapidly.

Murphy, always great at reading fucked-up situations, had positioned himself in the bow of the boat from where he could see all of us at the same time. He had his rifle pointed down at the deck, but both hands were still on it. It was clear that it would take only a fraction of a second to bring it back to a firing position.

In the seat amidships next to Rachel, one of her buddies sat himself down, glancing alternately at me and then at Murphy, while Rachel engaged the propeller and started the boat moving toward the end of the cove. Freitag, looking like somebody had just flushed her pet goldfish, dropped onto a bench seat across the stern next to the other guy who was busying himself with suspicious sideways glances at me.

I was standing on the deck in the center of the boat, suddenly trying to decide which of the two guys we'd just rescued was a bigger threat. That's to say that I wasn't certain that either of them was, but I was getting a bad feeling.

Accelerating the boat, Rachel glanced at each of her friends. "You guys okay?"

Nods only. No verbal response.

Bad sign.

I shot Murphy a quick look to emphasize my suspicion. He winked. He knew. His voice boomed, "Here's the deal, motherfuckers. Me and my boy Zed just saved your dumb asses. So if you want to keep giving us the stink eye, you can get out and swim home."

"Murphy." Rachel scolded.

I moved over to stand right behind Rachel's seat, keeping my back to the water on the boat's starboard side.

The guy in the seat on the port side looked at me, then turned to Murphy, and with no intonation at all said, "Thank you."

Murphy acknowledged with a nod and looked at the other guy.

"Thanks." He leaned forward, put his elbows on his knees, and his face in his hands. He muttered, "We're dead."

A little pissed, I asked, "What?"

The guy didn't respond.

Freitag answered for him. "He thinks you're going to infect him."

"Hey, dipshit." I said to the guy, "If you haven't gotten the fever yet, you're not going to."

The guy on the port side replied, "You don't know that."

"Oh jeez." I rolled my eyes. "Well, if you were worried about getting infected, you should have just stayed home. Why were you even out scavenging?"

The guy on the port side told the guy in the back, "You only get it if they bite you."

Murphy laughed out loud. "Where have you guys been, watching reruns of old zombie movies?" He looked at Rachel. "What are you doing with these hillbillies?"

The guy on the port side shot Murphy a dirty look.

Rachel, taking control, said, "Everybody stop. Just stop. I swear." She turned to look at each of us. The boat was out into the lake by then, so precise steering was not required. "Murphy, these are my friends—Bill, Karl, and Freitag."

With a dramatic roll of his eyes, Murphy said, "Oh yeah, we know Freitag."

To the man sitting next to her, Rachel said, "Bill, you're probably immune. That nurse who showed up a couple of days ago said the virus was airborne—"

Talking right over Rachel, Bill said, "You can't trust just anybody who says they're a nurse."

"A nurse?" I asked.

Freitag answered. "Your red-headed boss showed up a couple of days ago."

"Steph?" It was hard to smile with my mouth hanging agape.

Rachel said, "You know each other?"

Freitag added, "And the codger sergeant."

"Dalhover," I confirmed.

"And two of those girls from the riverboat."

"Amy and Megan?"

"Yeah."

Rachel looked at Murphy. "Those are the people you're looking for?"

"Yeah," Murphy answered. "They were headed for Monk's Island."

"That's where we are," she said.

"Dammit!" Bill got pissed. "Rachel, you can't just tell anybody where we are."

In a stern, "don't fuck with me" mode, Rachel pointed at Murphy and told Bill, "That's my brother. I'll tell him whatever I want to tell him, so you'd better figure out a way to deal with it."

Bill turned to look at the water, and after a moment he muttered, "I didn't know it was your brother."

"He, not it," Rachel corrected. "Murphy is a person."

Cowed, Bill sulked with his mouth shut while the occupants of the boat silently appraised one another. Nothing was said for a good long while, until Freitag voiced out loud a question she'd probably been silently asking herself since the moment she got into the boat. "What did I do in a previous life to deserve this?"

Murphy heard her and laughed.

I couldn't help but offer up my opinion. "It's what you did in this life, is my guess."

Freitag, with her vicious tongue, shot back, "You've got no room to talk, Mr. Fuck You Canoe."

I smiled at the memory of the moment when I told Freitag that she'd shot a hole in the canoe that I left her. It was one of the highlights of my post-apocalyptic life. I said, "As far as I'm concerned, we're even."

"Like I believe that."

I reached out an empty hand. "If you'll promise not to fuck with me anymore, I won't fuck with you. Like I said, we're even."

Freitag looked at my extended hand, clearly reluctant to put her own hand into the trap that she thought it represented.

"Up to you," I added.

Just as I was about to withdraw the offer, she stood up, wobbled a bit with the rocking of the boat, and grabbed my hand in her tiny grip. She didn't smile. She wasn't angry. Maybe resigned. "Even." It was a hard thing for her to say.

"Even," I confirmed.

She let go and sat back down.

I looked at Murphy. He was amused and disappointed. That made me wonder.

Bill asked Freitag, "What's that about?"

"Long story," she said.

Chapter 7

In the wee hours of the night when we neared Monk's Island, a row of seven school bus-shaped silhouettes floated a short distance offshore. I wondered if those were the rental houseboats that Megan mentioned back when we'd all been on the riverboat on Lake Austin, talking about coming to Lake Travis for refuge. It looked like the group staying on Monk's Island had beaten us to it.

A ski boat motored slowly toward us from the island. I couldn't tell how many people were inside, but rifles bristled on its silhouette.

Rachel reduced our speed.

Bill pointed a thumb at Murphy and in a defeated voice said, "They're not going to let us come back because of them."

Rachel shut Bill up with a harsh look.

Murphy adjusted his grip on his rifle and looked at the boat out in front of us.

If Murphy was nervous, that was all the indication I needed. I looked down at my weapon, checked the safety, and ran a hand across the magazines in my MOLLE vest, trying to recall which ones were empty. I had a system for that, but I had gotten confused during the firefight in the cove. Now I didn't know where the empty and full magazines were.

"Murphy," Rachel said. "It's okay. They probably saw extra people in the boat, and they're coming out to check on us."

"Uh-huh." Murphy's tone made it clear that he didn't accept Rachel's assessment.

Rachel pulled the throttle back and let the boat drift to a stop in the water. She turned the engine off.

I glanced around. Bill was nervous, and judging by the way he was looking at me, it was clear that if trouble started, he was going to make a move on me. Unfortunately for Bill, just a few feet in front of me, he was at a range I could still hit with my M4. Karl still had his face in his hands. Freitag just looked bored.

The boat from the island got within twenty or thirty feet of us. It throttled down and came to a stop in the water nearby. Three armed men stood behind two seated people. A woman's voice called across, "Rachel, who's with you?"

The rifles pointed at us.

Rachel said to me and Murphy, "Keep your weapons down. Don't aim at them, please. They're just being careful." Then, Rachel called back, "Gretchen, it's my brother and a friend of his."

"Really?" Gretchen's voice carried a degree of disbelief. "Did you find everything we needed at the pharmacy?"

That seemed like an odd question.

Rachel answered, "We got everything we needed at the pharmacy."

Tension seemed to disappear instantly on the other boat. Rifles lowered and the engine revved to bring it toward us.

Rachel looked up at me, "A code phrase."

Bill hissed, "Don't tell them that!"

"Bill, be quiet."

"We can't trust them."

Rachel nodded her head toward Murphy. "What part of 'he's my brother' don't you get?"

Murphy grinned, "Yeah, hillbilly."

Bill shot Murphy a dirty look. The other boat floated up beside us. The people on board saw mine and Murphy's white skin. That made them nervous. Rachel stood up. "Gretchen."

Gretchen, an Amazonian goddess of a woman stood up, taller than any of her men. "We saw that you were coming back with more people than you left with. That's why we came out to meet you."

"Of course," Rachel answered.

Bill stood up, unable to contain his anger over the situation anymore. "They're infected. They're both infected."

"Shut up, Bill." Rachel, nearly as tall as Murphy and muscular for a woman, looked ready to make sure that he did.

Bill looked back at Rachel.

Rachel said, "Bill, I'm in charge. You know how we do things. Now stop being a stupid ass."

Bill dropped to his seat, muttering, "They're going to infect us all."

The guys on the other boat were getting a little nervous with their rifles.

I called across, "We're Slow Burns. We got the virus, but we're okay. We got better. We're normal."

"Normal?" Gretchen smiled broadly. "Were you always an albino?"

"Mostly normal," I answered.

Rachel looked at me with an expression that made it clear that she was indeed in charge and that I should let her do the talking. After that, Rachel conveyed the story about what transpired in the cove, emphasizing that Murphy was indeed her brother.

When Rachel finished her story, Gretchen thanked both Murphy and me for what we'd done. "Here's the way it works here. I'm in charge. I've got some people who help me. Rachel is one of them."

Murphy laughed out loud. "The women are taking over the world."

Gretchen looked at him with a stern face. "Is that a problem?"

With a big grin, Murphy shook his head. "No ma'am. I'm cool with it. I'm just sayin', is all."

Gretchen pointed at a lone houseboat anchored a good distance from the row I'd spotted a few minutes before. "When people come back from scavenging, we quarantine them there for twenty-four hours to make sure they don't bring the infection onto the island. When new people come, we quarantine them a little longer while we're deciding whether to let them join us."

I looked at Freitag. I didn't mean to. It just kind of happened. I asked, "Are you picky about who you let in?"

Freitag scratched her nose with her middle finger while she looked at me.

I suppressed a laugh.

Gretchen said, "We're not trying to build an exclusive country club, if that's what you're asking. We've taken in everybody who has come so far. We're trying to do our part."

Murphy said, "Cool."

Gretchen looked at Murphy. "Don't get too excited. You guys are the first—what did you call them—Slow Burns?"

"Yes," I confirmed.

"Only normal people have come so far. We'll all talk about it. I'm not going to make any promises about whether you'll be accepted to come onto the island."

"We're not contagious," I protested.

"We're not staying, anyway." Murphy told them.

Rachel was taken aback. "What?"

Gretchen said, "The quarantine boat is over there, if you want to get on it."

Bill was back on his feet and pointing at Murphy. "I'm not ·getting on that boat with Them. If I'm not infected already, I don't want to get that way."

Gretchen was clearly disappointed. "Don't then, Bill. You can stay in a ski boat anchored over there as close as you feel comfortable. They can stay on the quarantine boat if they want to. They saved your life. I think you owe them at least that much."

Bill muttered, "We'd 'a got out."

Chapter 8

It was weird, I mean, it was really weird. I was sitting on the end of a couch in the living room of a houseboat. Murphy sat at the other end, in an apparent talking race with Rachel, who was in a comfy-looking chair near his end of the couch. All of the windows were open and a comfortable breeze was blowing through. Better yet, the screens kept the mosquitoes outside. I felt safe and anachronistically normal.

Freitag had gone down a narrow hallway and laid claim to one of the bedrooms, probably asleep already. Some fifty yards away from our spacious houseboat, Bill and Karl were in quarantine on their ski boat, discontented and being quite verbose about it. But it was their choice. So fuck 'em.

Through the open windows I heard a boat motor up alongside. Talking jumbled to incomprehensibility with the noise of the boat engine and splashing waves. Several pairs of footsteps clomped along the deck outside. I looked at the door that faced that deck and was not surprised when it swung open. I was surprised when Steph came into the living room, followed closely by Dalhover. My mouth probably fell open as I struggled for something witty to say.

Steph hurried across the living room as I stood up. She threw her arms around me and we shared a long hug. She shuddered as she buried her face against my shoulder. Any ambivalence I had about sharing what I knew about her fiancée disappeared. Better to let her think that Jeff Aubrey died at the hospital.

With red-rimmed eyes, Steph pulled away and stepped over to give Murphy a hug—less affectionate, but a hug just the same.

Dalhover slapped me on the shoulder. "You made it."

Seeing an extra helping of sadness in his eyes, I said, "I'm glad you guys did, too."

He leaned in close, "There are some things you need to know."

"We saw."

Dalhover's face asked the silent question.

"We were almost back. We were on the mountain. We saw what happened on the boat."

Dalhover slowly shook his head. He had more regret in his voice than I thought possible. "We did what we could."

I put a hand on his shoulder. "I know. I know."

Dalhover looked at Murphy and turned back to me. In a just-you-and-me tone, he said, "I'd 'a thought he'd take it harder."

Softly, I answered. "You know Murphy. He cries his tears and moves on. He loved her. I mean, he really did."

Dalhover nodded, slapped me on the shoulder again, and stepped over to shake Murphy's hand and pass along his condolences for Mandi.

Gretchen came in through the still open door. A wiry, tall man with John Lennon glasses followed her in, closing the door behind him. He said, "You don't want to let the mosquitoes in."

Seeing the questions on all of our faces, Gretchen said, "I'm here now, so I'll have to stay the full twenty four hours. I hope you don't mind."

Steph nudged me in the arm and said, "She's the boss."

Gretchen announced, "I wanted to talk to you about this Slow Burn thing before we decide to let you guys on the island. The people there are afraid of the virus. I need to find a way to ensure them that you won't be a danger."

Murphy, face strangely absent his smile, answered for both of us. "You don't need to worry about that. Me and Zed, we ain't stayin'. We just came to make sure our friends were okay."

Rachel was not pleased. "I don't know what you think you're thinking, Murphy, but we need to talk about this."

Murphy said, "Me and Zed got some killin' to do."

Chapter 9

While Murphy was getting his ear bent by Rachel, I made my way up to the sun deck on the houseboat's roof. Steph, Gretchen, and Paul all came along.

As I was taking a seat on one of the long vinyl couch cushions, I asked, "Any news from the outside world?"

"Some," Paul answered.

Gretchen and Paul sat on a couch along the starboard side. Gretchen said, "We had a man with a shortwave radio."

I nodded knowingly.

Paul said, "Walter had a place up the lake a bit."

"We talked about disassembling everything and moving it to the island," Gretchen said.

"I wish we had," said Paul. "He had everything set up at his house and had a generator, as well."

Gretchen said, "He'd go there once every three or four days, with a few of our people along for protection. They'd fire up the generator and try to contact anyone they could."

"It's much more complicated than you'd guess," said Paul. "Talking with someone five or ten miles away is easy, depending on your antenna. But talking to someone in—say—Dallas, or Florida, or South America, that's a completely different thing." Paul paused and started to slowly shake his head. "Unfortunately, they got overrun."

"The Whites," I said.

Paul nodded.

"Is the equipment still functional?" I asked.

Gretchen leaned forward. "Do you know how to operate a short wave radio?"

I shook my head. "I was just curious in case we come across another person who does."

"No one has been back there," said Paul. "We don't know what state it's in."

Steph joined the conversation. "Tell him what you told me."

Gretchen made herself comfortable in her seat. They'd managed to contact seven other groups of survivors in Texas alone. That sounded like a lot to me, though when one group turned out to have renovated an old titan missile silo out in West Texas, I wasn't surprised that they'd survived. There could be any number of groups whose doomsday plans actually worked out.

What did surprise me was the mention that some group was in Fort Hood, an hour north—at least back when we had a highway system—reconstituting a military and claiming to be the new seat of Texas government.

One group, thirty-six people, were on what they described as a tall ship, an old three-masted sailing vessel used for training some group that nobody seemed to know. At any rate, they'd set themselves up as some kind of census and data group, trying to assess the state of affairs, trying to figure out how many people had survived, who had what, who needed what, and who might need help. No mention was made of how help might be provided.

The upshot was that although we felt alone in a sea of the infected, we weren't. Others were finding ways to survive.

I asked, "So what's the deal here? Oh, and while I'm thinking about it, Gretchen, why are you in charge? I know why we picked Steph to be our boss, but what's your deal?"

Gretchen giggled a little before answering. "First come, first served."

"What does that mean?" I asked.

Paul said, "We were the first here on the island."

With genuine admiration, I said, "That was quick thinking, coming up with a safe place to ride this out and getting here first."

Paul and Gretchen both laughed, but Gretchen answered, "We were camping on the island when it started."

"Really? Camping in the middle of the summer? With the heat that had to be miserable. I thought sane people only camped in the spring and autumn."

Paul said, "I'm a geologist. I've been working on a speleological study of the Lake Travis area for the Texas Water Development Board all summer."

"A speleological survey?" I asked. "You explore caves for the state? I saw something about a UT advertising professor exploring Texas caves in a Southwest Airlines magazine once."

Paul shook his head. "Well, not exactly. I study the limestone formations and try to survey the underground structures for stability."

That had me curious. "Why here?"

"Do you remember hearing about what happened at Lake Amistad?"

"I'm not even sure where that is."

Steph piped in, "It's a man-made lake down on the Rio Grande, by Del Rio."

"That's right," Paul confirmed. "The limestone structures beneath the lake turned out to be less stable than anyone guessed. A sinkhole formed and pretty much opened a drain valve for the lake."

"You're kidding." I looked at Steph and then at Gretchen. "You're kidding, right?"

"Serious as a virus attack," Paul answered.

"No shit. What happened?" I asked.

"The lake level dropped by ninety feet in a single day."

"Holy crap."

Even unexcitable Steph muttered something to that effect, but put the pieces together faster than I did. "So wait, are you telling me that you're doing that speleological survey because you think that could happen here?"

Paul smiled and shook his head. "Nobody at the state—and I share this opinion—thinks there's any immediate danger of that happening at Lake Travis."

I asked, "Did anybody expect it to happen on Lake Amistad?"

"No." Paul shook his head. "It came as a complete surprise."

"So it could happen here." Steph asked, looking back over at Monk's Island, "And this place suddenly becomes open to attack."

That was a depressing thought. I'd only just arrived. In fact, I hadn't even officially arrived yet.

Paul stood up and paced around a bit. He waved a hand out at the water. "Lake Travis has been here for seventy years. There are one hundred and eighty-eight major reservoirs in Texas, and who knows how many smaller ones. I read one report that there are seventy-five thousand dams in the continental United States."

"That many?" Steph asked.

Paul asked, "And how many have you ever heard of that drained because of a sinkhole?"

Steph answered, "None."

"Exactly. The odds of it happening here are miniscule."

Just because I'm a contrary pain in the ass, I asked, "But how many of those dams were built during the Depression, or in the decades after?"

"I know where you're going with this."

Steph shook her head. "I don't."

"Me neither," said Gretchen.

Paul gestured toward me. "He's wondering if the lakes have aged sufficiently that the problem will start to show up with more frequency."

"Yes," I nodded.

"That is one of the reasons for the survey. More importantly, we want to examine the rock that the dam is built on. Having a sinkhole open up and drain the lake would be bad, considering how many people depend on Lake Travis for their drinking water. To have the dam fail would be catastrophic."

"And that could happen?" Steph asked.

"If the limestone under the dam was structurally unsound, yes. It could happen."

"What did you find?"

Gretchen said, "We're not anywhere near finishing our survey. So, no answers yet."

"Nope." Paul confirmed and sat back down.

"You know," I said, "That sounds like super interesting stuff."

Paul nodded. "But pretty much pointless now, don't you think?"

"What do you mean?" I asked.

"I think there will be little room in the days ahead for geological work. We'll all be farmers, or hunters, or soldiers, I guess."

"Or doctors," Steph added. "And nurses."

"Just the essentials," I agreed. "Getting back to the beginning, so you guys were camping on the island and when people started showing up after the virus hit, they voted you in charge?"

Gretchen shrugged, "It just kind of happened. The first arrivals just deferred to me on decisions."

Paul chuckled, "She's a take-charge type."

I looked at Steph, "Sounds like somebody I know."

Steph punched me in the arm.

"Hey, that's a compliment," I protested.

"Eventually, we voted," said Gretchen. "It seemed like the smart thing to do, having somebody in charge. And I won."

"By a landslide." Paul smiled at Gretchen.

"Congratulations," I said.

With a formal nod, Gretchen said, "Thank you. I owe it all to the little people."

We all laughed.

I asked, "So people just kind of trickled in as things got bad in town?"

Becoming more serious, Gretchen said, "Yes. We got six that first night after the riot at the jail downtown."

I was thinking about my escape from that riot with Murphy when I noticed Paul looked down at his feet and shaking his head. I asked, "What happened?"

Gretchen had a little difficulty with it. "There were six of them, a family with four children. The oldest of the kids was fifteen, the youngest was eight." Gretchen seemed to run out of words at that point.

I looked over at Steph. She was looking at Gretchen. I guessed she hadn't heard the story yet.

Gretchen took a big gulp of air as though that might make the story more palatable. "It was the fifteen-year-old that turned first. It happened late that night." Steph pointed at the silhouette of the old chapel at the top of the hill. "We were all sleeping in the church then. I was keeping guard. The family was exhausted. It seemed like the right thing to do to let them rest. I was outside, keeping an eye out for danger. Paul was inside."

Another long pause. It was Gretchen's and Paul's first one-on-one experience with the infected, and it had scarred them more deeply than subsequent experiences.

Paul stuck his arm out. He had a nasty, bite-shaped scar. "The fifteen-year-old attacked me."

Steph took hold of Paul's arm and examined the nearly healed wound. "You're lucky."

"That I wasn't infected?" Paul nodded. "Yes. I guess I'm immune."

I looked at Gretchen. "And you think you're immune, too."

She nodded. "I have to be, or I'd have caught it by now."

"How so?" I asked.

"Paul had to kill the boy to save his own life," she said.

"The parents got angry," Gretchen said. "They didn't behave rationally."

"I guess that's to be expected," I said. "That early on in the infection, I mean."

Gretchen looked at Paul. "The father had a gun, and he threatened Paul with it. Even though his son was there, with pale skin and blood all over his face from biting Paul. His father—"

"—Jim," said Paul. "His name was Jim."

"I'd forgotten." Gretchen admitted. "Jim was livid. He couldn't accept that his son had turned. Even though he was frightened enough about everything going on to bring his family out to the island, he couldn't accept the reality." Gretchen shrugged. "Maybe none of us could, at first." She pulled her hands together in front of her mouth, almost as though she were going to pray, as she thought about what to say next. "I thought Jim was going to shoot Paul. But I had a gun, too. We always have one when we're out camping—not that we ever needed it before—but just in case, you know."

Steph and I both nodded. Of course.

"I think that's the only reason Jim didn't shoot Paul." Gretchen pointed to another old structure up on the hill. "Jim took his wife and kids and went to the old stable and told us to leave him and his family alone."

"Yelled at us to leave them alone," Paul said.

Gretchen nodded emphatically at that. "He was so angry with us." Then she shook her head. "He made his wife hold their gun and picked up his son and carried the body with them to the stable. I begged them not to go."

"Why?" I asked. "It sounds like the best thing, given what happened."

Shaking his head, Paul said, "The other kids were infected."

"Oh, no," Steph said.

Gretchen said, "One of them appeared to be feverish. The other was lethargic. I tried to tell them, but they wouldn't listen. Jim was crazy over the death of his son by then. He was talking about revenge, and calling the police, and what not. He thought we just wanted to kill his kids." Gretchen stopped talking after that.

After a few moments, I ventured a guess. "And they turned. They turned that night?"

Gretchen nodded. "Paul and I didn't sleep after that. It was nearly sunup when we heard the ruckus from the stable. There was crying and screaming. There were gunshots."

"What happened?" Steph asked.

"The children killed the mother. The father shot the children. I think he was feverish by then. He shot himself."

In a lost voice, Steph said, "Oh, my God."

Shaking his head, Paul said, "Probably not an uncommon story."

We all agreed.

"We burned the bodies." Gretchen said, after we'd had a moment to assimilate the story's conclusion. She looked at Paul, and it was pretty clear that the two were close. "We both thought Paul was going to turn. He made me keep the gun after that. But I didn't want to be here, not in this world, without him. We don't have any kids. We never wanted any. We don't have any family that we're close to. We only have each other."

Tentatively, Steph asked, "If he turned, you were going to shoot him?"

Gretchen nodded.

"And then yourself?" Steph asked.

"Yes." Gretchen took Paul's hand in hers. "We didn't make any attempt after that to keep me from getting infected. I decided that if Paul was going to die, and I was going to die, then I was damn sure going to be affectionate with the love of my life." Gretchen leaned over and kissed Paul on the lips.

Steph smiled, but I could see restrained tears.

"Neither of us turned." Gretchen smiled. "We both got lucky with immunity."

"That's amazing luck."

"Better than winning the lottery." Gretchen said. "After that, we instituted the quarantine system for those coming on the island."

"And that worked?" I asked.

"There were some difficult moments. But people were more understanding about it than you'd think. Everybody knew it was for the safety of all."

"Wow." I shook my head. "Reasonable people."

Gretchen laughed at that. "I wouldn't go that far. But about the quarantine, they were reasonable enough."

"Reasonable enough," Paul agreed.

"Have you had any infected on the island since that first family?" I asked.

"Not a one." Paul answered. "But we were plenty worried before the flood."

I asked, "Because of the lake levels? Did it get that low?"

"Yes." Paul nodded emphatically. He pointed at a spit of land pointing down from the north shore. "This island and that peninsula are actually part of the same ridge. It dips down beneath the water out there but not by much. Before the flood came and refilled the lake, anybody could have waded across and never gotten more than chest deep."

I looked in the direction of the peninsula. The islanders were surviving by little more than luck. Perhaps that was the story for everyone.

Gretchen said, "Because of that, we try to keep hidden out here. We don't build cooking fires outside. We don't walk around outside during the day, at least not where someone onshore can see us."

"Sounds smart."

"We got lucky with some of our choices," said Paul. "They were the right ones and they worked out well. On the other hand, we don't know what we'll do about food in the long run. We can only scavenge along the shore for so long."

Gretchen ignored Paul's change in the subject and pointed at Steph, "And we got lucky with who came to the island. We didn't have anybody with any medical knowledge. But now we have Steph and Amy, two nurses. I don't know all of what we need to survive in the long term, but I have to think that having someone to treat the injured and sick could make all the difference."

"I'm just a nurse," said Steph.

"You're more than that," said Paul. "You're hope."

I liked Steph a lot, but I wasn't sure I'd go that far.

Paul went on. "We used to take for granted that if we got sick, we could just go to a doctor, get a pill, and get better. It wasn't always like that for people. It wasn't that long ago that influenza was a deadly disease. People got sick and died all the time. Minor injuries could lead to infection and death. We never had to think about those things because we had modern medicine. With the world like it is now, all of those seemingly minor medical problems become major again."

"I hadn't thought that much about it," I said.

"I don't know why," said Paul, "but the subject came up a lot when we islanders talked around the campfire at night. It worried everyone. You see, people today—ahem, yesterday —were all specialists. We did jobs and had skills that made us successful in the world we'd built. I studied rocks." Paul laughed. "Not much need for that now. People were financial analysts, computer programmers, insurance adjusters, all totally useless now. But doctors and nurses, those are professional skills that humans took thousands of years to develop, and that we can't afford to lose. They represent one of the major progressive steps away from barbarity and into civilization."

Chapter 10

Knowing that we had the whole next day to talk, Paul and Gretchen went downstairs to claim a bedroom. That left just Steph and me on the sun deck. The boat was silent, and I assumed by then that everyone else was asleep.

I was sitting at the end of a vinyl covered couch, and Steph was sitting on a twin of my couch, but set perpendicular to mine, leaving us close enough together that our knees were nearly touching. She asked, "Was Murphy serious about what he said?"

I raised my eyebrows to ask for clarification.

"About going out to kill Smart Ones? Is that what you plan to do?"

A path that had previously seemed so clear suddenly needed stuttered rationalizations. "We're not safe. We have to. You saw what they did to…to Mandi, to Russell."

Steph leaned forward and put a hand on my knee. "Zed, I hate them too. I really do. We all do. But there's nothing you can do about it. Chasing revenge around Austin until you get killed isn't going to accomplish anything."

"It's not revenge."

"How could it be anything else?" Steph wasn't going to let me by without expressing her disagreement.

"It isn't revenge."

"Then what is it? Are you the Valiant Null Spot? Are you going to save the world?"

I put a hand on Steph's. I put them both there and stared at the white fiberglass deck. I looked at the patterns of black grippy tape and looked for a good way to figure out what I was really feeling, the reason I really wanted to kill the Smart Ones, if not to indulge a desire for revenge. Finally, I said,

"I'll admit, it doesn't make any sense. When I take a clinical step back and examine it, it does seem pointless."

Steph laid her other hand on the pile of hands on my knee. "Then why do it?"

"I...I..." It was hard to deal with the truth of it. "I have a rage. I have this big black hole that I feel like I need to fill. I hate the Whites. I hate the Smart Ones. As irrational as I know it is, I think if I kill enough of them, maybe I'll fill the hole. Maybe I'll feel better at the end."

"You won't." But she said it not as an insult but simply as a matter of fact, as though my assertion was so ridiculous on its face that it needed no thought. It was just wrong.

I sat back in my seat and leaned my head back to look up at the stars. Timidly, I admitted, "I know."

"Then, why?"

"I don't know what else to do."

"Stay here with us. Don't endanger yourself for nothing. Stay here with me."

With me?

"I worry that I'm turning into a monster," I said. "I worry that this need I have to kill isn't pointless revenge. I worry that I want to do it because my brain is changing. I worry that I want to kill because I like it."

Steph sat up and pulled her hands to her own lap. She pulled her legs up onto the couch to sit Indian-style. "Is this about what happened with Nico?"

I shook my head. "I don't know. I think Nico was...He was just one in a long line. I've killed so many."

"But they were all infected. They were all dangerous."

I shook my head. "No. I don't think they were all dangerous." I told her about the thin, bald kid in the Children's Hospital, the one that looked at me and didn't resist when I hacked him down with my machete. I wondered if he had been as innocuous as Russell. I told her about the girl who was sitting on the rock outside the front gate at Sarah Mansfield's house. I'd heard her screams after the Whites chased her into the trees, and I knew she'd been a Slow Burn, just like me. I'd murdered her because I was too impatient, too stupidly certain about what I thought she was to figure out a way to discover the truth. "How many others have I murdered, Steph?"

"You can't think about it that way."

"And the worst part about it all," I said, ignoring her comment, "is that sometimes the only time I feel better is when I'm killing more of them. How fucked up is that?"

"Most of them, nearly all of them, are monsters, Zed. They'll kill us if they have the chance. You have to remember that. You're doing things that are hard because you want to keep the people that you love safe."

"Love?"

"Okay, like. Whatever."

I looked across the bow of the boat and saw Monk's Island, alone on the smooth black water. Softly, I said, "Love is fine. I'm tired of losing my friends. It hurts too much."

Steph rearranged herself in her seat, leaned forward, and put her hands back on my legs. "It does hurt. But we can't give up. We still have to try to be human. If we can't do that, what's the point of it all?"

"Exactly." I shrugged. "What's the point?"

Steph stood up, leaned over me, took my face in her hands, and kissed me on the lips. She sat back down, not taking her eyes off of mine. "Don't go. Stay."

I'd both been wanting and dreading that first kiss for weeks, but the rush of feelings didn't sit right with me. I deflected with humor. "Are you trying to manipulate me with your womanly wiles?"

Steph smiled and a few tears rolled down her cheeks. Shaking her head, she said, "Yes. Maybe I am trying to manipulate you, but please, please tell me you know there's more to it than that."

She was so beautiful in her severe, redheaded Steph sort of way. With that kiss she'd opened the door on the complex mess of emotions that had been troubling both of us. I said, "I think that kiss is the best thing that's happened to me... fuck it. Let's just say it's the best thing that's ever happened to me."

Silent tears followed one another down Steph's cheeks. "But?"

"I have to be honest with you about something."

Steph shook her head and laughed through her tears. "You're gay."

That was so unexpected, I couldn't help but laugh. "You can be funny."

"See, I told you." She wiped her cheek with her sleeve.

"No. I'm not gay."

"What then? Spit it out. I'm a big girl. Are you going to call HR and file a sexual harassment complaint?"

I favored her with a smile, but we were both past the jokes. "When Murphy and I went to get the suppressors, we were on the hospital grounds for a little while."

"And?"

There was no good way to say it. "Jeff Aubrey is still alive. Or he was, anyway."

Steph just looked at me for a long time after that.

I waited patiently, silently.

Finally, she asked, "Why didn't you bring him back?"

I shook my head. "I thought about it. I wanted to. Kind of."

"Kind of? So he wasn't one of them, was he? If he was, you wouldn't have had to think about it."

"No, I don't know what he was." It was my turn to lean forward and take Steph's hands in mine. "He wasn't like me and Murphy."

"What then?"

"I don't know. He wasn't right. He had a hard time with single syllables. I don't think he understood what Murphy and I were saying most of the time."

Steph was crying again.

"Steph, I don't know if he was dangerous or not. He didn't attack us, but Murphy and I are both Whites."

"Zed Zane, I hate this fucking world."

"I know."

Through her tears, Steph said, "It never stops hurting."

"I know."

Somewhere in the dark, we ran out of words and fell asleep on separate couches, with only our thoughts to hold us close.

Chapter 11

When I woke, my wrists were being bound behind my back. "Hey!"

Steph was cursing and struggling.

I rolled off of my couch and hit the deck while kicking out at a dozen legs that danced sideways to avoid my boots. Then they kicked back. A kick hit my thigh. Another hit me in the stomach and a third bruised my ribs before the bravest of my assailants dropped onto my chest and put a cold revolver barrel against my face. "Don't move, you white piece of shit."

I stopped struggling.

Steph shouted, "You assholes."

A man shouted, "Quiet!"

Everything on the top deck stopped.

Seething with fury, I looked up the barrel of the gun that was pressed into my cheek beside my nose. I memorized the face of the dark haired, mustached man who was using the weapon to hold me still.

"Don't move," he warned me.

Not yet. But one day.

The voice in charge said, "Take her down."

Steph struggled. Feet moved. In my peripheral vision I saw her being manhandled toward the stairs.

"Get him up," the voice ordered.

The man with the gun leaned close. "If it was up to me, you'd be dead already."

Interesting that he and I were both thinking the same thing.

He got off of my chest. I was rolled over and dragged to my feet. There were four of them up there with me, two handling me, the guy who'd been on my chest, and the last—who I guessed was in charge—a dumpy, older man with white hair and glasses with thick, black frames.

At the spiral stairs that led down to the main deck, one of my keepers led the way. The other held my bound wrists behind me. As we rounded the descent into the houseboat's main salon, Steph was being seated on a couch beside Dalhover. Rachel and Paul were on the same couch. Gretchen was in a chair at the end of the couch. Murphy was standing with his back to the wall at one end of the rectangular room with his hands bound behind him—apparently Whites like me and Murphy needed to be tied up. A man with a pistol stood a pace in front of Murphy, keeping the weapon pointed at Murphy's chest. I was urged to move in that direction.

Eight men and one woman all had weapons—several handguns, a couple of shotguns, some rifles, and mine and Murphy's M4s. The two guys that we'd rescued with Rachel were among them. That pissed me all the way off and then some, but rather than indulge the anger, I caught Murphy's eye. We were on the same page: escape.

The older guy who'd been giving orders up on the roof went to stand next to another dumpy, white-haired man that looked just like him, but with different glasses.

Gretchen was the first to speak. To her credit, she didn't sound angry. "What are you doing, Jay?"

Jay—apparently the twin with the different glasses—began to speak. "This has all got to stop, Gretchen." Jay's tone wasn't bellicose, not angry. He was just a nice old man talking to the grandkids.

With anger starting to show on her face, but calm still in her voice, Gretchen said, "We all talked. We all agreed. But you weren't happy with the majority decision, and now you're going to get your way by force, is that it?"

Jay stepped to the center of the room and looked down at Gretchen. "You think that because you pushed everyone to agree with you, they all did."

"They agreed with me."

Shaking his head, Jay said, "You bullied them."

"That's not true," Paul disagreed, loudly.

In the same loud tone, Jay's twin told Paul, "You don't see it, Paul, because you've been pussy-whipped your whole life."

Jay turned to his twin and raised a hand to calm him. "Jerry."

Jerry made a show of glaring once more at Paul before he looked back at Jay. And that was the pecking order. Jay was in charge. Jerry was the lackey.

"I don't do that," said Gretchen.

Jay dismissed Gretchen's argument with a wave of his gun. "We voted again after you came out here to camp with your new friends. And now you're out."

Gretchen shook her head. She was disgusted.

"Just like last time," Paul shouted. "Everybody knows that you just want to be in charge." Paul looked around the room for support. "That's all this is. Little Jay Booth trying to feel important."

Not one of Jay's armed men gave any hint that they'd heard Paul speak.

Not good.

Slowly, so as not to attract any attention, I wiggled my wrists and turned my arms to see if there was any way I might get my hands free. The guy next to me had a pump action shotgun. All I needed to do was get that in my hands.

On the coffee table in front of the couch lay my Hello Kitty bag next to Murphy's bag. If we could get a grenade or two out, we could make our escape, just as we'd gotten out of that dorm when dipshit-crazy Mark was threatening us. Only this time we wouldn't leave anyone behind with the whack jobs.

It felt like some kind of wire wrapped around my wrists. It was tight, but had been tied in a hurry. I felt it give ever so slightly as I twisted my wrists.

Looking at Paul, Jay asked, "Finished?"

Rachel sat forward and calmly said, "Jay, let's—"

"Not a word from you," Jay snapped.

Rachel froze and I thought Murphy was going to explode with anger and kill him, wrists bound or not.

"You're just Gretchen's silky-tongued lawyer mouthpiece." Jay pointed his pistol at Rachel's forehead. "Just say something else."

Murphy started to lean away from the wall. Jay turned to him. Back in the kindly grandpa voice, he said, "Go ahead."

Murphy was ready to kill, but chose wisely to do nothing.

Gretchen pulled Jay's attention back to herself. "What exactly is happening here? Why all the guns? What are you going to do with us?"

"You ask that like you expect me to say I'm going to kill you. You've watched too many movies. You need to go, that's all. You need to take your white monster friends and go away. They aren't coming to our island and you're not staying."

"Fine. Paul and I don't want to stay." Gretchen looked around at Murphy and then at me. "If you're just going to banish us then why are Murphy and Zed tied up?"

It was kindly Jay who spoke. "They're monsters."

"We shouldn't let any of them go." Jerry was agitated. "We should kill them all right now."

That sent a ripple through the room and it became apparent that most of them didn't mind participating in the coup. But they weren't up for murder, at least not the murder of Gretchen and Paul.

Jay read it all. He was smart enough to see exactly what I was seeing. He and Jerry both wanted me and Murphy dead, at least, but he didn't have the political support to have all of us killed. He said, "We'll put them in a boat and drop them off on the shore."

"Just drop us off?" Gretchen spat.

"Yes," Jay answered.

"Where?"

"Wherever you like."

"When?"

"Right now," said Jay.

"In the middle of the night?" asked Gretchen.

"Right now."

"Can we get our things from the island?" she asked.

"No," Jay told her. "Those things belong to the community now."

Gretchen shook her head. "And what can we take with us?"

"Nothing."

I looked at Murphy. He was still angry but keeping it to himself. I was still having no luck with the wires on my wrists.

"You're going to put us ashore with nothing," said Gretchen, "but you're not killing us?"

"What a load of shit." Paul didn't care about the risks of showing his derision.

"If you don't like it, you can leave anytime you want," said Jay.

"Leave?" Paul asked.

"Jump off the boat and swim to wherever you like." Jay smiled insincerely.

Jerry laughed out loud. He, and no one else, found Jay's little joke funny.

Paul glared at Jay, revealing all the hate he was feeling.

Freitag opened a side door and stepped in, a gun in her hand.

Fucking bitch.

I hadn't even realized she was missing from the group of prisoners.

"Let's not lollygag anymore." Jay turned to Freitag. "Is the boat ready?"

"Yes, sir," she answered.

Chapter 12

A thirty-foot cabin cruiser was tied alongside the houseboat. One of the men and the tough-faced woman from inside were already on the cruiser's deck, holding weapons at the ready. Jerry, with my machete in his hand, joined them. The rest of us were motioned to get aboard. Paul led the way, followed by Rachel, Murphy, and Dalhover. Accepting the situation as just another reset, with wrists still bound, I climbed onto the deck of the cruiser.

"You first." Gretchen motioned to Steph, then turned to Jay and asked, "What about Amy and Megan? Are you evicting them with us, or are you going to throw them ashore somewhere else where they can get killed?"

Jerry started to laugh again. Something wasn't right in that guy's head. I wanted to cross the four or five steps between us and shoulder him over the side. But that would probably get me shot by one of Jay's assholes, not to mention losing my machete on the bottom of the lake.

"Amy and Megan are staying with us," Jay told Gretchen. "Now get in the boat."

A bearded man with a big gut and a sleeveless t-shirt pushed the barrel of his shotgun into Gretchen's back. "Move, Queen Gretch."

Gretchen shot him a dirty look and stepped over the gunwale to get into the cabin cruiser. "Let's go, Steph."

Steph turned on Jay. "You're telling me that they decided to stay with you. Do they even know what you're doing here?" It was clear that Steph didn't believe Jay.

"Ask her yourself," Jay answered.

The man with the beard pushed Gretchen and she tumbled into the boat, falling at my feet.

"Asshole." I stepped toward the bearded dude.

He pointed the shotgun at my chest. "Uh-huh." He smiled. "It's a gun."

I wanted so badly to kick in his perfectly white, good dental plan teeth.

"What do you mean, 'ask her myself'?" Steph wasn't moving. She got up in Jay's face. "What's that supposed to mean?"

Jay nodded and a couple of his men took hold of Steph's arms. "You're staying with us, honey."

"Fuck you!" I shouted.

Something, a gun butt maybe, pounded me on the head, and I collapsed to the deck, seeing nothing but stars. Gretchen was on her feet and raising her voice angrily at Jay. "What do you mean she's staying? Jay, what the hell is wrong with you?"

"Amy and Steph are nurses." Jay wasn't the least bit ruffled by Gretchen's yelling. "They're the first two medically trained people we've come across. We need a doctor, but short of that, a couple of nurses will do."

"If you think I'm going to treat you when you get hurt, you're crazy." Steph left no doubt that she was serious. "I'm not about to help a bunch of kidnappers."

Jay shrugged and looked at her with sad, kind eyes. "It doesn't matter. I'm the guilty one here. I don't expect you to care for me when I'm sick. But those other folks on the island, they're good people. They don't have any guilt in this. You'll help them. That's all that matters."

Jerry giggled away, like this was just the funniest thing he'd seen in years.

I tried to get up to my knees, but the barrel of a gun kept me down.

"You cannot be serious about this." Gretchen's voice was back to a diplomatic level. "These people are together. You're just going to tear them apart to further your own goals?"

"You know the people on the island as well as I do, Gretchen," Jay said. "You know they could use a nurse to treat them when they are injured or sick. Do you think sending Steph out into the world with these yahoos is going to be best for her or us? She'll just get killed. We're going to value her, give her a safe place."

"You're a lunatic." Steph told him.

"Maybe," Jay answered. "But that's irrelevant. Take her back inside."

The two men holding Steph pulled. She struggled, but couldn't break away. She cursed at Jay, her captors, and everybody else. I was seething with anger and thirsting for revenge even before the door shut. But revenge would come later. First, I needed to be free.

Chapter 13

We prisoners were crammed in below decks on the cabin cruiser. A padded bench wrapped around inside the bow, and it was clearly designed to convert to a bed. The space was cozy for a couple looking for romance out on a weekend cruise. For us, it was tight.

On the fourth highest of five steps leading down from the outside deck, Freitag stood with a rifle in her hand pointed tensely at where we were seated on the benches. Jerry and two others were up on deck. A few small lights illuminated the darkness in the back of the boat, and I saw Jerry standing in the stern. One of the three was just outside the open door and one was at the helm.

What were they going to do with us, I wondered. Were they really just going to free us? Run along now. Shoo. Don't come back. It didn't make sense. If they planned to let us go, really, why not just give us a boat and tell us to hit the road? There were plenty of boats moored around the island. They wouldn't miss one.

If they feared that giving us a boat would only give us a way to return to extract revenge for their kidnapping of Steph and Amy, then how would they keep us from finding one of the thousands of boats tied off around the lake and doing just that?

The look in Jerry's crazy eyes told me all I needed to know about what he wanted to do. He wanted to kill me and everybody else with me. Jay couldn't do that with everyone looking on. But he could pretend to let us go, only to have us killed somewhere out of sight by his most loyal of thugs.

That did make sense.

The cabin cruiser bounced over a wave, and Freitag, in adjusting her balance, stepped down to the third step up from the bottom. I glared at her, telling myself for the hundredth time that I should have killed her when I had the chance. There was no depth to which she wouldn't sink.

For no apparent reason, Freitag slowly stepped down one more step closer to us.

From the back of the boat, Jerry leaned over for a better angle into the cabin and called, "You all right there?"

"Yes, sir." Freitag called back without turning.

Jerry stepped out of view toward the back corner of the boat.

Freitag glanced back over her shoulder and quickly moved down to the last step.

Being that close, she wasn't far from where I sat on the end of one of the padded benches. I thought through a scenario to free us. I could wait until we hit the next big wave. Like all of us sitters did each time we hit a wave, I'd bounce up a bit. My motion would be natural, expected. But instead of being a victim of gravity and momentum, I'd use it to my advantage. I'd push with my legs and jump toward Freitag. She was five feet from me, and by the time she realized I was coming at her, she wouldn't have time to react.

I could plow into her stomach, shoulder first—my only available weapon—and knock the breath out of her. One of the others could take her gun. One of them could free me and Murphy. But that's where the plan fell apart. Jerry and his thugs would hear the struggle below. Then we'd be trapped below deck with one weapon, trying to get our hands untied when three guns fired on us.

I looked at my companions. How many of us would die when that happened?

Did it really matter how many of us died? The question was how many would live? If we did nothing, we'd all be doomed. I looked around at my fellow prisoners, wondering which of them had also figured that out.

Freitag glanced nervously over her shoulder. She was the only one of our captors that we could see.

I waited. I focused on the rhythm of the waves. I turned to Murphy and caught his eye.

He was up near the bow, furthest from the door, furthest from Freitag. I motioned toward Freitag with my eyes.

With a barely perceptible motion, he nodded. He understood. More importantly, he agreed. He was smart, and he was intuitive. He knew what fate awaited us.

Turning back, I noticed that Dalhover was staring at me. He'd caught the exchange between Murphy and me. He shot me a bare nod. He was on board, and his hands weren't bound. We had a chance.

Without any urgency, I turned slowly back to Freitag and fell into the rhythm of the waves.

There would be no mercy this time. Not for her. Not for any of them.

I felt a pattern in the waves. It seemed like one out of every eight or ten we hit was larger than the others and would bounce us all a little higher off of our seats. As we came over one of the big ones, I started counting the small ones. I was going to make my move on the next big wave.

Freitag's expressionless doll face made a change.

I counted through two waves.

She was troubled. Her forehead wrinkled, and her eyes seemed sad.

Another wave.

Another.

Her left hand let go of her rifle's barrel. My excitement ticked up a dozen notches, but I tried not to let it show.

We bounced over another wave.

Almost there.

Freitag's hand slid into her pocket.

It was going to be easy, at least the Freitag part. Just a few more waves.

The hand came back out of the pocket with a lock-blade knife.

Before I formed a guess as to what she planned with the knife, she caught Dalhover's eye and tossed it to him. She turned to me and said, "Don't kill them."

I was dumbfounded.

Dalhover opened the knife and bounced behind Murphy to cut his bonds.

Freitag looked up over her shoulder. Just loud enough for us to hear, she said, "The boat will come to a stop soon. Hurry."

I turned in my seat so that Dalhover would have easy access to the wires binding my wrists. As soon as my hands were free, I was up on my feet. I stepped quickly over and put myself against the wall beside Freitag. Dalhover jumped to the spot on the other side. We weren't visible from outside the cabin.

"What is this?" I asked.

She simply said, "Now we're even, okay?"

"Even?"

"Yes," she said. "So fuck you, too."

The boat's motor quieted as the helmsman throttled down.

I said, "Thank you."

Bobby Adair

Dalhover handed the knife to me and said to Freitag, "Give me the gun."

Chapter 14

Murphy was beside me before I knew he had moved.

Dalhover had the rifle in his hands and was ready to spring. Freitag held her position with her back to the stairs.

The engine noise had decreased to a low rumble, and the boat slowed to a drift.

From above, I heard the sound of Jerry's laugh. I smiled. He was about to be surprised.

"Send 'em up," Jerry called.

Freitag remained frozen, pretending not to hear.

"Send 'em up." More loudly.

Still, Freitag did not move.

Footsteps sounded on the stairs above. "Can't you hear me?"

Dalhover swung around in front of Freitag, using her for a shield as he held the rifle over her shoulder, pointed up the stairs. His shout at Jerry to freeze was so loud that Jerry would have been startled into inaction, even had he not seen the rifle.

I peeked around the corner. Jerry was indeed frozen, with surprise in his eyes and his mouth hanging open. He had a pistol in his hand, pointed down at the stairs. My machete hung from his other hand.

"If you move even the slightest bit, you're dead. You understand me?" Dalhover's voice was frighteningly harsh. "If you think there's any chance that I can miss blowing your head off from this range, you're a fool. You got me, Jerry?"

No one spoke, but feet were shuffling on the deck.

I squirmed around the corner, holding the handrail with one hand, leaning far forward and keeping well out of

Dalhover's line of fire. I reached out to Jerry and laid a hand on his gun.

"Let him have the gun." Dalhover ordered. "Tell your people if I hear them move again, I'm shooting. Do it."

In a wavering, weak voice, Jerry called, "Don't move."

I pushed the pistol into Murphy's hand. "You know I can't hit anything."

Murphy grinned and took the weapon.

I reached back up and took my machete. Rearranging ourselves, Murphy aimed the pistol up the stairway.

Dalhover moved so that Freitag could come all the way into the cabin. "You come down here, Jerry."

I couldn't see the stairway, but I heard no movement.

"You can walk down here or fall down."

"You don't need to do this," Jerry pleaded.

"Now."

A stair creaked. Another creaked.

Dalhover backed into the cabin.

Murphy scooted back a bit, and Jerry stepped onto the floor. Murphy grabbed the back of his neck and drove his face to the floor, placing the pistol against the back of his head.

Dalhover called up. "You two. Lay your weapons on the stairs where I can see them."

"No," a man's voice called back down. "I'll shoot your ass."

Murphy used the barrel of the gun to persuade Jerry to make a guess on what to do next.

Jerry guessed right. He called, "Do what he says, Gerald. Just do it."

"Do it, Gerald." Dalhover called.

Muffled voices conversed above, but I couldn't make out what was being said.

Murphy harshly nudged Jerry with the pistol barrel again.

"Do it now!" Jerry ordered.

"Good man," Murphy said to him.

I heard the sound of metal being laid on the deck. It was one of the guns. Another followed.

"You two," Dalhover called, "go to the stern. Face away from me. Put your hands on the gunwale."

Murphy kneed Jerry in the ribs.

Jerry called, "Go to the stern."

Feet moved on the deck.

"Don't move." Dalhover started up the stairs.

Murphy looked at me, passing responsibility for Jerry.

As he got up to follow Dalhover, I dropped a knee between Jerry's shoulder blades and laid the machete blade across the back of his neck.

"Don't hurt me," Jerry pleaded.

Five minutes later, we were all on the deck. I looked around at the lake to get my bearings. We were nearly a mile from either shore, far up the lake from Monk's Island, and around several bends. No one still on the island had any chance of seeing or hearing what had been planned for us.

Hefting my machete, I looked at Jerry, Gerald, and the girl kneeling in the stern as they leaned over the gunwale.

Freitag must have seen the way I was looking at the three, because she guessed my thoughts. "You promised not to kill them."

Implicitly, maybe. I looked at the three. Crap. "Sure. But they were going to kill us."

"No, they weren't," Paul assured me.

I pointed my machete at the water around the boat. "Don't you wonder why we were stopping in the middle of the lake?"

Paul looked around. His face went slack.

Gretchen asked, "Was that the plan, Jerry? Were you going to kill us?"

"Of course not."

"Why were we stopping in the middle of the lake?"

Jerry turned to look up at Gretchen.

"Stay on your knees," said Dalhover.

From an uncomfortably twisted position, Jerry asked, "How could you even think that?"

Gretchen repeated her question.

Gerald snapped, "We were looking for a marina."

"A marina," Jerry confirmed.

Gretchen looked around.

"Man," Murphy said, "they're lyin'."

Freitag said, "We can't kill them. Let's put them ashore somewhere."

"Or let 'em swim." Murphy was shaking his head and pointing at the water. "That's what they were gonna do to us. If they didn't shoot us first."

"As much as I want to kill them, we can't." Dalhover made it clear that debate on the matter was closed.

"I agree," Gretchen said.

Murphy shook his head. Mostly to himself, he muttered, "That's a mistake."

"Shit." With the bulk of his heavy body already on the gunwale, Jerry pushed with his legs and slithered into the dark lake.

"Dammit." Dalhover glared at Murphy.

Murphy said, "I wasn't gonna shoot him, Top."

Gerald decided that distraction was enough to try to save himself. He rolled over, swept his leg across Dalhover's ankles and knocked him off his feet.

Rachel shouted, and Paul stepped back.

Gerald was on Dalhover in a flash, trying to wrestle the rifle out of Dalhover's hands. Murphy jumped into the fight.

Gretchen shouted, "No!"

Another splash.

The girl was over the side.

While moving over to get my hands on the barrel of the rifle at the center of the wrestling match I said, "Let 'em swim."

Murphy hauled back and punched Gerald in the back of the head.

I got my hands on the end of the barrel, and though I didn't have control of it, I was able to keep it pointed into the deck as the three struggled.

It only took another few moments.

Bleeding from his mouth and nose and drawing his breath in deep gasps, Gerald fell back against the stern, while Dalhover stood up, rifle in hand.

Murphy stood up, ready to punch Gerald again.

"Gerald, you didn't need to do that," Gretchen said to him.

Gerald glared back.

"Oh, my God," Rachel shouted, "Where's Jerry?"

I looked out at the water. I only saw one swimmer.

"He can't swim," Paul said.

Another one?

"Where is he?" Gretchen turned around and looked toward the bow.

I looked around. All of us did, except for Murphy. His job was to keep Gerald in place, and by the look on Murphy's face, Gerald had better not try anything else.

"Oh, Jesus fucking Christ." I'd seen enough James Bond movies to know that Jerry was hiding under the boat or something like that. "Turn off the engine."

Paul was closest to the helm and did as asked.

"What are you thinking?" Gretchen asked.

I pointed at the water along the boat's hull. "I'll bet he's hiding underneath and coming up for breaths."

"That's stupid," Dalhover told me.

I asked, "Where is he, then?"

"Bottom of the lake." Dalhover wiped some blood away from his mouth and looked down at Gerald in a way that should have given the man cause to worry.

Gretchen looked up and down the length of the boat. "Let's check. Paul, you and Rachel go and look over each side of the bow." She stepped over to the port side. "I'll take this side. Zed, you take that side. Dalhover, will you look over the stern?"

Shaking his head, Dalhover leaned over the back of the boat.

Murphy leaned close to Gerald. "It won't bother me to shoot you if you decide to get froggy."

"Froggy?" Gerald was confused.

"If you jump," Murphy explained.

Not even knowing why, I told Gerald, "Murphy is a comedian."

"Nothing back here," Dalhover announced.

Rachel said, "Nothing here."

"Clear," said Paul.

"We'll keep looking for a few minutes. "I doubt Jerry can hold his breath for long."

Gerald said, "He's not under the boat."

"And how do you know that?" Gretchen asked.

"Because that dude's crazy."

"Yet, you sided with him."

Gerald looked at Murphy with plenty of hate in his eyes. "You were going to let these fucks on the island."

"Don't you understand that you're immune?" Gretchen asked him.

"Nobody knows that for sure," Gerald argued. "We might all still get it, and you would have turned us all into monsters."

Murphy shot me a look. "Told you, Zed."

I huffed and flatly said, "Yeah, you told me. Everybody hates us."

Dalhover glanced at me and almost smiled. "If you whiners don't be quiet about that shit, I'm going to hate you, too."

Damn, even he had a sense of humor.

From the front of the boat, Paul mused, "Ignorance. Nothing ever changes."

Gretchen asked, "Does anybody see anything yet?"

Nobody did.

"We'll give it another few minutes, just to be sure." She was sad about that.

I wasn't. It saved me the trouble of killing crazy-ass Jerry and dealing with the guilt I'd feel about it later.

"If you're going to kill me," Gerald spat, "just do it."

Gretchen wasn't impressed with Gerald's machismo. "You watch too many movies. Nobody wants to kill anybody."

I said, "Hey, that chick out there looks like maybe she's getting into trouble."

Dalhover looked. "Dammit."

From her side of the boat, Gretchen announced, "Jerry's not here. Paul, will you come back here and drive the boat? We need to go get Melissa before she drowns."

Paul hurried back. Rachel followed and went down into the cabin.

"Looks like crazy Jerry drowned himself." I looked at the others for consensus on that.

Gretchen shook her head. "I was hoping we could trade him for Steph."

Shit. She was right. We could have. I looked back at the water, hoping to see Jerry coming up for air.

The cabin cruiser's engine started and Paul steered it toward Melissa. Rachel came out of the cabin with a couple of life preservers. She tossed one in Gerald's lap and moved to stand beside him. Paul was guiding the boat so that when we came up beside Melissa, she'd be on our side.

I asked, "Gretchen, we can trade these two for Steph, right?"

She shook her head. "I doubt it."

"Jay will go nuts when he finds out about Jerry," Paul said. "He'll want revenge."

"Are Steph and Amy in danger?"

"Hurting them won't make any sense." Gretchen sat down in a seat by Paul. She reached out and took his hand in hers. "Jay is crazy, but he's smart. The whole reason he kept Steph and Amy is because they're nurses. They're valuable."

I asked, "What about Megan?"

"He won't hurt a child."

I couldn't tell if Gretchen was certain or whether she was hoping.

Paul slowed the boat.

Rachel tossed the life preserver to Melissa. "Grab it."

Melissa did, looking up at me with fear in her eyes.

I shook my head. That was disappointing.

Paul asked, "What do we do with them?"

Gretchen's mind was somewhere else by then. Maybe she was thinking about our chances of starting over somewhere safe. Maybe she was thinking about what might happen to Steph and Amy when Jay found out about Jerry.

Rachel said, "They both have a life preserver. They can swim back from here."

Wow. She had a pragmatic edge, just like Murphy.

She saw me looking at her and smiled. "They won't drown."

I said, "I think we should take them back and try to trade them for Steph and Amy."

"No," Gretchen answered. "That really won't work. Honestly Zed, once Jay hears that Jerry is dead, he'll stop being rational. He'll want to kill us all. He won't have any interest in negotiating."

"Well, I'm not leaving her there." I looked at each of them and let them see my defiance.

"Nobody says you have to," Paul said. "Going there now won't do anybody any good. That's all we're saying. But nobody's your boss; you can do what you like."

Gretchen stood up. "We shouldn't go back." She pointed at Melissa. "Get her in the boat. We'll skirt the shore until we see a canoe or something with none of the infected around. We'll drop them off, and they can find their own way back."

Rachel put herself in charge of getting Melissa into the boat.

Chapter 15

We found a kayak in a boathouse filled with somebody's water toys on the north shore an hour after the sun came up. In that kayak, Melissa and Gerald were paddling away in the distance, and our cabin cruiser was drifting maybe a hundred feet from shore.

With one problem solved to nobody's satisfaction, I announced, "I don't know what any of you guys have in mind, but I'm going to go get Steph, and Amy and Megan if they want to come along. I don't know how I'm going to do it, but I'm going to do it."

Murphy looked at Rachel and then back at me. "I'm with Zed."

"Me, too." Dalhover didn't look up. He was watching the pair paddle away.

All eyes fell to Rachel, who was looking at Murphy. "I'm not losing you again, Murphy. I'm sticking with you."

"I guess that leaves us," Gretchen said.

"You two aren't locked in with us if you don't want to be," I said, "You had it pretty good on your island, I guess, before we came along. I don't want to cause you any further trouble."

Gretchen looked at Paul. Paul looked at each of us, but settled on Rachel. "I trust Rachel's judgment. Rachel trusts Murphy." Paul nodded to me. "Murphy trusts you, and you trust Dalhover. It's the transitive property of trust."

Murphy laughed. "Oh, God, not another professor.

Paul looked a little hurt.

"Don't mind him," I said. "He doesn't like big words."

Rachel laughed.

"Hey." Murphy feigned offense.

Gretchen, choosing to be the adult, said, "It'll be better for us all if we stick together, if we can all work together."

"Another female boss," Murphy concluded.

Gretchen laughed and looked at Rachel. "Is he always this way?"

Rachel nodded.

"I don't want to be anybody's boss."

Murphy reached over and gave Gretchen a friendly punch on the arm. "I'm just joshin' ya. You seem a lot like Steph, a natural in-charge type. I'm good with it."

"I don't care who's in charge or anything like that," I announced. "We can do anything you guys want. I don't care. I only want a couple of things. I want to get Steph, and I want to find a safe place to go and get away from all this shit."

Rachel pointed at Gretchen. "She does a good job at keeping everybody organized and keeping everything running smoothly."

Paul said, "I'm biased. She's been my boss for twenty-seven years. I don't want to be retrained."

"Fine." Gretchen looked around at us. "Zed, we'll find a way to get the girls back."

"I have a way," I said. Whether it was macho bluster on my part or matter-of-fact confidence, I continued. "You guys can drop me off near the island after dark. I'll swim over there with my machete, take care of anybody who disagrees with me, steal a boat, and leave with Steph, Amy, and Megan."

Murphy looked at Gretchen, "I'm not saying he can't do it. He finds ways to make shit work out for him, but I think he watched too many action movies in his formative years."

Rachel laughed at that.

"Zed," Gretchen said, "Let's work together on this, okay? We'll help you get the girls. There's no urgency though. If you go tonight, Jay will be expecting you. Let's wait, they're in no danger. Remember, Jay values them. Let's take care of priorities first. Let's get a relatively safe place to stay. Let's get some food. And when the time is right, we'll go get the girls. Okay?"

I hated being patient, but Gretchen was right. "You're the boss."

Chapter 16

Those among us who'd spent any time with Jay Booth were certain of one thing: he'd blame us for the death of his brother, Jerry, no matter how honest Gerald and Melissa were when they related the story of his brother's demise. It was also taken as a certainty that Jay would want revenge. With few weapons with which to defend ourselves, we fled, depending on Lake Travis's two hundred and seventy miles of shoreline, wrapped in countless curves and coves, to give us plenty of places to hide.

Gerald and Melissa would spend the better part of their day paddling a kayak back to Monk's Island. Once they arrived, Jay wouldn't waste any time getting into the islanders' fastest ski boat with his most loyal henchmen, bringing revenge in our direction. With that in mind, the cabin cruiser's big engine rumbled under the deck and we split the water, racing up the winding length of the lake.

I was sitting in the back of the boat, eyes closed, the wind buffeting me while I seethed. I hated Jay for what he'd done to us the night before. It irked me to think about what he might be doing to Steph. I hated running away.

Murphy sat in the back of the boat with me. Unfortunately, so did Freitag. Dalhover was rummaging around in the cabin, seeing what he could find. The others were gathered at the helm, making a plan. I was making my own plans, thinking about the best time and the best way to get back on the island, perhaps administer a little rough justice to Jay and his buddies, and rescue Steph.

Murphy, never content with quiet time, said to Freitag, "Don't get me wrong on this. I'm thankful and all for what you did. I just don't get it. Why'd you help us? I thought you hated Zed."

Curious about the answer, I listened, but Freitag said nothing.

Murphy asked again, "Man, you might as well spill the beans."

That was apparently all the prodding Freitag needed. In her delicate, vulnerable voice—a guise, I was sure—she asked, "Am I in danger now? Did I make a mistake?"

I said, "Don't buy it, Murphy."

"Buy what?" he asked.

"She's playing her helpless act on you," I answered. "She's a lot tougher than you or me."

Murphy looked at Freitag. "So, you're tough?"

"No," she answered.

"Yes, she is," I said.

Freitag turned angry dark eyes at me. She was regretting her choice to help us.

"Look," I said, "I'm not being mean. You don't need to play the woe-is-me game. I think you have a talent for manipulating—"

"You are a pig." Freitag turned in her seat so that she could look out behind the boat. "I should have let them kill you."

"Listen." I waited for Freitag to look back at me.

She didn't want to.

I tried to take any sense of confrontation out of my tone. "Please turn around. Let's talk."

Without saying a word, Freitag turned, making it seem as if she'd been tortured into compliance.

I said, "Thank you for helping us. Thank you for helping me."

Freitag nodded, but just barely.

Continuing, I said, "I don't mean to insult you. I really don't. I think you're really good at hiding behind a vulnerable façade, but—"

Freitag frowned and started to turn back away.

I reached over and put a hand on her arm.

She looked down at it as though I was diseased.

I guess I was. I pulled my hand back. "You don't need to play games with people to get your way. You don't need to pretend you're something you're not. All I was saying is that you're a lot tougher and smarter than you give yourself credit for."

"So you're going to say nice things, so you won't feel guilty because I just saved your life."

"No," I shook my head. "That's not it at all. I still think you're mean, ruthless, and vindictive, but that doesn't mean I can't see your positive characteristics, as well."

Murphy laughed loudly.

Freitag spat, "And you're a reckless, egotistical cockroach."

Murphy laughed again, "Zed the cockroach. This is some funny shit."

"A cockroach?" I was offended.

"Because no matter what anybody does," she said, "you just crawl out of the rubble like nothing happened."

I thought about it for a minute. "So that's a compliment?"

"If it makes you feel good to be called a cockroach, then yes."

"Jesus," I said. "If you hate me so much, why'd you help us?"

Letting go of her control, Freitag raised her voice, "You may think you're some high and mighty good person, running around and trying to be the hero all the time, but you don't see that other people are good, too."

Murphy laughed some more.

I nodded. "Okay. So you're a good person. Is that what you're saying?"

"I just saved your life." Freitag sneered so expressively that I thought she might lean over and bite me. "You hate me and that's fine. But you saved my life in the cove last night. I just repaid the debt, that's all. We're even."

"Okay, but I don't hate you. Why do you hate me?"

"For what you did to Harvey."

"Who the fuck is Harvey?" I asked.

"You chopped off his hands," Freitag spat, "with your stupid little sword."

"Oh, Bird Man," I said. "He shot Murphy in the head. What the fuck was I supposed to do?" I'd raised my voice. My anger was slipping out. I took a deep breath. "I'm sorry. I didn't mean to yell. But you know what happened. You know it was a bad situation."

Freitag looked at the deck and then back up at me. "I can't forgive you for it. And I don't want to."

"Fine. Now that we're even, do I need to worry about you fucking me over again?"

"No."

"Why?"

"Because." Freitag looked at me with open hate on her face. "You're a piece of shit. You always will be. But I know you won't fuck me over first."

"And how do you know that?"

"Because you could have killed me in that house when you stuck me with that canoe with the hole in it."

Murphy laughed. "That was a funny story."

"I told you," I said, "I'm not a murderer." Though just saying it I knew I was trying to convince myself as much as her.

Dalhover came up out of the cabin with a handful of items, one of which was a hammer. He crossed the deck and extended the hammer handle to Murphy. He said, "I thought you'd like it."

Murphy accepted the hammer. "Not as good as my hatchet, but it'll do. Thanks, Top."

Dalhover nodded and turned to say something to Gretchen.

Freitag said, "I would have killed you if the tables were turned."

"No, you wouldn't have," I responded, shaking my head. "You may think you're that kind of person, but you're not."

"You don't know me very well."

I looked her up and down as though I was going to read some information from her clothes, from her shape. Mostly I was just thinking. I said, "You could have killed me when you ditched me down the river."

"I thought I was killing you."

"No, if you'd really wanted to kill me, you could have shot me, or let me jump in the water to swim out to the boat and run me over. If you'd wanted to kill me, you could have."

"Maybe I'm just not very good at killing."

I sat back in my seat. "I think you're just not as bad as you think you are."

"You don't know anything about me."

"I know," I countered, and then asked, "Are we good?"

"We're fine. Just don't ever try to touch me again."

I reached a hand over the stern, cupped some water, and made a show of scrubbing my hands together in front of her, because I'm just that mature.

Chapter 17

We'd been on the water for maybe an hour and were cruising slowly past a marina hidden in a cove, looking for a suitable place to hide the cabin cruiser and ourselves. Conversation in the back of the boat had come to a halt after the hand-washing display, and my mood was sinking as I ruminated over the things that were bothering me. Primary among them were Steph and what Jay and his macho dipshits were up to with their hillbilly hunting rifles and their pigment-based sense of superiority.

Memories of what had happened to Amber haunted me. I never got past the guilt of leaving her in that dorm with that band of fucktards. The more I thought about it, the more I wondered if that was exactly what I was doing to Steph, leaving her alone in the hands of fucktards who were going to harm her. The more worked up I got, the more I believed I could wrap a Rambo bandana around my head, sharpen my machete, swim out to Monk's Island, and kill bad people until the wrongs were righted.

I jumped to my feet suddenly enough that everyone in the boat looked at me, which was just what I wanted. I said, "So, here's the deal. I've thought about this. I don't care what Jay is or isn't expecting. I'm going there and I'm getting Steph, Amy, and Megan, too. I don't give much of a fuck about what Jay thinks he's going to do about it."

"That's a bad idea," Gretchen said. "I think it's best if we wait."

"I understood your argument the first time," I told her. "Repeating it isn't going to change my mind. I'm going to do this. I'm not asking for any help. I'm not asking any of you to take a risk and come with me. I'm going to do this because I have to. It's that simple."

Everyone was silent, probably still thinking about what, if anything, should be said to me about my announcement.

Dalhover, who'd been leaning against the windscreen, said, "You're just going to head over there with no plan at all, no weapon to speak of except that machete, and hack your way through twenty or thirty people, all of whom might want to shoot you. Is that your plan?"

I wasn't about to accept the condescension. "I don't have to have a plan to decide to do something. I just have to decide. I'll figure it out along the way. Who's there on the island, Gretchen, a bunch of housewives and accountants? Does anyone there have any military experience? None of the guys that took over the houseboat looked military to me."

Shaking his head, Paul said, "No, no. You can't just go over there and kill people to get what you want. We know those people. They're good people. Some of them are our friends."

"Some of them might be good people." I looked at Paul and then at Gretchen. "But the ones that put us on this boat, the ones that decided that we needed to die, those aren't good people. I don't know how many on that island are good and how many are bad. I really don't know much of anything about what happened on your island while we were quarantined on that house boat, but enough of them backed Jay that he didn't have any qualms about coming out to the houseboat with murder on his mind."

Gretchen turned away. Paul put an arm around her.

Then I felt a little bit bad. "Look, Gretchen, Paul. I don't want to hurt anybody but Jay, and maybe some of the dudes on that boat. But I'm not letting them do whatever it is they think they're going to do. Because I know that whatever Jay is thinking, in the long run, it'll turn out badly for Steph and everybody else on that island. Jay needs to die."

Murphy said, "You're getting a list."

Shaking my head, I said, "I've only got two on my list: Mark and Jay."

"Here's what I think," Dalhover said. "I'll help you, Zane. But we have to do this smart. The last thing we need to do is get Steph, Amy, or Megan hurt."

"Thanks." I gave Dalhover a nod.

Murphy said, "I'm in."

Rachel said, "If you're going, so am I."

"No, you're not," Murphy told her.

Rachel stood up, nearly as tall as Murphy and, in her way, just as formidable. "I don't know who you think you're talking to, but if you think you can tell me what to do, you don't know me as well as you thought you did."

I don't know why—maybe I'd seen too many movies. I looked at Freitag.

She shook her head and said, "You must be dreaming."

I shrugged. I didn't expect her to lend a hand. In fact, I didn't think I needed anybody's help. I was more than ready to do it all by myself.

Dalhover said, "Now that we're all on the same page…we can't go off on a Zane crusade right this minute. We have to plan and do this smart."

Bobby Adair

Chapter 18

We docked the cabin cruiser in an empty slip next to a houseboat among dozens of other boats. That kept it pretty well hidden. Of course, the smart thing to do would have been to sink it, erasing any clue as to our whereabouts. That thought never occurred to any of us at the time.

Murphy was the first one off the boat, and I was right behind him. Several Whites were hiding in the morning shade under the dock's canopy, probably wondering what the cabin cruiser was and whether the people getting off of it were of the tasty variety.

Murphy and I were the first two off the boat for a reason.

A long, straight dock ran down the center of the marina, and the Whites were at the far end. Murphy and I headed right toward them. As we neared, they first seemed curious. They stood up and postured aggressively, hoping to drive us off, as whatever was left of their brains made the determination that we were coming for them. By the time we were a dozen steps away, the Whites were afraid and backpedaling until their heels were hanging over the water.

Murphy took a businesslike approach and raised his hammer as he got within a few steps. I had my machete up, ready to hack when the first one lunged. I was certain that one would. They were simple-minded beasts, and backed into a corner, would turn on us.

But they didn't.

First one, then the others, turned and dove into the water.

"Motherfucker." Murphy was surprised.

I looked at Murphy and agreed. "Motherfucker."

"Fucking swimming Whites," he said. "That island's not going to stay safe."

"No." Watching the Whites swim slowly and clumsily across a hundred yards of water toward shore, I said, "This changes everything."

Running footsteps on the boards behind us reminded me that talking out loud was almost always a mistake. I spun and raised my machete. A White was only a few dozen feet away and running at full tilt.

Murphy stepped back a bit, knowing what was coming.

Just as the White got within reach, I swung my machete around in a fast arc that ripped through his throat. The White tumbled to the boarded walkway, bouncing his face on wood as he came to a rest at my feet. Blood gurgled out of his open throat while he twitched and tried to move.

"Might as well get the rest of 'em." Murphy called up the dock, "Hey, buddy! We're right here!"

Murphy's hollering had the desired effect. Another White came running from the far end of the dock. Four more popped up from places where they'd been hidden on the decks of boats.

"You got it okay?" he asked.

I gave Murphy a glance. "As long as I don't have to shoot any, I'm fine."

"If you get in trouble, I'll jump in. Cool?" replied Murphy.

I readied my stance and held my machete back, ready to hack.

The Whites tumbled out of their boats and rushed toward us. The one from the far end of the dock began sprinting in our direction. Murphy's words had him convinced that we were edible despite our skin color.

When the runner got within reach, I swung my machete around and caught him across the throat just as I'd cut his predecessor. I had to step aside as his momentum carried him through the place where I'd been standing. He tumbled into the water.

The other Whites were busy doing me the favor of not coming together in a gang but at intervals of twenty or thirty feet, leaving me plenty of time to dispatch each before the next arrived. The last of them was a young blonde woman in one of the tiniest bikinis I'd ever seen. She was also the wiliest of the bunch.

My throat-slashing technique worked perfectly on all except her. When I swung, she was ready. She ducked under my blade and plowed into me with all of her momentum.

I fell, losing my machete as I hit the deck. She was immediately clawing and biting; whether trying to kill me or eat me alive, it didn't matter. I was punching wildly and pushing, trying to keep her teeth off my skin.

Murphy grabbed a handful of her long, oily hair, pulled her head back, and punched her hard in the temple. That stunned her for a moment, and Murphy punched her again, and a third time. Her eyes rolled back and she went limp.

"Fucking bitch." I crawled out from under her.

Murphy smashed her face into the dock a few times and rolled her into the water. She splashed and floated face down.

"You all right, man?"

I looked down at myself. "Embarrassed."

"That you got tackled by a chick?"

"That I got taken down by somebody whose IQ is a hundred points lower than mine."

Murphy chuckled. "Or both."

Still checking myself, I nodded and bent down to pick up my machete. Looking up, I saw Rachel up on the deck at the bow of the cabin cruiser, worry on her face.

Murphy raised a thumb to indicate that we were okay.

She nodded, looked around, and squatted on the boat's deck.

I followed Murphy over to the cabin cruiser. To Rachel, he softly said, "The marina is clear for the moment. Me and Zed'll go check that brown houseboat up there. Get the others." Murphy looked at me. "You ready?"

Smiling, I said, "Ready to get beat up by another blonde?"

Murphy chuckled, and we jogged half the length of the marina's main dock to arrive at the stern of a houseboat similar to the one we'd been quarantined in the night before. Showing its age, its paint was oxidized and its metal fittings were rusted, leaving thin trails of orange down the sides of the boat.

Murphy stepped off the dock and onto the houseboat's stern. I jumped across beside him.

Looking at me, he asked, "You wanna knock?"

I stepped over to a closed door and did so.

We waited. No sound came from inside.

I knocked again. I looked up and down the dock to see if any other attention was being garnered.

Nothing.

"Try the door?"

I tried the knob. It was locked.

Murphy looked around. "I don't want to kick it in. Let's check around."

There was no side deck on the boat, so I climbed a stairway that led to the rooftop deck, but there was no door down from there to the boat's interior. "No way in up here."

Murphy looked around again. "You see anything?"

I shook my head.

He jumped over to the dock and walked up along the walkway beside the boat, reaching across to check each of the windows he passed. He cursed quietly under his breath after trying each one. They were all locked.

When he was walking around to the other side of the boat, I heard the sound of boat motors. "Hurry, dude. I think I hear something."

Murphy looked up at me with a question on his face.

"Boats," I told him in a harsh whisper.

He ran around to the other side of the houseboat. I climbed down the stairs, crossed the deck, and hopped over to the dock. When I went around to the boat's port side, I saw Murphy's legs sticking out of a window as he tried to crawl his way in.

Figuring he had that problem solved, I ran down the dock until Rachel and I made contact. I pointed toward the lake as I ran.

She understood immediately and jumped down from the bow to gather up the others.

The sound of high-revving boat motors grew more distinct. I looked toward the end of the cove and wondered how much time we had before Jay's boats arrived.

Feet hit the wooden dock behind me. Fully expecting those feet to be one of the cabin cruiser's occupants, I glanced over my shoulder. It wasn't one of my new friends. "Damn."

Just a dozen feet behind me, a strong-looking young man with short hair and white skin was looking at me, trying to figure out if I was food or friend.

"Hey, dude," I said.

That was enough. He rushed at me and reached for my throat. I ducked under his arms and sliced his abdomen open as he ran by. He fell to the deck, writhing, feebly wheezing his pain with what little breath he could muster. I stepped over and hacked at the back of his neck, bringing his misery and noisy death to an end.

When I looked up, the rest of the boat's passengers were running up the dock. I waved them forward and ran to the houseboat, jumping over to the houseboat's deck as Murphy swung the back door open. A moment later, Freitag rushed past, followed by Rachel. Gretchen and Paul, older and slower, came next. Dalhover, self-appointed rearguard, was last. Murphy closed the door behind us.

Once inside, Dalhover found a window through which to peek and see up the cove. Murphy found a spot at another window.

"How did they get here so fast?" Gretchen softly asked anyone who would listen.

"Jay is crazy," Freitag said, as if that was sufficient to answer the question. She started peeking through curtains.

Rachel said, "My bet is that when Jerry didn't come back when Jay expected, he sent a boat out to see what happened."

"And they came across Gerald and Melissa paddling back in that kayak." Paul cast a worried look toward the windows. The sound of the motorboat engines was audible through the houseboat's thin walls. "It was the right thing to do, but we spent too much time finding a boat for those two. We probably should have left them on the shore somewhere."

"You survive. You help your loved ones. Fuck everybody else." Even as I said it I knew I was being a hypocrite. I'd broken those rules and suffered the consequences too many times. "That's just the way it is now."

Paul looked at me and his mouth twisted as though he was chewing on a bitter grapefruit rind.

He seemed like a nice man, so I kept my "fuck you" to myself. He'd spent the whole epidemic on the island, trying to build an idealistic, mutually beneficial, post-apocalyptic utopia. The problem with any utopia is that it discounts the vile ability of humans to turn it into the same ugly world they create in every utopia. Jay and Jerry had just given Paul his first lesson in that course of study, and Paul hadn't understood any of it yet.

"Jay is a hothead," Gretchen said. "He will race his boats all the way to the next dam. That's the way he thinks."

"So we're safe, then?" Paul asked.

The engines of the boats were louder inside than our voices, but they revved just as high. Murphy, Frietag, and Dalhover all crouched.

Dalhover, in a hushed voice said, "They're at the end of the cove."

Everyone froze.

"They aren't slowing," Murphy said.

More than one breath of relief escaped into the air.

The sound of the motors whined lower.

Dalhover changed his angle on the window. "They're going by."

I looked at Gretchen and said, "You were right."

"Some people are easy to predict," she said.

"But you didn't predict that he'd mount a coup and try to kill us," I said, some anger coming out in my tone. I was immediately ashamed for having said it. "That wasn't fair. I'm sorry."

Gretchen looked away.

Paul looked like he wanted to slap me. Had he been a younger man, he might have.

Freitag said, "You'll get used to him. He's an ass."

Well, fuck her. I gave her the meanest look I could put on my face. "Or you can ditch me somewhere for the Whites to eat while I'm doing you a favor."

"Kiddies." Murphy's sounded like a dad threatening to stop the car and spank the children in the back seat.

"I knew Jay and Jerry were—" Gretchen took a moment to look for the right word. "Unusual."

Rachel laughed nervously as she looked at one of the windows. "They're more than unusual."

"Nobody could have guessed they would plot to kill us," said Paul.

"Look," I said, "I'm sorry about that. I'm just angry because he kidnapped the girls. I know this kind of stuff is hard to see coming." Involuntarily, I looked at Freitag, but turned away before she saw it. For the moment, we were on the same side, even—or so she said. But I feared she might be as crazy as Jay and Jerry, and any insult might tip the scales of her stability in the wrong direction. That made me nervous.

"They're gone," Dalhover announced.

Everyone relaxed.

Turning back to the room, Dalhover said, "They'll be back. They're hauling ass up the lake trying to catch us before we get wherever they think we're going, but they'll be careful on the way back and search for us. They'll come into this cove, and they might find the boat."

After a short pause, he added,"They'll have more guns than we've got."

"Do we hide here?" Gretchen asked, "Or do we go onto shore and try to find a place?"

I looked down at the bloody machete, still in my hand. "There are Whites around. Plenty, I'd guess. If they see us making for a house, we might be double screwed. They'll trap us inside, and if there are enough of them around when Jay's men find the cabin cruiser, the Whites might give away our hiding place. I can't imagine that will turn out any way but badly."

"He's right," Dalhover told everyone.

"He likes being right," Freitag sniped.

I ignored her.

"What are our choices then?" Paul asked. "Do we stay here and hope they don't find us when they come back? Is that our only choice?"

I looked around at the room. Each of them was looking for better answers from the others. But none of us had a better idea.

Crap.

Hiding in the houseboat didn't seem like a good idea. I turned to Murphy. "Do you know how to hot-wire a car?"

Grinning, he asked, "Why does everybody always ask the black dude that question?"

"Oh, Jesus," I said, looking over at a shrugging Dalhover. "Here's what I think. We see if we can find the keys to one of these boats and get out of this marina while Jay and his nutjobs are chasing their tails up at the other end of the lake."

"Yes." Paul was nodding enthusiastically. "We've got a window of time in which to get away. We can head back down the lake while they are going up. They'll never know. Then when they get here on the way back and find the cabin cruiser, they'll think we're around here. We'll have lost them."

Yeah. Isn't that what I said?

Bobby Adair

Chapter 19

The sound of boat engines faded to nothing.

Rachel, Paul, and Gretchen stayed on the houseboat. Dalhover and Freitag went to work together to search the boats in the marina to see if they could get one started. Murphy and I headed up the dock toward the marina office. The hope was that we'd find the keys for the boats there.

Murphy hefted his insufficient little hammer. "I'll feel better once I get a rifle back in my hands."

"Soon enough." I hoped. I looked around for signs of Whites.

We were crossing a long walkway that led from the boat slips to the shore.

Rubbing his hand over his head as he looked around, Murphy sighed and said, "I'm having second thoughts about going to hunt Smart Ones."

I stopped and looked at Murphy, shaking my head. "What the fuck, dude? I thought we agreed on what we need to do after we get through all this bullshit with Jay."

"C'mon." Murphy pushed me forward. "We got work to do."

"Why?"

"'Cause we need a boat."

"You know what I'm asking." I was mad.

"You said so yourself, didn't you? What Would Murphy Do?"

"I thought Murphy would kill some motherfucking Whites," I said. "Last I heard, that's what Murphy would do."

"It was at the time."

I stopped again and planted my feet on the dock. This needed to be resolved. "What about Mandi?"

Murphy stopped and turned on me. For a second, he was an angry beast. I flinched. But Murphy's temper flare passed as quickly as it came. He slowly shook his head. "If you want to chase off after the Smart Ones after we get the girls, I'll go with you. I think it's a stupid idea, but I'll babysit you so you won't get yourself killed while you're being angry and stupid."

"What changed?"

"Nothing changed."

"A few days ago, you wanted to kill them as badly as I did."

"I still do," said Murphy.

"Then what the fuck, dude?"

Murphy's face turned sad and he looked at the water, his thoughts getting lost in the lake's cold depths. Then he looked across to the shore as though he'd just remembered that he needed to look out for Whites. "Is this the best time to talk about this?"

"Just tell me what changed, and we'll go."

"I can't go back there," he said.

"Where?"

"You remember how I told you I was, back after I killed those three…kids behind the 7-Eleven?"

"Kids?"

Shaking his head, Murphy said, "They were just teenagers."

"Murphy, don't make them more vulnerable in your memory than they really were. You know what they did to Keisha. You know as well as I do that if they did that to her and laughed about it, who knows what they did to other people? They were vicious monsters long before the virus ever showed up. They deserved what they got."

Murphy nodded.

We started walking toward the marina office again.

Murphy said, "It took me a long time to get right after I killed those boys."

"Guilt?" I asked.

"No," Murphy was having a hard time with it. "I was in a dark place. It's like I didn't have a soul anymore."

I knew that feeling.

"You joke about my philosophy," he said. "I know you think it's some kind of simple bullshit to make myself smile."

I stopped then. "No. Honestly, Murphy, I don't. Yeah, it seems too simple to be real, but it works for you. You're happy. Do you know how many people in this world are happy, or were happy before all this shit went down?"

Murphy shrugged, and we started walking again.

"Pretty much none of them."

"I feel like going to kill the Smart Ones, no matter how bad I want to—" He struggled for a moment and changed course. "I've got so much hate in my heart right now, Zed—" Murphy drew a long slow breath. "I don't know if I can be both."

"Both?"

"Me, the person I am now, the person I've been since I got right with all that shit about killing those three punks. Or that other guy, the angry one that needed his revenge. I can't be both."

Bobby Adair

The marina office was a square little building a short way up hill from the edge of the water. It had grids of windows stretching across three sides, leaving the marina and the entire cove visible from the counter inside. When we got there, the door was open. The doorjamb was broken and the strike plate was on the floor among splinters from the wood that had held it in place. Someone had already forced his or her way in. The office stank.

That gave Murphy and me pause as we stepped across the threshold. Papers were scattered on the counter and the floor. A desk behind the counter was in disarray. Murphy leaned over the counter and shook his head. "Dead guy."

I leaned over to look. A body with a big chunk of skull shattered open lay rotting on the floor. I said, "Somebody ransacked this place."

Murphy pointed to a tall, flat metal cabinet on the back wall. The sheet metal around the lock had been pried apart, leaving a wide rent.

I turned to look out through the windows. "I'll keep an eye out for them. You check for the keys."

"Probably right inside that cabinet." Murphy shuffled through some office supplies scattered on the floor and stepped around the counter.

"Two of those Whites we chased off the dock are out there, watching us."

"How close?" Murphy asked.

"A ways." I scanned across the marina. "I don't think they want anything to do with us, but they sure seem interested."

The metal cabinet door swung open on creaky hinges. Murphy said, "Jackpot."

Jackpot? That was Mandi's word. She used it all the time. I thought it best not to mention Murphy's use of it. Off to my left, a tall White came out from behind some kind of building that probably contained a repair shop. He was looking at something out on the docks. No good was going to come of that. "Murphy, hurry it up."

"Man, I don't know which keys are for which boat."

I glanced back over my shoulder. Rows of keys hung on hooks beneath three digit numbers. "I'll bet those are the slip numbers."

"Like that does me any good, professor."

The staring White had two other companions, and one of them was looking back in the direction from whence they came. My guess was that more were on the way. At least they were all of the clothed variety.

"Just grab four or five, and let's go. There are some Whites out there getting really interested."

Keys jingled.

"Interested in us?" Murphy asked.

I watched another couple of Whites come out from beside the building. All of them were staring at the docks. I looked over at the docks, but couldn't see what they were seeing but it didn't take a genius to know it was one of our people who had their interest.

Murphy shuffled back through the papers.

The Whites took off at a sprint for the dock, and several more that I hadn't seen followed them out from behind the building.

"Shit." I ran out through the door.

The Whites were fast and were going to reach the long wooden walkway that stretched out to the boat slips before me. Halfway down the slope, Murphy ran past me with his hammer swinging in his fist. I tried to keep up.

Seven Whites were stretched out in a widely spaced line, clomping on the deck when Murphy reached the boards just behind the last of them. I was still a good ten paces behind Murphy. I bounded onto the dock as Murphy reached the first of the running Whites. He swung his hammer at the side of the man's head, knocking him off balance. As Murphy passed the reeling White, he pushed it into the water.

The White was flailing at the water and starting to howl when I passed him.

Murphy caught up with another White and shouldered her hard from behind, bouncing her face on the dock as she rolled off the left side and into the water. Two down, five to go.

I made up a few steps of the distance between me and Murphy.

A loud banging of wood on wood rang across the water from the right. That had to be the sound that had gotten their attention.

The first of the infected in our line made the right turn off the walkway and onto the main dock, followed closely by the second.

Murphy closed in on a pair of Whites running side by side.

A third made the turn.

I shouted, "Hey, motherfucker!"

The two Whites in front of Murphy turned as they tried to stop. Murphy barreled into both of them. One fell off the dock. The other hit the dock, banging his head, losing his senses.

The other three Whites that had already made the turn to run up between the boat slips were too focused on the noise they'd heard ahead of them.

Murphy ran on past the White he'd just knocked down, and I swung my machete to slice at his head as I passed. The blow caught him under the jaw, and while it probably wasn't lethal at the moment, it would be. Whether I'd hacked all the way through the jaw or not, it was broken. The White would bleed out from the wound or starve to death in a month or two. Either way, it was out of the day's fight.

Murphy rounded the turn onto the wide dock between the boat slips. A few seconds later, I did too.

Far down on the right, the houseboat that kept Rachel, Paul, and Gretchen hidden floated as innocuous and boring as every other boat in the marina. The tall, infected man leading all of us along passed the houseboat without showing an iota of interest.

The loud bang pounded from somewhere far down toward the end of the dock. It had to be Dalhover or Freitag.

Murphy caught up with an infected woman and pounded her in the back of the head as he passed. She tumbled. I clipped the back of her skull with my machete as I went by. She wasn't likely to get up and join her two compatriots either.

The tall one cut hard to his left and jumped off the dock, over a gunwale, and landed on the deck of a blue-hulled cabin cruiser.

The infected woman following came to a stop on the dock at the stern of the cabin cruiser. She looked down at the water between the dock and the boat's hull, fear on her face. From inside the cabin cruiser, fists pounded on wood.

The woman, too fixated on the terrifying water, looked up at the sound of Murphy's running footsteps just a moment too late. He body slammed her full-on, and she flew off the dock, bounced against the walkway between the cabin cruiser and the sailboat in the slip next door, and sank into the green water. She didn't resurface.

Murphy put a hand on the gunwale and jumped into the boat.

Not sure I could make the jump, I ran around to the side and leapt onto a set of four stairs up to the height of the boat's gunwale.

Murphy grunted something harsh and mean just as his hammer thudded wetly into a skull.

But that wasn't enough to kill the White. Bodies hit the deck and a struggle ensued.

I reached the top step and evaluated what I was seeing, even as I jumped into the boat. One White was leaning back against the door to the cabin, clutching his head, but he wasn't the tall one—where did he come from? The tall one was on top of Murphy and seemed for half a second to be getting the best of him.

Unfortunately for that White, he never saw nor expected my machete. I hacked a deep gash between his shoulder blades.

Figuring that was all the help Murphy needed, I turned to the White sitting on the floor, grasping his head. He was just trying to get his feet under him, and I put an end to that with a chop into his already damaged skull.

When I turned back around, the situation had reversed. Murphy was on top of the White who was wriggling in an expanding pool of red. Murphy pounded his hammer into the White's skull again, and again, and again, until the struggling stopped.

I looked around, breathing rapidly, trying to find any other threats that might be running our way.

Nothing was moving on the dock. I didn't see anything on the shore.

"There's an extra one," Murphy said, coming to his feet and pointing to the White I'd hacked by the boat's cabin door.

"I guess he was making the noise," I said. "I thought it was Dalhover or Freitag, being stupid."

"Not stupid." It was Freitag's voice, coming from the other side of the door. "Trapped."

Chapter 21

Murphy and I went to work searching the boat slips for numbers that matched the tags on the key rings Murphy carried. We found a match and I said, "Talk about luck."

Murphy climbed over the side and into a long monster of a speedboat with two enormous outboard engines on the back. Grinning, he said, "I'll bet this is the fastest boat on the lake."

"Just see if the key fits."

Murphy dropped into the seat at the helm. Keys jingled. One slipped in the ignition switch. He turned and shined his Christmas present smile at me. "Heh, heh, heh."

"I'll get everybody else." I took off at a sprint toward the other end of the long dock, keeping an eye on the walkway that led to the shore. Nothing there except a few downed Whites, one of whom was still rolling and moaning. That would soon attract more infected.

As I was nearing the houseboat, Dalhover's head leaned out of the door on the back of the boat.

Coming to a stop, I urgently waved at him to come.

The head disappeared back inside. The door flung open, and Freitag ran out with Rachel right behind. I took another glimpse at the walkway. Gretchen and Paul came out, with Dalhover taking up the rear, as usual.

As Freitag neared, I pointed at Murphy's new toy, "It's the big two-engine thing, three from the end."

She slowed just enough to understand and raced on.

"Thanks," Rachel said as she ran by.

I started to backpedal as Paul and Gretchen neared. "Hurry. There's no telling when they'll show up." Of course, "they" could have meant the Whites or Jay's henchman.

"Go," Dalhover told me. "I'm with them."

I nodded, turned, and sprinted back down the dock.

When I got to the boat, Rachel was standing behind Murphy's seat. Freitag was in a seat beside him. For such a large boat, there wasn't much deck space, pretty much just a couple of couch-sized seats, one behind the other. We were all going to have to get chummy. I got onto the front couch beside Freitag.

She was just as happy about the arrangement as I was.

"Start it up," I said to Murphy.

"You got it, boss." Murphy turned the key.

Nothing happened.

"What's the matter?" Freitag asked, panic pushing her thin voice up an octave.

"Murphy?" Rachel asked, putting a hand on his shoulder and leaning in.

"You've to be fucking kidding me." Clearly violating the touching rule we'd agreed on, I reached across Freitag's lap to get the extra keys from Murphy.

He misunderstood my intent. "I got this man. Give me a sec." He was calm, but urgency was slipping toward panic. We both knew that being exposed, things could quickly go badly for us. The shores were full of Whites, and they might have already spotted our uninfected companions.

I quickly said, "Just give me the other keys while you work on getting this thing started."

Paul was helping Gretchen onto the back of the boat.

Murphy handed me the keys.

Still leaning over Freitag, I looked at the numbers, pushed a few into her hand and said, "You check those two. I'll check these two." I jumped up and hopped over the gunwale, landing loudly on the dock. I was running toward a ski boat four slips over when I heard Freitag's tiny feet land on the dock behind me.

Still, no sound came from the big engines on the stern of Murphy's useless toy.

"Hurry," Dalhover said to me as I cut the turn onto the main dock and headed toward the end. He readied his rifle and stood high on the back of the boat.

Glancing to my left as I ran, I saw what his concern was. A mob of twenty or thirty Whites was tentatively crossing the marina's parking lot, closing in on the long gangway that led to the main dock.

I reached the boat at the end of the row of slips, and my first thought was junk. My second thought was to wonder why it was still afloat. Its paint was faded and flaked. Everything metal looked to be rusted to the point of uselessness. Shreds of a canvas cover dangled from places where it had once been secure.

Without slowing, I jumped up to step on the upper edge, and as I was landing in the boat, I saw that the place where I expected a deck to be was a hole instead, a hole where an inboard motor should have sat beneath a deck panel. Both were gone.

I rolled as I fell, and instead of breaking my leg in the hole, I hit the deck on my back, knocking the wind out of me and earning a few more bruises. Cursing and jumping to my feet, I clambered back over the gunwale and onto the walkway between the two slips. From down the dock, a little boat engine zinged to life. That had to be Freitag.

Good enough. I ran back over to the main dock. The Whites from the parking lot had lost all of their caution upon hearing the zinging little engine. They'd spotted our group and figured out quickly enough that most of us were edible. They were running toward the walkway.

Dalhover hollered a warning.

Gretchen and Paul were climbing their way slowly back out.

Running past Freitag's boat, I was immediately concerned whether it would hold all of us. It was an old ski boat or fishing boat, or something. I cast a quick glance back at the Whites. My concerns about Freitag's boat had suddenly turned irrelevant. We didn't have time to be picky.

Paul was reaching over to hold onto Freitag's little boat when Murphy's two big Mercury Marine engines roared deafeningly over the water, stunning me, Dalhover, and all of the Whites. Unfortunately, the Whites recovered first and came charging at full speed. They were pouring onto the walkway, and the boat's engines were so loud that I couldn't hear their feet or their howls.

When I looked over at Paul and Gretchen, they'd changed direction and were running back to get into Murphy's speed machine. The engines' power was comforting and enticing.

I ran past the bow of Freitag's boat and waved at her to get out.

Without any resistance she abandoned her newfound captaincy and climbed out of the boat.

Whites were on the main dock and coming toward us. Dalhover had loosed the rope at the stern of Murphy's boat, and he turned to climb in. I ran up along the starboard side of the boat and hacked through the rope that had the bow tied tight. I tossed my machete up onto the expansive bow deck and jumped, catching a section of chrome railing and pulling myself up.

Dalhover's rifle was firing. The boat was already moving out of the slip, and everyone inside was hollering at Freitag to hurry as she ran onto the walkway along the path I'd come, Whites on her heels. Without slowing, she reached the end of the dock and jumped for the boat. I reached out to her, catching her hand as she flew toward me.

The engines revved, and the boat accelerated.

Freitag's feet swung out over the water and her face turned to fright. I fell to my belly, and her feet dipped into the water as I reached over with my other hand to get a grip on her that wouldn't slip. As the boat made a turn away from the docks, the chasing Whites poured off the end of the dock and into the water, trying uselessly to catch us.

Dalhover yelled something, and as soon as Murphy understood, the big engines revved higher and the boat ripped across the cove, nearly dragging me into the water on top of Freitag.

"Don't let go of me," Freitag begged.

"I won't."

Hands grabbed at my belt and somebody jumped on my legs to hold me steady.

"We're good," I said to Freitag.

A moment later, an arm reached over my shoulder and grabbed a handful of Freitag's shirt, pulling her up on top of me. I caught a knee in my face as Dalhover dragged her farther into the boat.

Dalhover let go of Freitag and Rachel got off of me.

I rolled over onto my back. "Thanks."

Without any of the vitriol that I'd come to expect, Freitag said, "Yeah, thanks."

We threw up a thirty-knot wake as we flew out of the cove and into the lake.

I sat up, and looked at the Whites far behind us, swimming stupidly toward us or turning back toward the dock. "That was exciting."

Rachel laughed and Dalhover almost smiled. And for the moment—and it always ever just seemed like a moment—we were safe.

Over the wind and rumble of the engines, I looked at Dalhover. "My curiosity is nagging me, so I've got to know. What happened?"

Dalhover looked back into the marina as the boat picked up speed. We turned in the opposite direction that Jay's henchmen had gone. He glanced at Freitag. "You go ahead." Dalhover got up, cautiously climbed over the windshield, and got down into the cockpit beside Murphy.

I looked at Freitag.

Rachel asked, "What did happen? We couldn't see anything from inside the houseboat. We heard the banging, and it wasn't long after that all the running and shouting started."

"Yeah," I nodded. "I'll say."

With our eyes on her, Freitag said, "We were checking the boats one at a time, looking around inside for keys or anything else that might be of use. We got to that cabin cruiser, and I went down the stairs and opened the door to the cabin. I guess by then I was getting lazy and—" Freitag glared at me.

I understood the warning and kept my comments to myself.

"—I wasn't expecting anything to be inside. Not really. I peeked and didn't see anything, so I swung the door wide open and went on in. Sergeant Dalhover was at the top of the stairs, asking if the cabin was clear. I was halfway across the cabin by then, and something shrieked behind me."

"A White?" I guessed.

Freitag nodded.

"Right there in the cabin?" Rachel asked.

Freitag nodded again. "I frightened him as much as he frightened me. He was sitting in the corner to the right of the door. I never saw him until he screamed. Then he jumped up and rushed through the door."

"How did Dalhover get inside?" I asked.

She shrugged. "When the White screamed, I tripped and fell as I was turning around. I heard Dalhover shout something. I heard them fall, and when I got back up, Dalhover was on the floor and kicking the door closed with his feet. I guess the frightened White ran into him as it tried to get outside. They scuffled, and by the time the White figured out that we were just what he'd been waiting for, it was too late."

"That's crazy." Rachel smiled, and her smile was just as big and shiny as Murphy's.

Freitag said, "That's when the White started to pound on the door."

"You probably should have just shot him through the door," I said.

"We talked about that. We didn't know which would bring more trouble, the noise of the gunshots, or the White pounding on the door."

"Good point." I nodded.

"We all made it out." Rachel summed up, or perhaps just changed the subject, before Freitag and I went back at one another's throats. "That's the important thing." She looked over the bow that was starting to bounce on the waves.

I said, "Murphy needs to slow down, or we need to get in the cockpit with the others."

Freitag got up on her hands and knees and made her way toward the windshield to climb over. Rachel and I followed.

Bobby Adair

Chapter 22

An hour later, we were idling into a cove just a few miles across land from Mansfield Dam, but because the shape of the lake was dictated by the river which had been dammed to make it, we were still ten or fifteen miles away by water. Monk's Island was at least five miles further up the lake.

Like all of the docks and boathouses on the lake, they weren't built on piers. They floated with the drastically changing level of the lake, which might vary by thirty or forty feet throughout the course of a year. The benefit of that for us at the moment was that during the drought, all of the boathouses in the cove had been re-anchored farther and farther from the houses of their owners as the lake receded. When the floods came, with no one left to reposition them, they simply floated up from their current positions. Of course, many broke loose and floated freely. Some floated, still anchored to the lake bottom, but at a good distance from the shore.

Murphy pulled the boat up next to one such boathouse floating near the center of a cove. It had been built to house three boats behind garage-style doors, all three of which were closed when we arrived. He looked around for consensus and received shrugs and nods. One boathouse was as good as the next.

Looking at me, Paul asked, "Anybody want to swim under and see if there are any Whites inside?"

I accepted the task and stood up to climb over the windshield to the long bow deck. "I don't mind going, but just so you guys know, for the future, when you're in the water, the Whites can't see enough of you to figure out if you're one of them or not. At least the ones we've been dealing with downriver thought anybody swimming was food."

"Really?" That surprised Gretchen.

Having the luxury of being on the island since the infection started, the islanders had little experience with the Whites. I figured none of them would last long onshore.

"I'll go, then," Paul said, jumping to his feet.

I shrugged. "Come along if you like."

Dalhover gave Paul a dismissive look as he stood. "I'll go."

Though the two were of the same age, Paul had spent his life in academics, and while he wasn't overweight at all, he didn't look like he was up to any strenuous task. Dalhover looked like any middle-aged man, beaten down by life and, at a glance, unable to even change his own car tires. But I knew he wasn't that. He was hard, athletic, and accomplished in the suddenly valuable skill of butchering hostile former human beings.

I was happier to have Dalhover along.

With my machete in hand, I jumped into the water and let my momentum carry me down. Dalhover splashed in, and side by side we swam beneath the wall of the boathouse. In the shadow beneath, I saw the hull of a small boat in the first slip. It left plenty of room around its sides for us to come up inside.

We surfaced together at the stern of the small boat, far enough from the walkways on either side that we couldn't be reached by any White who might happen to be there. I inhaled quietly as I looked around, listened, and sniffed the air: nothing but dim light, lapping water, and motor oil.

Dalhover silently moved through the water over to the walkway along the wall. Once there, he pulled himself up with a degree of silence I could only envy. I was never quiet going into or climbing out of the water.

Leveling his rifle to point up the dock, he slowly looked around the dark room. No Whites stood or squatted on the docks, and the only other boat didn't seem to have anyone on it. He looked down at me and shrugged.

Good so far.

Making a splashy noise, I climbed up on the dock beside him. I hefted my machete, showed it to Dalhover so that he understood my meaning, and scooted around him on the dock so that anything coming at us from any other part of the boathouse would come to me first. I said, "Hey. Anybody in here?"

Nothing responded.

In a louder voice, Dalhover rasped, "Come out if you're in here."

We waited.

"I think we're good." I walked slowly up the dock, eyeing every shadowy corner as I moved. "Let's check it out to be sure."

"Right behind you."

We worked our way past the old wooden ski boat that we'd come up beside, passed a couple of windsurfing boards hanging on the wall, and moved over to the slip on the far side of the boathouse. I leaned over to get a good look inside that ski boat and saw that it was empty. Dalhover took his time examining storage shelves and cabinets built into the wall.

He said, "We're clear."

"Yeah."

He crossed the dock to a door on the backside of the boathouse and fumbled with the lock until it opened. He peeked outside, looked back at me, and uncharacteristically smiled.

That got my interest, so I crossed the decking and took a look. "Nice."

On the backside of the boathouse was a wide covered deck, a table big enough to seat eight, several pool loungers, a barbecue, and a small refrigerator.

After looking around to make sure that nothing on shore was showing an interest, Dalhover walked over and opened the fridge. The smile returned. "Beer."

I laughed. "You just made my day." I hurried down the length of the deck, got to the corner of the boathouse, and motioned to Murphy to bring the speedboat around. The engines rumbled slightly louder and Murphy navigated the boat around and parked it along the deck, which, as it turned out, blocked the view of the outdoor deck from the shore.

Unfortunately, the fridge held nothing but beer—some kind of edible food would have been nice. The beer was the temperature of tepid coffee, but pickiness over which kinds of calories to ingest in the late morning was a luxury that none of us could afford. So we all got a little buzzed.

I maybe got a little more buzzed than I should have, but I didn't have any plans until the sun went down. Bedsides, I had a mountain of memories that I wanted to forget for a while. After drinking my brunch, I laid down for a nap. Dalhover, Paul, and Freitag all chose to keep watch. Maybe overkill, but what else were they going to do?

Murphy, Rachel, and Gretchen were talking nearby about something that sounded more and more like burbling, random syllables as I drifted off to sleep.

Chapter 23

"Hey, Sleeping Beauty."

I opened my eyes. Murphy was leaning over me in the dim light and nudging me none too gently.

"You gonna sleep all night?"

Blinking the sleep out of my eyes, I said, "I feel like a hammered turd."

Murphy chuckled. "Too many beers."

"I wish." I sat up. "Too many hard miles lately. I need some down time."

"I hear ya, man, but you wanted to get this Steph thing rolling."

Sitting up introduced me to a headache. I rubbed my temples. "We need to. I just need a sec."

"Cool, man." Murphy sat down on the dock beside me and leaned against the wall.

"What time is it?"

"A little after nine."

I looked around in the dimness. One flashlight was in the far corner of the boathouse, sitting on a wire shelf, pointed at the floor. It made a good night light—not bright enough to attract any attention from outside but enough so that I could see two shadows standing at the windows, peeking through the shades.

Murphy noticed that I was looking at the guards, "Freitag is outside on the deck, keeping watch."

"Everybody else is asleep?"

Murphy pointed to the other side of the boathouse. Shadowy people sat on the floor by the shelves, talking softly. "They're worrying over what we're about to do."

"Did you get any sleep?"

"I crashed for a couple of hours." Murphy pushed a beer can into my hand. "Second breakfast. It's all we've got."

"It'll have to do." I popped the tab on the aluminum can. "We can't live on this stuff."

Murphy chuckled softly. "Lots of people do. At least it's not light beer."

"Thank God for that," I agreed.

"It's not ideal, but we could probably survive on warm beer for maybe four or five days."

I shrugged and took a long, hideous drink of warm beer. "We should probably pull it out of the fridge and store it in a net in the water. I hate warm beer."

"Tell the boss."

"Is Gretchen the boss?" I asked. "Is that what was decided?"

"More or less. But you know, man. There's nothing formal, so don't start getting your panties in a wad about it."

"Dude," I was offended. "I didn't say anything. I just wasn't sure."

"I know how you are, man. Finish that beer. You need some calories, and the alcohol might take the sharp edge off that stick in your ass."

I rolled my eyes and drank some more. "Have you ever tried this whole friendship thing before?"

"No, you're my first friend." Murphy chuckled again and gave me a friendly push on the shoulder. "Lighten up, man. Shit could be worse."

"I hear you. Sorry." I lifted my beer and looked at the label. "Coffee would be better."

Murphy shrugged. "When you're done whining, we need to talk about what we're going to do."

"We know what we're going to do. We just need to do it. Is everyone still cool with it?" In truth, I didn't care how cool they were. It was dark outside. I had calories in my belly and a machete to do my dirty work.

"Worried, but cool enough."

I sat up straight and looked worriedly at the flashlight in the corner as a new thought occurred to me. "What happened with Jay's thugs? Did they come back?"

"Dalhover said one of the boats did a quick run-through of the cove just before sundown. They weren't very thorough. He thinks they found the cabin cruiser in that other marina and probably saw the dead Whites. Jay probably thinks we got munched there, or we got away. Either way, they weren't looking for us here, not really."

That was a relief. I said, "Cool." I had no doubt in my mind that crackpot Jay was still fuming over his revenge, but he probably figured we were a problem that wouldn't trouble him further.

Murphy opened up a beer of his own.

"You know, that thing with finding Rachel was a nice surprise," I said.

"Yeah," Murphy nodded. "I never thought I'd see her again."

"How's she been? How's she dealing with all of this?"

"Better than you, if that's what you're asking."

"What does that mean?"

Murphy grinned. "You brood too much."

"I'm trying to follow the Murphy plan. How'd she get all the way from east Austin over here to Monk's Island?"

"Luck."

"What kind of luck is that?" I asked. "Oops, I took a wrong turn on the way home. What's this lake doing here?" I laughed.

Murphy put a finger to his mouth to keep me quiet. The boathouse walls weren't insulated. Sound would carry across the water. In a soft voice, he said, "That's almost what happened."

"Whatever. Really, how'd she get to the island?"

"A friend of hers from the office has a house out here on the lake. They wrapped up some big pain-in-the-ass deal at work and were blowing some vacation days waterskiing. When shit went down, she said she tried to call Mom but never got an answer. Her friends convinced her not to go home and check on her. They said it was suicide to try."

"It probably was," I said.

"True or not, it doesn't make the guilt go away." Murphy glanced at the others sitting in the shadows on the other side of the boathouse.

I asked, "Did her friends make it?"

"There were four of them. I guess one was her boyfriend."

"Interoffice romance?" I asked.

Murphy nodded. "I never even met the guy. They'd been dating for six months or some shit."

I nodded, knowingly.

"The boyfriend was the first of them to get infected. The others came down with the fever. Next thing she knows, she's in a big house on a cliff looking over the lake with three people passed out with the fever. The TV and radio were still working then, so she knew what was coming."

"She bailed out?" I hoped, for her sake.

Murphy shook his head as he frowned. "She stayed until the boyfriend turned."

"I don't see a happy ending."

"She found a gun in the house. She had him locked in the wine cellar."

"The wine cellar?" I asked, with an inflection in my tone that implied something, though I didn't even know what it was. I was just trying to lighten Murphy's mood.

"All rich white people have wine cellars." Murphy put on a false smile. The joke wasn't worth a laugh.

I said, "I'll bypass the stereotype and ask how you felt about your sister dating a white guy."

Murphy punched me in the arm. "You know that's bullshit, right?"

"I know." Letting the mood fall back into seriousness, I asked, "Did she have to shoot him?"

Murphy nodded.

"And the other two?"

Murphy shook his head. "After the boyfriend, she packed up all she thought to carry, loaded it in a boat, and headed out. She ended up on Monk's Island."

"How's she dealing with the boyfriend thing?"

"She's a tough girl."

"I gathered that." I finished the last of my beer and crunched the can. "When do you want to head out?"

Murphy nodded toward the others who were still awake. "Everybody wants to talk first."

Bobby Adair

Chapter 24

Murphy looked at me with a face that told me to be quiet and keep my thoughts to myself. He'd been around me enough to know my moods. He could see that I was pissed. I was apt to say any number of stupid, insensitive things that wouldn't make anything any better. Being a good friend, he was trying to keep me from doing that.

Sure, our new friends needed food. We all needed food.

But I'd run on an empty stomach for so many days that the concept of three meals a day had not only stopped being a luxury, but had also stopped seeming like a necessity.

In my head, a grub run was just one more obstacle.

I wanted so sorely to go and kill those Smart White motherfuckers all over Austin, but I needed first to get Steph out of Jay's hands—hands that in my imagination, grew more lecherous with each passing hour. On top of that, I had to—well I didn't have to, I agreed to—follow Gretchen's advice, which was to follow Dalhover's plan as a safer way to pull off Steph's rescue.

Everybody thought my Rambo plan was—well, they didn't say half-baked, but I saw it on their faces.

Peer pressure. Ugh!

But putting off Steph's rescue meant pushing back my Smart One hunt even further. And it all started with logistical problems. The consensus in the group was to make our first step raiding the houses on the hills above the cove for food and—with any luck—weapons. I'd argued that beer was, in fact, just liquid bread, with a nice buzz as a fringe benefit. Nobody agreed. They all blabbered on about the benefits of real food.

Did it make sense?

Yes. It did. But that just pissed me off all the more.

To Gretchen, Paul and the others, Dalhover said, "We'll leave two of the guns with you."

"Why does Murphy have to go again? That's what I don't understand." Rachel was not happy about the plan and didn't mind letting her anger show.

In another pointless attempt at placating her, Murphy said, "We've talked about this plenty. You know it makes sense for me and Zed to go ashore. The Whites don't see us the same way they see the rest of you."

"How many stories have you told me already about the dangerous exploits of Mighty Murphy and his sidekick the Valiant Null Spot?" Rachel topped it off with a belittling laugh. "And I'm supposed to believe you're going to be safe."

"Let's not pretend you're telling me what to do." Murphy had come to the end of his patience. The volume of what he said next made that clear. "I'm going."

Rachel understood that whatever else she had to say on the subject was wasted breath. She crossed her arms and glared at me instead. Like it was my fault that Murphy was coming along. Well, maybe a little.

Getting back on track, Dalhover said, "I'll have one rifle. Zane has his machete—"

Murphy raised his hammer. "It ain't perfect, but it'll do."

"Do you think that'll be enough?" Gretchen asked. "Should you take another rifle?"

Dalhover shook his head. "Another rifle won't help. Besides, if we run into trouble, we'll run down to the water and swim back."

"Murphy can't swim." Rachel's anger hadn't abated.

"I'll be fine," Murphy told her.

Exasperated with the whole process, I finally said, "Can we just get in the boat and go? All this talking is pointless. We know what we're going to do."

"It never hurts to plan," Paul said.

"Fine, when you guys are done, I'll be in the boat." I walked to the other side of the boathouse.

They kept talking.

I peeked out through the front window where Freitag was keeping watch. She said, "It's clear."

"Okay." I lifted the handle on the garage door in front of the slip that held the bass boat. I stopped and looked up at the electric garage door opener and said, "Crap."

"It's okay," said Freitag. "Sergeant Dalhover disengaged the mechanism while you were sleeping. It should come right up."

"Thanks." I lifted slowly, doing my best to minimize the noise.

Cool, fresh air blew in off the water as the door rose. By the time I had it all the way up, the discussion had ended, and both Dalhover and Murphy were getting into the boat; Dalhover at the stern, Murphy in the middle. That left the bow for me.

I asked Freitag, "Will you close it when we go?"

She nodded.

I took my spot in the front of the boat and turned back to Dalhover, who flipped a switch on the silent, electric trolling motor. The boat moved slowly out of the boathouse.

Once out in the water, Dalhover angled the boat to point the bow at the shore and reversed the direction. Freitag tiptoed and reached up to the garage door handle and brought it slowly down. The others stood on the dock with their emotions on their faces.

Bobby Adair

Chapter 25

We left the bass boat anchored in waist-deep water a dozen feet from shore, cautiously crossed a hundred yards of sloping backyard, and let ourselves in through a back door that had previously been kicked in. After closing the door behind us and positioning ourselves in the living room for what we thought might be a good defense, Murphy called into the dark house, "Anybody home?"

The house was quiet. But the smell of old rot let us know that death had visited well before us.

He called again, of course. "Anybody home?"

We listened to the silent house for a minute longer.

"C'mon." Dalhover led the way toward the kitchen.

Despite the back doors having been broken through and the smell of the rotting corpse somewhere inside, everything about the house appeared to be in order. Once in the kitchen, Dalhover positioned himself in a corner between the sink and a Cuisinart appliance so he'd have a view of both entrances. He readied the rifle at his shoulder and said, "I'll cover. You guys search."

Murphy was closest to what appeared to be a pantry, and he peeked through its open door. "Somebody beat us here," he said.

I crossed the kitchen. It was dark in the pantry, but the shelves were empty. Everything was indeed gone. "Let's check the cupboards."

We worked our way around the kitchen, but found nothing but dishes, coffee cups, pans, utensils, and cookbooks. Not even spice bottles were left.

When I found myself in front of the refrigerator, I glanced at the others. I didn't want to leave the house empty-handed. "This probably won't smell good." I yanked on the door.

Before I could see inside, I knew already that it was pointless. There was no immediate clinking of bottles and jars as the door swung open. It had been emptied of anything salvageable. Only the rotting items remained. I closed it before too much of the stink clung to my clothes.

Murphy was disappointed.

"Do you want to check the rest of the house?" Dalhover asked.

I peered into the darkness through one of the kitchen's doors and shrugged. "If someone beat us here, it may be a waste of time."

"They may have missed some things." Murphy was talking himself back into optimism. "There was a set of steak knives in that drawer. Those will be useful."

"Any weapon is better than none," I agreed.

"Zane, you lead the way." Dalhover pointed the barrel of his rifle at one of the kitchen doors. "Let's stick together and do this quickly."

Chapter 26

With only the steak knives in the bag, we crossed through the trees toward the second house on our search.

Murphy whispered, "It's weird how some parts of town don't seem to have any Whites."

"I wonder why?" That got me thinking about the peculiarities of the infected behavior. I wondered if there was something significant to learn about the empty areas. I especially wondered if there was something in these areas that repelled the Whites, and if so, was that something that could be replicated?

"Stay quiet," Dalhover told us. "Keep looking."

Yes, Dad. But again, he was right.

When we came out of the trees, we weren't far from the next house, and Dalhover stopped and dropped to a knee with his weapon at his shoulder, scanning back and forth across the house.

That alarmed me and Murphy both. We both dropped to our knees on each side of him.

Murphy whispered first. "The ground floor windows are boarded up. The top floor windows are open."

"You think somebody's here?" I asked.

Dalhover shrugged. "Somebody tried to fortify it."

Dalhover gestured for us to follow him back into the woods.

Once we were far enough in that we couldn't be seen, he said, "Whether there's anybody in there now, there was somebody in there, somebody that planned to survive this thing. My bet, they are the ones that ransacked that other house and probably all the other ones around here."

"Yeah," Murphy agreed. "So if we want to find anything, it's already in that house."

"But?" There was definitely a "but" in the situation, and I needed to know that I wasn't the only one thinking it.

"But," Dalhover answered, "we might find a frightened person or group in there who will shoot us if we get too close."

Chapter 27

Murphy was tall, and with his fat melting away and uncovering powerful muscles, he could intimidate without having to say anything. Dalhover looked like a transient who collected money at an intersection and lived under a bridge. Not the sort anyone would welcome. But I was thin, pale, and still bald from the day when I'd been initiated into the naked horde in a creepy hair-pulling episode. I looked more like one of the crazed Whites than Murphy.

We had no good choices when deciding who to send to the front door to knock.

In the end, I went. Though we only had one gun with us, Murphy and Dalhover could both shoot. More precisely, they could hit what they shot at. What was I going to do if the chosen door knocker got into trouble on the porch, throw my machete across the yard and frighten someone when it clinked against a brick wall?

So I left Dalhover and Murphy in the bushes and crossed the yard. After stepping up onto the patio, I knocked and stepped back from the door and just a little to the side. It didn't make sense that someone would unload a shotgun through the door to kill me for knocking, but I did look like a virus-laden monster, and I did have an overactive imagination.

I took another step back from the door and another to my left. No point in making it easy when the shooting started.

Hearing nothing but crickets, I looked over my shoulder and spotted Dalhover where he'd concealed himself behind some cacti and big landscaping stones. I shrugged.

He pointed at the door again. So I knocked again, already doubting anyone was inside.

Crickets kept chirping.

I stepped up to the door and pounded loudly three times, stepped to the side, out of prime shotgun range, and waited.

I was not rewarded with an answer. I looked around, back at the tree line, up the driveway, and at the corners of the house. Habit. I tried the doorknob. It was locked. Oh well. "Hey, if there's anyone in there, let me know, okay?"

Murphy chuckled.

I pointed my middle finger at him and continued calling at the closed door, "I'm planning to come in upstairs and climb in through a window. If you want me to go away, now would be a good time to tell me."

No response.

I turned my back to the door so that Murphy and Dalhover had a clear view of me. I pointed up.

We'd agreed beforehand that if no one answered, we weren't going to bust down the door. The house, while being no real protection from the naked horde, looked secure enough to protect us from the disorganized infected that were always about.

Dalhover pointed to his left and moved back into the woods. Murphy followed. I sat down on a wicker chair at the corner of the wide porch and watched. Well, I couldn't see them in the darkness once they got back in the trees, but I heard them moving. When they were in position where they had a view of the side and back of the house, it would be my turn to get to work.

As they crept through the woods, much more audibly than I'm sure they thought, I listened for any sounds from inside the house. Still nothing. If there were people inside, what could they be thinking? I shook my head for no reason other than to participate in the dialogue in my imagination.

There wasn't any reason for the residents not to say something. They were either long gone or dead.

The sounds from the woods stopped. Murphy and Dalhover were in position. Dalhover would have the rear and one side of the house covered. If anyone showed themselves with obvious ill intent, Dalhover wasn't likely to miss. He'd put a bullet where it needed to go.

I walked around to the side of the house to a spot near the corner, where the patio roof attached to the house. A thick steel gas pipe ran up the wall, probably to provide gas for an upstairs laundry room. At least, that was my guess. Building codes back when the house was built required a pipe of monkey bar thickness on mounts that kept the pipe physically separated from the house by—as luck would have it—just enough space for me to wrap my fingers all the way around. How I learned that I could use a gas line to scale an exterior wall to gain access to upstairs windows and roofs is one of those details easily explained by my delinquent youth.

Once I laid a hand on the pipe, it took all of ten seconds to climb onto the patio roof that spanned the back of the house. Six windows were open across the back upper floor, letting a cool breeze blow in off the lake. I chose the closest to the corner of the house for letting myself in. I drew my machete and used the tip to pry up the edge of the screen. It popped right off. I set it to the side for reattachment later. Not many luxuries were left in the world, but screened windows allowed for mosquito-free sleeping. That was an underappreciated luxury in the recently passed land of air conditioned rooms and permanently closed windows.

Curtains billowed into the room, obscuring the deep shadows within. I poked my head inside. Just to the right of the window stood a tall chest of drawers. With a headboard against the wall to the right, a twin-sized bed stuck out into the room, unmade. Across the room, sliding closet doors were closed. A door in the far left corner exited, presumably to a hall.

I sniffed the air. No death. That was a relief.

Feeling pretty safe, I leaned back out, turned around, and stuck a leg inside. Bending over, I stepped inside and stood up.

Looking at the bedroom door as my eyes adjusted to the darker room, I nearly pissed myself when something metallic pressed against the back of my neck as a voice softly said, "Don't move."

Chapter 28

Then I got mad. "God dammit. I fucking knocked. Why'd you let me come in if you were going to put a gun to my neck when I got inside?"

He said, "Don't alert your friends, or I'll shoot."

"What, so you can shoot them too? Well, fuck you. I don't like this world anymore, anyway. I need a rest." Then, without turning, I hollered, "Don't come in. Fucktard has a gun on me."

The man behind me cursed, hit me on the head, and pushed me forward.

I guess he'd planned to knock me out, but all he did was make me angrier as I stumbled forward. "Damn, dude."

I pulled my machete out as I caught my balance and spun to face my assailant. The quick move surprised the guy, who'd apparently been hiding on the other side of the dresser. At least, it surprised him so much that he didn't shoot. I swung the blade down hard at his wrists with the full intention of cutting off a hand just as I'd done to Bird Man, or whatever the fuck his real name was.

But, as the blade was coming down, I saw the stark white face of the man who held the gun and I stopped just as the blade touched his forearm. I stepped to the side and pushed down, letting the machete's edge convince the man that lowering his weapon was a good idea. "Drop it."

"No."

I shook my head. "Really? If I was going to hurt you, don't you think I would have just chopped your fucking hand off?" Yeah, I know, idiotic logic to use on a man I was currently threatening, but neither of us stopped to question whether I was making sense. "Now drop the gun."

It fell to the carpet.

"Step back into the corner, Dipshit."

Before stepping, the man glanced at the bedroom door, which was behind me by then.

Crap.

I quickly raised the blade and pressed it to his throat.

A woman's voice from behind me said, "If you think that's going to keep me from shooting you, you're an idiot. I don't even like him."

"Whatever," I answered, more confidently than I had any reason to be. "If you were going to shoot me, you would have already done it."

"Lower the machete," she ordered.

I leaned forward, putting my weight on the blade that was pressed against Dipshit's throat. "You're not shooting me already, so I'm guessing that's because you think Dipshit here will get cut. So I think I'll just leave it here. Come around here where I can see you."

"You may think that you're in charge, with your stupid little sword—"

"Ask Dipshit if he thinks my stupid little machete is sharp enough to cut his throat out."

Dipshit said, "It is."

Feet moved on the carpet.

With her weapon aimed at me—no surprise—a woman moved over to the other side of the bed where I could see her. She said, "Okay, asshole, what's your plan? Because if you think there is any circumstance under which I'm giving up this gun, or even lowering it, I've got news for you. You're the dipshit, because you don't know anything."

"Let's see," I said. "I know you don't want Dipshit to die. You don't even want to take the chance. So he's your brother or your boyfriend or some shit. Good for me, I think. There's also a pretty good chance that if you shoot that gun at me, you'll miss."

"I'm ten feet away from you, asshole. Why don't you lower your machete and take that bet?"

I cut my eyes quickly in her direction. "You're just as infected as me, but a Slow Burn, since we're talking."

"A Slow Burn?" she asked.

"You know. Infected people like us, who didn't turn."

"I'm already bored," she said, pulling a face.

I said, "You're kind of a smartass bitch, aren't you?"

"Hey," said Dipshit, offended.

"Be cool, Dipshit," I told him, pressing the blade just a tad. Why? Why not? He at least needed to be totally convinced that I had him under my power.

"Steve, stay calm," the girl said. "Don't worry about him."

Without turning his head, Steve looked at the girl. "You don't have a giant sword at your throat."

"Machete, Dipshit." Sometimes being an ass just comes naturally to me.

"Jesus, Asshole, does it matter?" The girl's voice was louder, her words more angry. The stress of the situation was getting the best of her.

"Look," I said, "Let's all take a deep breath, okay? I don't want to cut Dipshit's throat, or I would have done it already." I glanced at the girl, "You don't want to shoot me, or you would have done that already. Maybe none of us has bad intentions. Is it possible that we're all good folks who've stumbled into a bad situation?"

The girl said, "You broke into our house, Asshole."

"Jesus. Really? I knocked on the door like ten fucking times."

"Three."

"Whatever. Does it matter?"

The girl glared at me.

"When you and Dipshit raided the other houses around here," I asked, "did you knock or just break in?"

"Stop calling him Dipshit, Asshole."

"Tell you what, I'll stop calling Steve Dipshit if you'll stop calling me Asshole."

"Why don't you just leave?" she asked.

"I'm not totally against doing that," I said. "But while you have that gun pointed at me, I'm not going to lower my machete."

"So if I lower the gun, you'll lower the machete?" she asked.

"I'd prefer that you put it down," I said.

"I told you there's no way that's going to happen."

"And how do I know you won't just raise it and shoot at me once I lower the machete?" I asked.

"That's a chance you'll just have to take. Like you said, I probably can't hit you anyway. Be a man, Asshole. Take a chance. You've got balls, right?"

I figured I take another tack and try to defuse the situation. "My name is Zed."

"Did you make that up to sound like a badass?"

"Really? You're going to make fun of my name? Are we back in third grade again?"

Dipshit—I mean, Steve—said, "Angie, lower the gun, please. Zed, she won't shoot you."

"How do I know that?" I asked.

Steve said, "She's not like that."

"Yes, I am." The girl raised her voice to make the point.

"I think you're not going to shoot, because you're as likely to hit Steve as me if you shoot that thing." I took a deep breath and then took a chance. "I'm going to lower the machete. I don't want to hurt Steve or you either, Angie. I was just looking for some dinner."

"What about your friends outside?" she asked.

"What? I can't have friends to cover my ass? You have Steve, right?" I lowered the machete and let it hang straight down. "Thanks for not shooting me. Would you lower the gun please?"

Angie looked at Steve. Steve nodded. Angie glanced at the window, looked at me, and then looked back at Steve. "Don't try anything." She lowered her weapon, but kept both hands on it.

Not even aware that I'd been wound tight with the tension of the situation, I felt myself relax a bit. "Thank you."

Steve said, "If you want some food, we can give you some before you go."

"We can't just give food to anybody who breaks in," Angie argued.

"We have enough for a while," said Steve.

"So you guys probably already raided most of the houses around here?" I asked.

"Yes," Steve answered.

"Don't tell him that," Angie said, not at all pleased that Steve was divulging secrets.

"Listen, I'll be happy to have whatever you can spare. The only thing I've found in the last twenty-four hours is warm beer. It's better than nothing, but me and my friends could use a little solid food. But before we go too far with this, I need to lean out the window and wave to my friends to let them know I'm okay, or they'll worry. Cool?"

Angie stepped to her side to get a better view through the window on the side of the room. "Just so you know, if you signal them to come in here, you'll be the first one shot."

"You'll be dead before you raise that gun." Dalhover's voice startled all of us. With the barrel of his rifle aimed at Angie's head, he stepped out of the hall and into the room. "Drop it."

Angie face showed so much anger I thought she might try to raise the gun and shoot at Dalhover.

"Don't," I said, as calmly as I could.

"Please," said Steve, "drop the gun, Angie. We weren't going to hurt him." Steve looked at me with promises of revenge in his eyes.

"Be cool, Steve," I said. "Nobody's going to get hurt." I nodded toward Dalhover. "He's just protecting me."

Dalhover, in a voice that made it clear that compromise wasn't on the table, said, "Lay the weapon on the bed. Do it slow. Do it now."

Angie did as instructed.

"Murphy," Dalhover called.

Murphy leaned in through the window that I'd climbed in.

Dalhover said, "Get their weapons." To Angie he said, "Back up against that wall. You, too, Steve, step back to the wall."

Murphy climbed in the window, moved around me, and gathered up both of the weapons.

I said, "You guys are like ninjas."

Dalhover glanced at Murphy. "Cover them."

From his position standing at the foot of the bed, Murphy raised a pistol and pointed it at both Angie and Steve. I stepped around behind him.

Dalhover turned around, sidled up behind the doorjamb, and pointed his weapon down the hall. "How many more are in the house?"

"Three," Steve answered without hesitation.

Angie glared at Steve. Clearly she didn't want us to know that. She looked at Dalhover, "They'll come up here and kill you. You better leave."

"Uh-huh." Murphy's tone made it clear that he didn't believe her.

"Let's all be calm, okay?" Steve asked. "You don't need to worry about the other three."

Angie hissed, "Steve."

Steve shook his head. "They're different. They're harmless. Please, don't hurt them."

"Harmless?" I asked. "Are they kids or something?"

"No." Steve shook his head and looked at the floor. "The virus, it changed them."

I looked at Murphy. "Like Russell, you think?"

"Or Nico." Murphy frowned and glanced toward the door.

Dalhover said to Murphy, "Give Zane a gun. Zane, you keep an eye on them. Murphy, you come with me."

"You got it, Top." Murphy handed one of the weapons to me and turned to follow Dalhover who was already moving up the hall.

Holding the pistol in the general direction of the wall where Angie and Steve were leaning, I said, "Why don't you two at least sit on the bed and get comfortable?"

Defeated or pragmatic—I couldn't tell which—Steve sat on the bed and leaned against the headboard.

Angie was defiant. "I don't think you can hit me if you shoot at me."

Steve said, "Angie, just because you can't shoot doesn't mean he can't. Just sit down and be quiet."

Angie took a half step at me.

I said, "Nope. I can't shoot for shit anymore. But you know that, don't you, Angie? Or at least you're guessing it because you can't shoot. So if you want to run over here and do something stupid, go ahead. I'll probably miss you." I raised my machete. "But that's why I carry this."

Angie's face turned to fright before she masked it again in defiance.

"Don't hurt us," Steve implored.

Angie sat on the bed.

"Like I said, nobody wants to hurt anybody. I was just looking for some food."

"Then let us go," Angie told me.

"When Dalhover finishes downstairs, okay? I'm sure he just wants to make sure that nobody is going to shoot at us when we're leaving."

"I'm sure." It was sarcasm. Angie just wasn't the trusting type.

"Yeah, whatever." I looked at Steve. Angie could be ignored now that she had no pistol in her hand. "You guys are both infected, but like me."

"I guess," Steve answered.

"Was Angie always a bad shot or is that recent?" I asked.

"What do you mean?"

"Has her marksmanship declined lately?"

"I think it's been getting worse all along," he said.

"Don't tell him that," Angie told Steve.

Steve rolled his eyes. "And she's got a shorter temper."

"I hear ya," I said. "I can't shoot worth a shit anymore either. I'm starting to think the virus is deteriorating my eye-hand coordination."

Steve nodded.

Angie looked away.

"Did you both get infected at the beginning? I mean, what's your deal here?"

Angie turned to Steve. "Don't say anything."

I rolled my eyes again. "Like I said. We'll go. We were just looking for some food, that's all. We're not looking to hurt anybody."

Chapter 29

Downstairs in the living room, Dalhover took the pistol that I'd been holding, removed the magazine, checked that the chamber was clear, and handed the weapon to Steve, who was sitting in a big leather chair at one end of the coffee table. Opposite him, in a matching chair, Angie fumed and pretty much kept quiet. On the couch between them, three mute Slow Burns sat with blank expressions. One was a teenage girl. Another was in her mid-thirties. The third was a young man about my age. They were all some version of Russell, harmless and near useless.

Dalhover put the magazine on the mantle behind where Murphy, he, and I were standing. He said, "We're going to leave. We're not going to take your weapons or rob you of your food. If you could do me the favor of telling me if there are any houses left bordering the cove that you haven't ransacked yet, I'd appreciate it."

Murphy removed the magazine from the pistol he had and laid it on the mantle.

"You're just going to leave us?" Angie snapped.

Nobody paid her any attention.

Steve said, "We've hit every house that borders the cove except that big one out on the point." He pointed. We all three looked, but of course, saw nothing but plywood where the sliding glass doors used to be.

He said, "It's that big Mediterranean house with all the statues and terraces and stuff."

"Why not there?" Dalhover asked.

"It's full of them."

"Whites?" I asked.

"Yes," Steve nodded. "Too many to worry about dealing with."

I asked, "Are they trapped inside or do they live there?"

"I think they're trapped inside. They don't ever come out."

Dalhover asked, "Besides climbing out a window, is there a door on the first floor that we can leave through?"

Steve shook his head. "No, we come and go the same way Zed came in. You guys are really just going to leave?"

Making a show of starting to go, Murphy said, "Man, let's get out of here. I'm already tired of this shit."

"Good, go," Angie told us.

"Wait," Steve said, standing half way up before Dalhover motioned for him to sit back down. "Do you guys know anything about what's going on? You're the first people we've seen in—"

"What about those assholes in that big boat?" Angie asked, reminding Steve with all the spite she could squeeze into her tone.

"We're those assholes," I told her. Turning to Steve, I said, "There's a pretty good group of people out on Monk's Island, but they don't take kindly to folks like us, if you know what I mean. So I'd steer clear of them if I were you, Steve. Angie, you might want to go out for a visit."

Steve ignored my jab at Angie and asked me, "Are there a lot like us?"

"No," I said. "We haven't met many."

Murphy laughed. "More like none, unless you count crazy-ass Nico."

"We've come across all kinds, but none that are as normal as we are," I said.

"Is the...what about the government, the Army?" asked Steve.

I shrugged.

Steve looked at Dalhover.

He shook his head and shrugged.

"What does that mean?" asked Steve.

"We're not aware of anything or anybody getting through this. Last I heard, New Zealand was doing okay because they quarantined early. But who knows? They might be overrun with Whites by now."

"I'm not asking about rumors from the other side of the planet." Steve looked at each of us. "Is it anarchy out there now? No government? No Army? No civilization? Is no one coming in to pick up the pieces?"

I passed along the information I'd heard from Gretchen and Paul on our abbreviated night in the houseboat, and then asked, "What's the last thing you heard?"

Angie sat up in her chair and started to say something, but convinced herself to be quiet and slumped back down.

I was getting more and more convinced that she was going to become a problem for Steve. "Do you guys have a thermometer?"

"No. Why?" asked Steve.

I said, "You might want to scavenge one when you're out. Check each other. When your temperature gets too high, you kind of lose it."

"And turn into one of them?" Steve asked.

I cut my eyes in the direction of Angie and nodded.

Dalhover asked Steve, "When was the last time you talked to anyone?"

"Before the power went out," he answered.

"Have you guys been here the whole time?" Dalhover asked next.

Steve nodded and pointed at the young girl on the couch. "I found her wandering when I was scavenging a couple miles from here, trying to keep hidden from the crazy ones. I figured early on that the power was going out, so I figured I'd find a place by the lake."

"This place?" I asked.

"Yes, there was a guy here already, Manny. He was like us —what'd you call it—a Slow Burn. He took us in and we started scavenging what we could when there wasn't any of them around."

"What happened to Manny?" I asked. "He's not here."

"Shot. He was down by the shore getting water from the lake one morning when some guys came by in a ski boat. He called and waved them over. I don't know if they couldn't hear him over the sound of the engine or what. When they got close, they shot him, like five or six times. Like after he fell they were just being mean or something."

"Did they come ashore after that?" I asked. "Did they find your house?"

Steve shook his head while his eyes fixed on some distant spot. He was still having trouble with Manny's death at the hands of the guys in the boat. "No. The infected heard the shots and came running out of the trees from every direction. When the guys in the boat saw the infected coming, they shot a few more times and left. I don't know why they shot Manny. They just shot and laughed and shot some more. I think they were just shooting because he had pale skin, and that was their idea of fun."

Disturbing. I couldn't help but glance down at my own white skin. I wondered if it was the guys in Jay's bunch that did it.

"And those were the last people you saw, before us?"

"Yes." Steve pointed at Angie and the others. "I took each of them in when I came across them."

"How'd you know they weren't like the Whites?" I asked. That was a point I needed to learn about. Ever since killing that girl outside the walls at Sarah Mansfield's house, I wondered, when I killed a White, whether I was actually murdering a Slow Burn.

"They didn't behave like the others. They seemed different. I took a chance that they were like me."

His process seemed like guessing to me. I said, "Be careful with that, dude."

Chapter 30

By the time we left, we were getting along with Steve fairly well. Even Angie toned down her anger and was tolerable. We worked out a trade: Steve fed us and gave Dalhover enough food to feed the others in the boathouse for a couple of meals. In trade for that and two more days of food that would come when we fulfilled our end of the bargain, we'd give Steve an M4 from our stash, along with a thousand rounds of ammunition. Since we had a dozen weapons and thousands upon thousands of rounds back in the Humvee that Murphy and I had acquired from the dead snipers, it seemed like a reasonable trade.

After we ate, Murphy and I escorted Dalhover down to the cove, saw that he got into the boat with no problems, and said our goodbyes. He had his tasks, we had ours. Murphy and I were back on foot and headed toward the dam. We crossed between the houses, got to the road, and started to follow it away from the lake.

"What time is it?" I asked.

"Late," Murphy told me.

"Dude, you've got that big super-fly watch. Just tell me."

"Two a.m." he said.

I looked at the trees on both sides of the road. I listened. "I'm thinking it's a two- or three-mile walk to get to the dam."

"Or four or five," Murphy grunted.

"Maybe. When did you turn pessimist?"

"Hanging with you," he said, without any humor.

I pointed through the trees to our left. "That group of naked bald ones that had Rachel trapped in the cove was off that way somewhere."

"I don't hear anything."

"They were rowdy because they had Rachel and the others trapped in that marina."

Murphy rolled his eyes. "It was like two days ago. I remember. I'm just saying, I don't hear anything now. Either they're all napping in the trees around here, or they aren't hassling anyone right now."

"Dude, what's up your ass?"

Murphy didn't say anything. He just kept walking.

After a while, I said, "I think we'll probably make better time if we just stay on the road. What do you think?"

"It doesn't matter."

I asked, "Are you in a bad mood about something that I don't know about?"

Murphy ignored my comment. "If we stay on the road, it'll be easier to see where we're going, and it'll be easier for Whites to see us. If we go through the woods, we'll make more noise, and we'll be easier to hear. There are pros and cons both ways. In the end, it doesn't matter. Either we'll run into Whites or we won't. You never know where those dudes are gonna turn up, except it'll be exactly where you don't want them."

I nodded. "You're right about that."

We walked by moonlight for several silent hours, watching the dark shadows in the trees and by the houses. We didn't hear or see a single White. We didn't see evidence that anything was still alive. We saw broken windows and abandoned cars. We passed ransacked houses, businesses with furnishings on the lawns, desks and chairs upside down in parking lots. Trash bins were spilled. Empty boxes tumbled with the breeze. The smell of rot floated on the wind. It felt like we were walking across the corpse of the world, and the deadness wore on me more and more every time I stepped over the bones of someone not as lucky as myself.

We reached a tall hill just south of the river with a view of Mansfield Dam's tall face just off to our left, and a view of the river snaking off to the southeast, forming the upstream end of Lake Austin. We sat down and rested, with only another hour of darkness left to keep us hidden.

After taking a long drink from my water bottle, I said, "I wonder if, when the naked ones come through an area, they pick up all of the Whites and make them tag along."

"Or kill them and eat them."

"Yeah, I suppose that could be true. I wonder if that's why some parts of town seem to be free of them or anything else."

Murphy stood up and stretched. "So maybe instead of going out to hunt them, you need to be thinking about letting them kill each other off, like that dude said they would. Maybe you should just let them do their business without your help."

"Is that what they did for you when they climbed all over the riverboat and—" The look on Murphy's face told me I'd said enough.

He put his water bottle in his bag, very pointedly not saying a word to me, and started hiking down the slope. We weren't going to cross over the dam as we'd done on the first night. Neither were we going to cross the tall 620 bridge behind the dam. That would leave us too exposed for too long. We were going down the steep mountain all the way to the old concrete bridge that stood just a few feet above the river's surface below. We'd cross that. On the other side was the crumbled boat ramp where we'd tied our ski boat to an old piling.

We didn't speak as we made our way down the steep slope between the trees, slipping on the loose limestone enough times to scrape our elbows and knees. Murphy even banged his head once, but kept pounding out a brisk pace as though nothing had happened.

It wasn't until we were crossing the low bridge with our boat in sight that I said, "I'm sorry."

"I know."

"You're bleeding on the back of your head," I said.

Murphy reached up, touched the wound, and looked at his hand. "I know."

"You're probably going to need stitches."

"I know."

"This isn't like you," I said. "Stop saying 'I know'."

We were halfway across the bridge, as visible as we could possibly be, and Murphy turned toward me and stopped.

"I said I was sorry," I told him.

"Sometimes you say shit and you don't stop to think how it affects other people."

"I'm sorry about the riverboat thing. I know you had a hard time with it."

"I did. I need to move forward. I don't need you blindsiding me with your snarky shit little comments just so you can be right about some stupid ass thing that nobody cares about. You got me?" Murphy turned and stomped off.

I didn't follow; I'm not sure if I was being obstinate and getting myself ready for an argument, or whether I was concerned enough that I needed to get Murphy to talk about what was going on in that big white head of his.

After a dozen steps, Murphy spun and said, "You gonna stand there, or are you just being a dick?"

"Is that it?" I asked. "Is it me who's being the dick here?"

Stomping again, Murphy came up to me, raised his fist, and though I saw it coming from ten steps away, I didn't do anything to avoid it. He punched me in the face so hard that I didn't even feel it.

When I opened my eyes, all I saw were stars, not the little ones that float in front of your eyes after you've been bonked in the head, but actual stars in the night sky. I was lying on my back on the bridge. As I sat up, I saw Murphy sitting on the edge of the bridge where a railing would have been on a modern bridge; I sniffled and realized that my nose was bleeding.

I touched my face and saw the blood on my hand. I spit it out of my mouth. Oddly, I wasn't angry. In years past, I'd have been up already, punching, kicking, and cussing. That was kind of my thing, fighting for no good reason at all. I spit more blood out of my mouth, sniffled up a bit more, and stood. I was a little wobbly, but that was passing.

Murphy was a good dozen paces down the bridge, frowning at the water flowing below his feet as though the rest of the world had ceased to be a problem. When I walked up and got close, he said, "If you need to hit me back, you go ahead and do what you need to do. I won't punch you again."

Instead, I laughed and sat down beside him. I spit out another gob of clotting blood. "You know, you told me about a hundred times you were gonna punch me in the face. I thought you were joking."

With sad eyes, Murphy smiled and looked at me. "That's true. But I was kidding. I'm sorry 'bout that, man."

"What are friends for?"

"Not for that."

I shrugged. "Maybe sometimes. Why don't you tell me what's going on?"

"This shit is just hard sometimes."

"What do you mean?"

Murphy rubbed his big hands over his face. "Everything."

"Yeah?"

The water below our dangling feet was gurgling, and the sound seemed to have Murphy's full attention. "Where do I start?"

"Anywhere. Mandi." I shrugged. "You're not past that yet."

"That's part of it. No, I'm not past it. I—" Murphy bit back his emotions.

I gave him a few minutes.

When he spoke again, he said, "It's like I traded Mandi for Rachel. I know one has nothing to do with the other, but it feels like that, like I pissed God off so much about something that now he doesn't want me to be all the way happy, just kinda part of the way there."

"You know that's not true."

"No, I don't." Murphy exhaled a long breath, as though blowing out all the stale air trapped in his lungs might take his troubles with it. "All the killing is wearing on me."

"The infected, you mean?" I asked.

"It doesn't bother you?" Murphy asked.

"Sometimes. Less now than before."

"I kinda figured you were some kind of black-hearted zombie killer and didn't care much about them."

"You know that's not true," I said.

Murphy shrugged and looked around for a bit. "It doesn't bother me that much when we're in the shit, you know, and they're coming at us, and it's us or them. But sometimes, it's kind of a rush. I'm getting addicted to the excitement, I think."

I nodded. I knew all about that.

"So when you drag me off to go do some crazy shit, part of me wants to say 'fuck you'. Part of me doesn't want any part of the killin'. 'Cause you know, every time we head out, somebody's gonna get killed."

"Seems like that sometimes." And it did.

"Part of me wants to go out and get that rush," said Murphy. "It's addicting. But part of me wants to go out and just kill those fuckers because I've got this anger 'bout what happened and all, and I just want to kill as many of 'em as I can."

I was definitely with Murphy on that one.

He said, "Like that day when we were up there on the ridge testing out those suppressors, we didn't need to stay out there and kill all of those Whites. They used to be people, just like us. But once I started shooting, I wanted to kill every single one of them. I wanted more of them to come running up the block."

"I don't think that's unnatural," I said. "Given the circumstances, I think that's normal."

"But that's what you don't get."

"What's that?" I asked.

"You don't have a problem being a black-hearted killer. You're different." Murphy looked over at me, and his eyes looked sadder than when he started. "It's like there's some black hole in you that's full of crazy shit, and it doesn't matter how many dead Whites you throw in there. It'll never be enough. So when you want to go off on a killing rampage, I think you should. It might be the only thing that ever fills all that up. It might be the only way you're ever going to get past whatever all that anger shit is that you're carrying around."

Murphy's guesses were hitting so close to home that I couldn't come up with a smart aleck response to deflect the conversation.

"But I can't do that," he said. "I mean, I'll go. I'll watch your back. I'll go all the way down into your black hole with you, if that's what you want. But for me, killing those three dumb-asses behind that 7-Eleven was enough for me. I got all of my hate out of my system then. I figured that out. I told you that. But now, it's like every time I kill a White, especially now, I know I'm not doing it to survive. I'm doing it 'cause I hate 'em. Every time, it's like I'm digging my own black hole in my soul, and when it gets deep enough, I'm gonna fall in and I'm never gonna come out again."

Murphy was done. I was left without anything to say.

Shit.

After a while, as we realized neither of us had any more to say, we got up. We walked through the trees over to the old boat ramp. We waded through the water in silence, got into the boat, untied it, and headed downriver.

Chapter 31

The sky in the east was starting to glow when we tied the boat to a tree pretty close to where the riverboat had initially run aground during the flood. I didn't say anything about that. What was the point?

We left the ski boat and started our long slow hike up the mountain as the sky slowly turned orange, and the clouds glowed silver. Murphy led the way, hammer in hand. Despite our conversation on the bridge, he was ready to smash a skull.

After nearly an hour of uphill walking, we reached the back fence of the house where we'd stashed the Humvee and our weapons. The slope there was steep, and rather than hop over and try to make our way up the dew-slick grass, we used the fence for support and walked along it until we reached the house.

Then it was an easy walk across ground that grew more level with each step. When we passed the corner to the front of the house, Murphy stopped and his shoulders sagged. Stepping up beside him, mine did too. It was a gut punch. The garage door behind which we'd parked our Humvee, loaded with weapons and the last of the silencers, was open. The Humvee was gone.

All of the black-hearted rage that Murphy talked about, all of that darkness that at the time seemed like something that needed to be sloughed off for the sake of happiness, came screaming to a head as I ran out into the center of the courtyard, swinging my machete at nothing — cursing, yelling, and stomping.

In getting those weapons, we'd paid too high a price. But those weapons were my hope for rescuing Steph.

I ran over to the open garage on the ridiculously small chance that the Humvee was sitting hidden behind another of the doors. Of course it wasn't, but in my rage-impaired brain, anything was possible. I ran into the house through the open door, just knowing that I would find one of the guilty thieves inside. I needed to kill, to hack something to pieces while it begged for its life.

I raced up the stairs. I checked the bedrooms and bathrooms. I looked in the closets and under the beds. I found nothing.

My search ended with me standing in front of an empty pantry. A few days before, enough food had been in there to feed our new group for at least a week. I screamed my anger into the emptiness.

Chapter 32

People are good and people are bad, sometimes one right after the other, sometimes simultaneously. Sometimes, it's hard to tell which is which. When my tantrum came to an end and I was spinning up black fantasies about how I was going to disembowel, behead, and hack at the thieves who took my Humvee—my fucking Humvee—any thoughts I'd had an hour earlier about aspiring to be a good person were gone.

As I walked through the foyer, I grabbed an edge of the front door and pushed it with all the force I could put behind it. I felt the weight of its nine-foot-tall, five-foot-wide, glass-paneled weight fly. It slammed and shattered, dropping shards of glass all over the foyer and porch.

"God dammit. God fucking dammit."

I stomped forward, snorting and huffing like a distempered javelina and crossed the driveway to where Murphy stood. He hadn't moved since we spotted the open garage. He was fuming, eyes black, hand gripping his hammer under white knuckles, ready to pound the life out of something.

"I hope we didn't kill every White on this street," I said as I marched past Murphy, heading up the steeply sloping, cobbled driveway, "because I need to kill something now."

At the top of the driveway, I saw to my right the bushes in which Murphy and I had hidden the day we'd tested our suppressors, shooting at Whites up and down the street. Just in front of the bushes lay the remains of the only one I'd shot. His clothes were shredded and most of his flesh was gnawed away.

"Good," said Murphy, looking down at the carcass.

I glanced back. He was standing just behind me, looking at the mauled body. Whether it had been chewed on by coyotes, dogs, or Whites, I didn't care and probably wouldn't have known the difference. I'd already decided that the partially eaten body proved the presence of my prey. I cut hard to my left. Not that it mattered which direction. The house on the left was the first to catch my eye.

With Murphy stomping resolutely behind, we cut through a garden of cacti and decorative limestone chunks and kicked a lawn gnome hard enough to make it fly across the yard and bang that house's front wall.

I hissed, "We're here, fuckers."

But no fuckers came out to meet us.

The front door of the house was open, and that angered me further as I crossed the lawn and stepped up onto the porch. Once inside, I smelled the miasma of old decay. Blood stained the floors and spattered the walls, dry and brown and red. Furniture in the dining room was disarrayed. A couch lay over on its back.

Rats, maggots, and flies crawled over the dead, uncountable in the scattered mess of their bones except that three skulls were on the floor.

"Hey," I shouted into the house. No sound came back to me. The house was empty.

"Next door," Murphy said as he spun on his heel and headed back out.

Running a few steps to catch up, I said, "Works for me."

Instead of walking up to street level, we cut through the trees and underbrush that separated the two houses. Murphy pushed through, blazing the trail, and I followed.

When we burst out of the trees and back onto another lawn of crispy, brown St. Augustine grass carpeting ground still soft and muddy, our anger had dissipated an iota or two, but when I spotted another open front door, my anger found fuel to rekindle itself.

As we stepped up onto a large front porch, Murphy swung his hammer at the side of a five-gallon terra cotta flowerpot, shattering it and spilling dry black dirt into a mound that I tracked through on the way inside. The house had no smell of death, but it had been ransacked. Furniture was pushed over. Decorative items were on the floor, many broken. Paintings were knocked off the walls.

Seemingly frozen in indecision, Murphy came to a stop in the center of a patterned marble floor that gave him a view down two hallways, into the living room, and through the windows on the back of the house.

Standing beside him for a minute while I calmed a bit, I said, "We should check the house anyway."

Murphy nodded and crossed the living room. I followed him as I looked over the mess: books, couch cushions, vases, a flat panel television, and lamps. Nothing of any value.

In the kitchen, the story was the same. It was a mess. Silverware was scattered on the floor, dishes were broken. Any knife of a reasonable size was missing. The pantry was empty. Nothing else in the house proved to be of any use. All the bedrooms had been gone through. There were clothes, blankets, and pillows. I did have the presence of mind to liberate some pillowcases. Sturdy cloth bags always came in handy for something. In the garage, we found some garden tools, though nothing that could double as a good weapon. And in the space large enough for three cars, all were gone.

We left that house and headed to the next one down the street.

•

Bobby Adair

Chapter 33

The street followed the curve of the ridge, and we tromped through the trees and stomped down the dead grass of people's lawns, only to find each home thoroughly ransacked. And though we had no interest in taking a car, not a one was in a garage. None were parked in the driveways. None were parked up on the road. That was odd.

We'd been through maybe a dozen houses, each with a pre-apocalypse price upwards of a million or two. All were now in their first stages of decay with doors open, windows broken, everything inside strewn on the floor. Animals had moved in, some feasting on the remains of the dead humans inside. Many houses had water standing on the floor or soaked into the carpet. With the summer's heat gone, the thick humidity would leave that water there a long time before evaporating it. Black mold was already growing up the sheetrock walls of some of the houses. Eventually the wooden frames would rot.

Once every four or five years, hailstorms blew across the Texas hill country, dropping hailstones large enough to disintegrate the shingles on most houses. The houses not already rotting would start, once rainwater got in through the holed roofs. Before long, houses would collapse, leaving their brick facades to crumble. Weeds would grow up through cracks in the foundations that appeared as the supporting clay soil dried and shrunk.

The asphalt streets would slowly fall apart under the assault of plant roots, rain, and seasonal temperature shifts. Ten, twenty, or thirty years in the future, cedar and mesquite forests would reclaim the endless suburban sprawl.

As Murphy and I trudged up a steeply sloping front lawn, I wondered if I would live long enough to hunt in the forest that would eventually grow to replace the houses we were searching through. Up at street level, we turned and followed an unbroken curb as it arced around into a cul-de-sac, the terminus of the ridgeline.

"What do you make of that?" Murphy asked.

Cars parked haphazardly on the street and up on the curbs nearly filled the cul-de-sac. A path wide enough to drive through bisected the scattered mess of vehicles and led to a driveway that fell away down the slope, to a house under the roof peaks that were just visible out past the edge of the pavement.

"I—" I didn't know what to make of it.

Murphy stopped walking and turned slowly, looking at the trees all around. No houses were visible, only trees on undeveloped lots around the cul-de-sac, the scattered cars, and the driveway.

I said, "I'm guessing it's a White like that tattoo guy. I think something goes haywire in their brains and some of them need to collect shit."

Murphy grunted, nodded, and crossed the empty asphalt until he came to a late-model Japanese sedan. He laid a hand on its roof and looked around, still glowering.

We were near the center of the cul-de-sac, and being exposed was making me nervous. "We shouldn't be out here." I pointed to the shingled peaks out past the collection of cars. "I'm guessing the guy who rounded up all this shit is over there in that house."

"Yup." Murphy nodded, and kept nodding. He was coming to a conclusion that was getting more obvious with each nod. He pointed to the driveway. "I'll bet our Humvee is down there."

The self-evident deduction left me momentarily speechless. Yes. He was right. But that seemed at the same time too good to be true. I looked around at the trees again, looking for a trap. Nothing moved except branches swaying with the wind.

Murphy took a step toward the clear trail between the cars. I grabbed his shoulder and stopped him, feeling him tense as his temper started to flare. I said, "You're right. But let's be smart." I pointed at the trees off to our left and took off at a jog across the asphalt.

A moment later, Murphy joined me in the trees.

Still looking around at what I could see of the cul-de-sac, I said, "We've been acting like reckless dipshits all morning."

"Yeah." Murphy didn't take his eyes off the gap between the cars.

"It's going to get us in trouble if we keep it up."

Murphy agreed again.

"I know you whipped the shit out of that guy at the tattoo shop without any problem, but you know as well as I do that some of the these Smart Ones can be dangerous."

Murphy drew a long, patient breath and looked down at his hammer, obviously thinking about applying it to some Smart One's skull. He asked, "What are you thinking?"

I thumbed over my shoulder at the trees behind me. "We go down the hill a bit and work our way around that house and see what we can see. Then decide what to do."

"All right," Murphy said. "I say we stick pretty close to the road and see if we can get a look at what's down that driveway."

"You want to make sure the Humvee is there, first?" I asked.

"Yep."

Murphy started through the trees and I followed. We moved away from the pavement as we went, using the curve and slope of the ridge as our guide. Murphy hefted his hammer as he gingerly stepped between cedars. I held my machete in a comfortable, familiar grip, telling myself to proceed cautiously, but wanting to hack a White.

I was trying to get a glimpse through the trees ahead for anything that looked like a limestone wall or a shingled roof when Murphy threw up a hand, a gesture to stop. I froze in place.

My heartbeat spiked and I slowly raised my machete, ready to fight as I looked left and right, listening. But nothing was around us that I could see.

When I looked back at Murphy, he was pointing at something on the ground.

I looked down, but couldn't see it. I mouthed, "What?"

Murphy, with one hand still raised to hold me in position, bent his knees and lowered himself slowly until his pointing finger touched a thin wire running at shin height above the ground.

Holy shit!

Murphy saw on my face exactly what I was thinking, that the wire was part of a booby trap. He pointed along the wire, tracing its length. It came to a stop at an olive green box, partially hidden behind a sprout of branches at the base of a tree.

He pointed back in the direction we came from, motioned for me to stay where I was, and stood, taking great care to watch where he placed his feet. When he was up next to me, he whispered, "Follow me out. Stay close. Do exactly as I do. Don't wander off on your own path."

Without saying a word, I followed Murphy.

Chapter 34

The ground in most places among the trees was just a layer of dried cedar needle clusters an inch or two thick over sandy bits of limestone or hard rock. So, following our footprints out the way we'd come wasn't an option. There were no footprints, just trees that all looked pretty much alike.

A few steps back along our path, I grabbed Murphy's shoulder. He turned to me. I pointed in the direction we were moving and whispered, "What are the chances there are booby traps back that way?"

Murphy shrugged and looked around.

I said, "We could have been walking in a minefield since we entered the trees."

"I'm not sure I'd call it a minefield."

I rolled my eyes. "Does it matter exactly what it is?"

Still looking around at the tree trunks and across the ground, Murphy said, "This whole place could be full of traps, or that could be the only one. There's no way to know until we find some more or get blown up by one we don't see."

I turned back in the direction we'd originally been moving and looked deep into the trees. "Just luck."

"What's that?" Murphy asked.

"We're only alive because of luck," I said. "Again."

"What's your point?"

"One booby trap doesn't change anything." I pointed toward the place where the house lay out among the trees. "We have the same chance of getting killed by a mine no matter which direction we go."

Nodding slowly, Murphy said, "Yeah, I suppose you're right." His face stretched in a wicked grin.

"What are you thinking?"

"Bad thoughts." Murphy looked back at the mine strapped to the tree behind me.

I asked, "Can you disconnect it and reuse it?"

"I don't know, but I think we're on the same page."

I put a hand in my pocket and yanked out a couple of pillowcases, kept one for myself and handed one to Murphy.

He shook his head. "If I can disconnect them, you'll have to carry 'em. I'll need both hands to keep from getting blown up." Murphy pointed to pair of tree trunks that looked to be competing for the same spot in the ground. "Go stand behind those while I do this."

"But—"

"Besides getting blown up, what are you gonna do to help? Go over there where you won't get hurt."

Sulking, I walked over and put the double trunks between me and the booby trap. Murphy knelt down by the mine and leaned in close. With his back to me, I couldn't see exactly what he was doing.

It took only a few moments of work before Murphy started to laugh and waved me over.

Puzzled, I moved between the trees, keeping an eye out for any wires I might have missed on the way to my hiding place.

Once I was beside him, Murphy said, "Get down here. Look at this."

I knelt so I could see.

Murphy had the thin branches pushed to the side, exposing the whole mechanism. The wire was still taut. He pointed a finger at the wire and said, "Look around the other side of the trunk and tell me what you see."

I leaned around the small trunk. The wire that extended across the path was looped around the trunk. On the backside of the tree, held in place by the loop was some kind of clicking mechanism with a wire that ran up to an explosive device, a curved, green, rectangular container very roughly the size of a Pop-Tart box.

"So, you trip on the wire," I surmised, "the wire pulls tight, the clicker switch closes and the mine goes off." I looked at Murphy expecting a nod and a smile.

Instead, he was holding in a laugh. "Typical."

"Typical? What's that mean?"

"You don't know what this is, or how to use it?"

I was a little bit offended. "No, but how hard could it be?" As I was saying that, I realized that my guess must have been wrong.

Murphy's big fingers went to work with surprising dexterity on the thin wire, untying the knot that made the loop. "Untie the mine."

I fumbled with the wires.

Murphy had his untied in seconds and brushed me out of the way, having little patience for my difficulty. Again, it took only seconds, and the wire loosened and the green mine fell. I gasped and caught it before it hit the ground.

Murphy laughed. "It needs an electrical charge to blow. Dropping it won't hurt it."

"The fall won't set it off?" It was hard to believe.

"You could beat it with a hammer and it wouldn't go off." Murphy held his hammer out to me. "You wanna try?"

I shook my head.

He looked down at the mine I was holding gingerly in two hands. "Turn it over and see what it says."

Looking at him like he was keeping a secret from me, I turned the mine over and read it out loud, "Front toward enemy."

"It's an M18 Claymore directional mine." Murphy said. He held up the clicker. "This is the clacker. You gotta click it three times to make it go off."

"Three times?" I asked.

"This booby trap wouldn't work. You'd get one click when you tripped over the wire. The Claymore wouldn't go off."

I said, "I'm confused."

"Whoever set this up, it wasn't somebody who understood what he was doing."

"Not soldiers?" I asked.

Murphy shook his head. "Like you said up on the street, probably some knucklehead White with a car fetish."

That made me feel a bit better about sneaking up on the house. "So our Humvee might be sitting in the driveway and all we have to do is get in and drive off."

"Let's not get ahead of ourselves." Murphy looked at me seriously. "Just because this guy doesn't know how to set up a trap with his Claymores doesn't mean he isn't dangerous."

"Yeah," I agreed. "Where do you think he got the Claymores?"

"Probably the same place we got the grenades from."

"The munitions bunkers at Camp Mabry?" I asked.

Murphy raised his eyebrows. Where else?

"I hope he had as much difficulty with it." I put the Claymore, its wires, and clacker in my bag.

"Let me disconnect those clacker wires from the mine first," said Murphy. "Don't want you blowing us up when we're traipsing through the woods." I held the pillowcase open and Murphy reached in.

We collected two more Claymores while working our way through the trees on the way to a black metal fence that bordered an expansive property. Whether natural or excavated, the front yard was a half-acre of mowed—now dead—grass and flowerbeds, laid out in front of a ranch-style house that might have covered a half-acre all by itself. Across the front lawn, snaking between the flower gardens, a driveway was covered with cars. Some parked neatly, others halfway in the grass. By the front door sat two Humvees. Neither had a machine gun mounted on the roof. Out across the yard, halfway to the fence and visible from every window on the front of the house, sat another Humvee—our Humvee. The machine gun mounted on the roof was all the proof I needed.

"I can jump this fence and be inside in like, twenty seconds," I said. "You run back up through the trees and I'll pick you up in the cul-de-sac." I looked over at Murphy for agreement.

He was shaking his head.

I looked over at the house's dark windows. "Unless there's some kind of super sniper in there, he's not going to be able to hit me, as fast as I'll be running across the lawn. Once I'm inside, I'm home free."

Murphy's brow furrowed as he looked at the house and back at the Humvee. "Any decent shot will get you before you get halfway across."

I huffed and looked back and forth across the lawn. "I'll be halfway there before anyone even sees me."

"Maybe." Murphy scooted further back into the trees. "You wanna take that chance?"

Yes. Some days I felt invincible, though I had to constantly remind myself that my delusions of invincibility were driven primarily by anger and stupidity. Reluctantly, I asked, "What do you think?"

"No point in chancing it. If we wait 'til dark, we just hike across, get in and drive off. No danger. No risk."

I looked longingly at the Humvees, knowing Murphy was right.

He said, "Let's fade back in the woods a bit, walk around the perimeter, and see what we can see. We'll gather up as many Claymores as we can. I'm thinkin', in our future, shit that blows up will always be useful. At dusk, that'll be the hardest time to be seen running across the lawn. Depending on what we learn when we're checking this place out, that's when we'll steal our Humvee back."

Chapter 35

We started on a zigzag path through the trees, going up near the fence where we could see the house, then   back downhill and away. With much of the day to burn, we had plenty of time for our Claymore Easter egg hunt, and we found them with ease. The tripwires had been strung with some silvery wire that was pretty easy to see over the brown and green background, at least when you knew to look for it.

After I'd put a fourth Claymore into my pillowcase, we rounded a curve on the hill and found ourselves in a haze of smoke. Murphy stopped and sniffed the air, looking in the direction of the house. "Damn, that smells good."

I said, "I can't believe those fuckers are up there having a barbecue."

"We might have to steal some of that, if we can." Murphy hiked up the hill, following the smoke back toward the house.

I followed as the smoke drifted through the tree branches overhead.

Murphy looked back at me and whispered, "I'm surprised they're not drawing in every White in the neighborhood with that smell."

"What are they cooking?" I asked.

"What?" Murphy sniffed the air.

"They can't run down to the H-E-B to buy a brisket," I said. "So what do you think? A deer? A dog? Maybe a wild pig?"

Murphy shrugged. "There are plenty of wild pigs in the woods in east Texas."

"That's wishful thinking. If anything, it's deer, I'll bet." I took a look around us in the woods. Always checking for anything that might be sneaking up. "I've never seen a wild pig around here."

Murphy licked his lips. "I don't care if it's a deer, or a dog, or a cat." He started forward again.

The hill grew steeper the closer we got to the fence, and by the time we were at a level to see across the backyard, we were mostly invisible from the house, hidden by the slope. The backyard was only half as big as the front and was mostly covered by an expansive patio. On the near side of the patio, behind several cords of neatly stacked oak wood, I spotted the source of the smoke: a long barbecue smoker, chugging white clouds into the air. The tops of two heads were visible just on the other side of the smoker.

I nudged Murphy and pointed. He'd been looking across the pool to the other side of the yard and was frowning when he looked up. He said, "I see 'em. C'mon." Murphy took off, moving quickly across the slope, staying far enough down so that he couldn't be seen from the backyard.

I hurried after, curious what had spurred him to hustle.

We dodged prickly pears that were scattered between the cedars and stayed away from loose, gravelly spots in which we might noisily slip, bringing unwanted attention from the people who stole our Humvee.

Eventually, Murphy came to a stop and crouched down as he started back up the slope on his hands and knees. I did the same and we worked our way up until we were able to once again see the backyard. I looked across the width of a swimming pool, across the patio, and saw the smoker, still spewing pungently delicious white smoke that drifted lazily with the wind in the other direction. The two people who'd been tending the smoker were now absent. Back in the house, or so I guessed.

Murphy nudged me and pointed to our left.

Along the fence at the back corner of the yard stood a rectangular construct of chain link fence, sealed across the top with fencing material and partitioned into four equal parts, each with a closed gate. It was a kennel, but it didn't hold dogs, it held Whites. Some were standing, a few were lying in the dirt, but most were squatting and looking despondently out at the yard or into the trees.

Murphy scooted back down the slope a few feet. I stayed where I was, sneaking peeks at what I could see. "What do you think?" he asked.

"Why imprison Whites?" I asked.

Murphy shrugged and pulled a face. "Doesn't matter why, I guess. Every time we come across some of these Slow Burn knuckleheads, we see something new."

"Oh, shit."

"What?" Murphy raised his hammer and looked around.

"No," I said, "not that."

"What?"

"I'll bet they're livestock," I said, feeling disgust at voicing the thought.

"Livestock?" Murphy asked.

"I'll bet I know what's on that smoker."

Shaking his head, Murphy said, "No, that's disgusting."

I looked back in the direction of the smoker. "They've got some kind of meat in that smoker."

Murphy turned away and slowly scanned through the woods. "I find myself liking the world less and less every day."

"I hear you."

Murphy took a moment to think about the Whites in the kennels. "Barbecued Whites, I don't give a shit. That doesn't change anything for us."

"Okay."

Murphy pointed back up toward the house. "There're at least two of them up there."

"I wonder how they get them into the kennels," I said.

"Doesn't matter," Murphy said. "We probably need to steer clear of that kennel unless we want them making some noise when they see us. You never know what those fuckers will do."

"Okay."

"When you saw those two behind the barbecue pit, did you see any gun barrels sticking up or anything?"

"Nope," I answered. "Just the tops of their heads."

"Yeah, me too. So we don't know anything about them yet, except maybe what they like to have for dinner."

I asked, "So what are you thinking? Plan A? Go out front and wait 'til dusk, then steal our Humvee back?"

"Or we get out of here." Murphy rubbed a hand over his bald head. "We don't know anything about how many are in there, what they're up to, or what they're capable of."

"Is that what you want to do?" I was looking at the kennels when I asked the question, and I realized there was something odd about the occupants of one section. "Oh, shit."

Murphy was immediately ready to fight again. "What do you see?"

I waved Murphy back up. "Come take a look at this."

Murphy was beside me. "What?"

"Those Whites in the far section of the kennel." I pointed.

Murphy squinted. "It's hard to make 'em out with the Whites in the other cages in the way."

"Yeah." I turned and sat down on a flat piece of limestone. "Keep looking and tell me what you see."

"What am I supposed to see?" Murphy asked. After a moment, he said, "Wait."

"Yeah. That's what I thought. I don't think those ones are Whites."

I got up off my comfortable flat piece of stone, and together Murphy and I worked our way around the curve of the fence to a place that would give us an unobstructed view of the end of the kennel in question. It was only twenty or thirty feet away from us when we peeked up over the sloping edge of the backyard.

Shaking his head, Murphy lowered himself back out of sight. He took a deep, frustrated breath.

I knelt down beside him. "Looks like half a dozen naked girls with normal skin color."

"Of course," Murphy said, disgusted. "If you're gonna have a rape kennel, you gotta have 'em naked." He pounded his hammer into the dirt a few times.

"A rape kennel?" I asked. "You think that's what it is?"

Shaking his head again, Murphy said, "I don't know. Does it matter? They're people—normal people, girls—in that cage. This place is just as fucked as that tattoo parlor. Maybe more fucked."

I was as disgusted as Murphy. "You know what I'm thinking."

"Null Spot?"

I nodded. There was no point in pretending that I wasn't.

"Me, too," Murphy offered. "I want to smash somebody's head with my hammer right now."

I hefted my machete and agreed.

Chapter 36

We continued to work our way around the fence, keeping hidden in the trees and just down the slope until we came across a section of the property that was covered with oaks and barely visible from the house.

Murphy looked at me and said, "This is the place. You sure you wanna do this?"

"Stupid question, Murphy." I scrambled quickly up the hill, made short work of climbing the fence, and took up a position behind a thick oak tree while I waited for Murphy to catch up. I peeked around the trunk and saw a window on the side of the house. It was open; the sun glaring on the screen made it impossible to tell what was inside.

Murphy came to a stop beside me, panting. "I slipped off the fence and fell on my ass."

"You all right?"

"I'm good. You see anything yet?"

"Nope."

Murphy nodded his head toward the house. "Lead the way, Null Spot."

I sprinted to another thick tree trunk a few dozen feet ahead, came to a stop, and knelt. I looked past it at the window. Still only darkness within the house. A second open window revealed the same. I waved Murphy to come up beside me. The house was maybe another fifty or sixty feet away. Most of the covering oaks were behind us, between the fence and us.

I pointed at a series of three air conditioning units sitting on the ground, attached to the house by copper umbilical tubes and wires. Knowing it was just as dangerous crossing open ground on this side of the house as it was in front did nothing to quell my angry, fuck-it attitude. I took off at a crouching sprint, trying to keep the bulk of my body below the line of sight of anyone sitting inside one of those dark windows and casually gazing out.

Without incident, I came to a stop against the house's stone wall, between two of the air conditioner units. I pressed myself against the limestone and looked back at Murphy. If someone inside either window noticed me, Murphy would see a reaction before I would. He looked from window to window a couple of times before giving me a thumbs up. I motioned with an upturned palm for him to stay put as I raised my head up from my hiding spot and looked up and down the length of the wall. I listened, but heard nothing. I pointed at the window to my left and Murphy gave me a nod.

Off I went, creeping along the wall, careful and slow as I stepped through dry mulch, avoiding sprigs of crisp brown flowers and crackly brown leaves fallen off the shrubs. Once I was below the window, I came to a stop and listened.

I heard breathing.

Someone was breathing, heavily and slowly.

The faint sound of a big man sleeping is what I heard. Looking first left, then right, and seeing no dangers, I chanced a peek in the window, quick up and then back down.

A big man with pale white skin—skin just like mine—was asleep on the bed, on his belly, head turned facing the other wall. But at the foot of the bed—

I took another peek in the window, longer than before.

Coming back down, I was shaking my head. At the foot of the bed a girl sat on the floor, legs curled up against her chest, head between her knees, wrist cuffed to the bedpost. Her skin color assured me she was normal.

That made three bad guys, at least. Two were up barbecuing. One was sleeping late or taking a nap after his morning rape session. The world had truly turned into a fucked up place.

When I looked back across the lawn, I saw Murphy looking at me with wide curious eyes. I held up one finger and then pointed to the window. I closed my eyes and put my hands together, then leaned my head over to indicate sleep. Murphy nodded and set his face in a hard frown. He was apparently thinking what I was thinking. That screen was a thin defense for the sleeping man.

Thinking the house's occupants were sloppy in their security, I took off moving quickly to the next window, again taking care to avoid any dead garden plants that might give away my presence with an audible crunch. I stopped below the window, just as I'd stopped by the first one. I listened, heard nothing, and got sloppy myself.

Expecting nothing but an empty room or a sleeping man, I leaned over to gaze through the screen and found myself face to face with a surprised man on the other side of the screen, trying to get a look outside.

Startled, I jumped sideways and pushed myself against the wall.

"Hey," the guy inside the window shouted. "Hey." The screen bulged out on a feeble push but didn't give.

Shit. Shit. Shit.

Not being a fan of indecision, I put my balls on the table and made my bet, sprinting away from the window and arcing out from the wall, hoping that Murphy would figure out what I was up to in time to lend a hand.

The voice from the man in the room shouted back into the house. "We got infected in the compound!"

I made a hard turn left and angled toward the first window. Committed to my latest date with impulsive stupidity, I planted a foot and sprang at the opening, leading with a shoulder, and flew right through the screen. With a rattle of the screen's metal frame, I hit the floor on the other side.

Rolling over to my feet and onto my knees I found myself facing a wide-eyed girl, still cuffed to the bedpost. I jumped up and hauled my machete back over my shoulder for a swing. I stepped forward as the big white-skinned man on the bed was just sitting up. The last thing his bleary eyes saw was the backhand swing of my machete splitting his skull horizontally across the cheekbones. Blood sprayed across the wall and spewed onto the sheets.

The girl gulped, but didn't scream.

A commotion from the room next door accompanied the metallic sound of the screen being pushed out.

A man's voice hollered, "Billy, he's trying to get in your window."

I looked at the slumping body on the bed. Billy was too busy dying to listen to his buddy next door.

"Jake! Keith!" The shout was followed by two dull cracks: sound suppressed rifle shots. I don't know what made me madder at the moment, the fact that that hollering jackass was using my stolen rifle or that he was shooting at Murphy. Either way, I could still count, and I figured I had four—no, three—remaining adversaries, all armed with automatic weapons and all inside the house.

Bumping walls and scooting furniture from somewhere far across the expansive house told me I had some moments before I had more trouble than I could handle. For the moment, surprise was still on my side, but it was rapidly evaporating.

I ran into the hall and tore off at full speed toward another doorway. Caution was a commodity I couldn't afford. I cut the corner into the room and immediately spotted the backside of the man I'd met just a few moments before. He was standing at the window, weapon at his shoulder, looking for a target.

I saw his shoulders flinch and his head started to turn as my machete came down vertically into his neck, cutting down between his shoulder blades. He grunted under the impact and fell forward out the window as I yanked my blade free of the bone in which it had stuck.

Choosing to ride my frenzied wave of surprise, I ran out of the room, around a corner, and into a long wide hall that appeared to run the length of the house. I figured my best chance was to catch the last two before they figured out I was in the house. I accelerated to full speed.

Oops.

Two men half-stumbled and ran out of a side room and into the hall in front of me. Urgency changed instantly to fright as the guy in front saw me coming at him. I screamed my wildest White howl, realizing I'd never reach him before he managed to get his rifle up to put a few holes in my chest. In a desperate hope, I threw my machete and dove through a door on my left. Bullets sizzled the air in the hall. I tumbled over a chair, scrambled over crates and things I didn't have time to identify, and dove through another window screen. Coming down on a cactus plant, I howled and rolled into the dead grass even as I scratched at the ground to pull myself away. A moment later, I was on my feet and dodging between cars as I crouched and ran.

Not realizing how fast I was moving, or quite how I'd gotten away from the house, I found myself next to my Humvee and I grinned. I put it between me and the house as I looked through the windows to find my pursuers. Indeed, a man was poking his head and a rifle barrel out the front door. I slipped inside the Humvee, safe for the moment. I looked around inside. All of the weapons, ammo, and camping supplies were gone. Only canisters of fifty-caliber ammunition remained. Standing up inside the Humvee, I opened the top hatch and slowly climbed up to position myself behind the heavy machine gun.

My pursuer at the front door was looking around cautiously at the trees, bushes, and cars. I was guessing he thought I was just another brain-fried crazy White, not smart enough to open the Humvee door. Too bad for him.

My fifty-caliber machine gun had a belt dangling from it. The guys in the house had apparently gone to the trouble to load it for me. I pulled the handle back on the right side, stood up straight, and swung the barrel around at the house's front door.

My pursuer saw the movement. He looked right at me, his eyes went wide, and he ducked back behind the front door as I let go with a burst of a dozen rounds. Bullets shattered limestone blocks, some tore into the roof, and others missed the house altogether, but some of them hit the front door— only a few of them needed to.

In the distance, I heard howls. Not many, but enough. From the backyard, the Whites in the kennels grew excited when they heard the shots. I panned the big fifty back and forth across the front of the house, hoping the other white-skinned, knuckleheaded fuck would think his balls were bigger then my fifty caliber rounds.

No such luck.

With adrenaline pumping, waiting for something to happen was hard. It was also a bad idea. I didn't know where knuckleheaded fuck number four was. I did know that he had one of the sniper rifles that had killed Jerome in that intersection. If number four was good with his rifle, and if he had any smarts, he'd be sneaking around to get me in his sights. I immediately dropped down inside the Humvee. It was time to move.

Speed and surprise were treating me well enough so far. I got out of the Humvee and bolted for the shattered front door. The thick oak had split twice as it flew off its hinges, landing partially on top of Number Three. Blood was everywhere. The guy was dead. I pulled his weapon out of his hand and cursed silently. It had taken a round through the body right above the trigger. The suppressor looked to be in good shape and, in fact, became the handle for my new metal club. It wasn't much of a weapon, but it was something.

Beyond the front door and the foyer lay some sort of living room with couches, chairs, and coffee tables. It looked liked a college dorm for the messy boys. Empty food packages, cans, and bottles lay scattered everywhere. The place stank of beer, urine, and vomitus. I raised my new club baseball bat-style and ran across the foyer, aiming toward a wide doorway at the far side of the living room. As I passed across that long hallway someone yelled, "Freeze." Two gunshots followed, but I was already past the hallway and well into the living room. I came to a sudden stop and froze. That was Murphy's voice.

"Murphy?" I called.

"Was that you?" he called back.

"Yes," I said, irritation dripping from my answer.

"Sorry, dude."

"There's one more I know of," I called as I worked my way across the living room to the wide doorway I'd been heading for originally. I added, "He's got an M4."

"Not anymore," said Murphy. "I mean, he's still got it, but he's dead."

I relaxed a little.

Chapter 37

After I retrieved my machete and stole a pistol off a corpse, Murphy and I hurried through the rest of the house, room after room after room. The place had to have been ten thousand square feet. It looked like a doomsday prepper and hoarder got married and spread their crap all over the house. The four Slow Burns we'd killed had to have been going through the whole neighborhood, meticulously collecting cars, weapons, ammunition, food, and alcohol. Mounds of it were in nearly every room.

Once we were sure we'd gotten the last of them, we went back into the main room. Outside, the infected were probably on their way because of my choice to use the fifty-caliber machine gun. Inside, the normal girl was still handcuffed to the bedpost—or so I assumed—and there was still a kennel of women locked up out behind the house.

"Tell you what," I said. "Why don't you take one of the sniper rifles and grab a spot where you can target any Whites coming down the driveway? And you know they're going to come."

"Okay." Murphy knelt beside the body of the man I'd machine-gunned through the front door. Murphy checked him for spare magazines, but found none. "What about you?"

"I'll go unlock that girl in the bedroom and see what's up."

"Bring her back in here." Murphy pointed back at the main room. "If we need to bail out, I'd rather not have to come find you."

"Gotcha, boss." I took off at a jog down the hall that led to the back bedroom where I'd slain the first of the Slow Burns in the house. When I entered the room, the girl was sitting up straight and looking at me with a blank face. Considering the circumstances, she looked to be in decent shape—not beat up, not bleeding.

"You okay?" I asked.

She didn't answer.

"Do you know where the keys are for the cuffs?" I asked. I waited for an answer.

The girl sized me up, I guess wondering if I was a hero or the next shift. She looked beside the bed and toward a nightstand. "In the drawer, I think."

I stepped over to the nightstand and yanked the drawer open—junk inside slid across the wood. Indeed, the handcuff keys were right there. I retrieved them and went back to the end of the bed where I handed them to the girl. I stepped back and got both my hands back on my weapons.

The girl started to laugh.

"What?" I asked.

"You're afraid of me?"

I shook my head then switched to a nod. "You never know. For all I know, he was your fiancé and you were playing S&M games when he dozed off."

The girl got the cuffs off and rubbed her wrist before pulling her knees in close to her chest to cover her breasts. I realized I was looking at them.

"Sorry," I said.

She looked down at herself. "It's okay. Your looking at my tits is far from the worst thing that's happened to me today."

I stepped over to the closet as I looked across the floor. "Do you have any clothes?"

She shook her head and I opened the closet door to see if anything inside might work for her. A thick terry cloth robe was hanging on a hook on the back of the door. I held it up for her to see.

"Thanks." She reached out a hand as she stood up while using one hand to cover her breasts.

I turned away for a second then turned back to watch her. Her modesty wasn't as important as my safety. As she wrapped herself up in the robe, I asked, "What's the deal here?"

The girl looked at the guy's corpse on the bed. "You didn't figure that out before you chopped his head in half?"

I shrugged. "Mostly. We saw the girls out back in the kennel."

The girl looked through a back wall as though a window was there. "That's where they keep us until they need us."

"Need you?" I asked, stupidly.

"They do terrible things to us."

"You don't look bruised up or anything," I observed.

The girl put a hand to her cheek as though touching an old wound. Emptily, she said, "You learn to cooperate."

"I'm sorry. I didn't mean—"

The girl looked back at the bed and we stood in awkward silence.

"I need to know you're not going to hurt me," I said.

She looked me up and down. "I need to know the same thing."

I almost laughed. "Kind of a common problem these days, huh?"

She smiled. "Thank you for killing him. You did get them all, didn't you?"

"Were there four?" I asked.

"Yes."

"Then they're all dead." I used my machete to point through the open door. "My buddy, Murphy, is out there keeping watch for Whites coming up the driveway. He helped."

"Whites?" The girl asked. "Your word for the infected?"

I nodded.

"You're different than these," she observed.

I shrugged again. "I got infected, but I'm okay, mostly."

"Mostly?"

"It's hard to explain. My buddy, Murphy, he's infected too. C'mon, we need to get out to the living room before Murphy gets worried."

As we came into the living room near the shattered front door, I heard the distinct, but muffled, sound of Murphy's suppressed M4. He was just outside standing behind a car with his weapon laying across the roof. Looking up at the end of the driveway, I spotted three bodies, but nothing moving.

"Just three Whites came?" I asked.

"That's it." Murphy glanced back at me and then at the girl. "I'm Murphy."

"I'm Molly," she said. "Thank you." She walked outside and extended a hand to shake his.

Murphy looked at the hand. "You're not worried about catching what I've got?"

With a look of disgust on her face, Molly glanced down at the dead man on the floor just inside the door. "I'm sure I'd have caught it already."

"Guess not." Murphy reached over and shook her hand.

To Molly, I said, "You're probably immune. I think anybody who isn't infected by now has to be immune."

Molly just nodded and said, "I need to get my friends out."

"Oh," I looked toward the back of the house. "In the kennel. Sorry, I wasn't thinking about them. Do you know where the keys are?"

Nodding, Molly knelt down and felt at the pockets of the prone man. "He's probably got them." She pulled a jingling key ring out and lifted it for me to see.

"You want me to tag along?" I asked.

The girl looked at me, deciding how to answer.

"You should go with her," said Murphy.

The girl's expression became suspicious. I said, "No, she's cool." To her, I said, "If any Whites are out there trying to come over the fence, don't yell. Come in here and get me. Better yet—I handed her my pistol. "Use this, but only if you have to."

The girl looked down at the pistol, extended to her grip-first. She took it, and I clenched my machete, ready to swing it if she decided that she was going to shoot me.

She gave me a nod. "I'll be right back." She ran for the back door.

Murphy said, "There's nothing much happening here. I think we got lucky. Why don't you go stand by the back door and keep on eye on her or something? If I get in a spot, I'll holler."

Chapter 38

It was mid-afternoon before one of us went up to the top of the driveway to pull the sliding gate shut. The gate—like the black metal fence all around the property—was only six feet tall and wouldn't stop any determined mob of Whites, but it would keep out any that were casually passing by.

Some of the girls I'd initially spotted sitting in the kennel staring at the sky turned out to be dead. In total, there were four still alive. The first thing they did, even before food, was to bathe themselves in the pool through the water had turned green with algae. Afterward, they scrounged clothing from around the house and gorged themselves on a smorgasbord of canned foods and snack foods laid out on the dining room table. I'd already eaten by that time, so Murphy was taking a turn while I loaded boxes of food, ammunition, and weapons into the back of our Humvee.

Molly was helping with the chore and was handing me cans of fruit when she said, "I used to live about a half mile up the road."

"Uh-huh," I said, wedging items into the back seat as best I could.

"My husband, my son, and both my daughters turned," she said.

It wasn't an uncommon circumstance, so I didn't comment.

"My husband went first. I think he brought it home from work. That was in the beginning, a couple of days after the riot at the jail."

I was out of the Humvee by then, looking at Molly and thinking about my escape during the jail riot. "What did you do with your husband?" I asked.

She said, "He was sick for a few days before he went after my youngest daughter."

I was afraid to ask what happened there, but Molly wasn't afraid to tell it. "I guess I knew what to expect. I mean, it was all over the Internet by then. I just didn't want to believe it. I was downstairs in the kitchen when she screamed." Molly slowly shook her head. "I told Annie not to go upstairs into Daddy's room, but you know how kids are."

No. But I nodded anyway.

"I dropped what I was doing and ran upstairs. By that time I'd taken to carrying a gun—a silver revolver that Jim bought me for Christmas. He liked his guns a lot. I hated it. I was so angry at him for putting a gun under the Christmas tree." Molly laughed as a few tears found their way down her cheeks. "So, I had the gun. I got to the top of the stairs. Jim Junior was right behind me, and Sara was coming. The bedroom door was open and Jim was on his knees on the floor over Annie. His mouth was covered with blood. He looked like one of those mistreated pit bulls that just mauled some kid on the news."

I just looked at Molly. I didn't have any words of comfort for her. But she didn't need any. She just needed to tell her story, and maybe after enough tellings the pain of it would subside.

"I screamed at Jim to get away from her, but he just hunched lower and snapped his teeth." Molly slowly shook her head again. "Jim Junior was trying to get around me. I don't know what he thought he was going to do, but if he'd gone over to help Annie, Jim would have killed him too. Sara was screaming and screaming and screaming. I thought it would never end, and it didn't, not until I pulled the trigger." Molly fell silent.

"You shot your husband?" I asked.

Molly nodded. "I didn't even realize I had the gun up. It just happened. I didn't kill him with the first shot. It nicked his shoulder. But that only made him angry, and he jumped to his feet and came at us. I shot three more times." Molly looked down at the ground and her tears rolled off her nose and dripped into a tiny puddle between her feet.

When she looked up again, she said, "When I got to Annie, she was bleeding so badly. I...I tried to stop the bleeding, but it was gushing out of her neck." Molly gulped another breath. "She died right there in my bedroom."

I laid a hand on Molly's shoulder. "That had to be hard."

She nodded. "You know, the police never even came. I called them. I called an ambulance. Nobody came."

"I know," I said.

"Jim Junior got sick after that. He never woke up. He died with the fever, thank God." Molly shook her head and laughed bitterly. "How twisted is it when a mother is thankful that her son died of a fever?"

"It was better than the alternative." Out of curiosity, I started, "After they died—" I paused, not sure whether to continue with the question.

"What did I do with the bodies?" Molly finished for me.

I nodded.

Another bitter laugh that verged on tears. "That's not the kind of problem I ever thought I'd have to solve."

I shook my head, thinking back to Freitag's friend with no hands who we went to dispose of downriver.

"I couldn't keep them in the house," Molly said. "I couldn't bury them. We've only got a few inches of soil in our backyard, and then it's just limestone. I wrapped them in layers of garbage bags and duct tape. I didn't know what else to do. I left them by the back fence under some blankets. I took some rocks that bordered the garden and put them on the blankets to keep them from blowing away."

Given the constraints, that seemed like a pretty good solution to me.

"A week or so later, they disappeared."

At first that surprised me, until I realized the bodies had probably been dragged off by hungry Whites. "Was the fence knocked down?"

Molly nodded. "For a while it was only me and Sara. We did okay, considering. We were getting low on food, and I knew I needed to go see what I could find in the neighbors' houses. I didn't know whether it was more dangerous to leave her at home or bring her with me. But she was too frightened to stay by herself. She convinced me, and I brought her along. I told myself I had plenty of ammunition, and we'd be okay." Molly shook her head again as she relived her choices. "We weren't. It happened next door at the Buckley's house."

Molly took another moment to collect herself, and I waited patiently while she did.

"The front door was locked, and I didn't think I could break it in."

I looked Molly up and down. She weighed all of a hundred and ten pounds. She was probably right.

"We went around to the back yard. I opened the gate. I was so stupid. I should have checked first if anything was back there. They were. They rushed out at us, three of them, like they'd been waiting there for us all along."

"Some of them can be pretty efficient predators," I said. "They may have heard you coming and chose to be quiet and wait, hoping you'd open the gate and come in."

Molly shrugged. "It all happened so fast. I had the gun in my hand, and I was shooting even as I was falling. The infected were clawing and snapping. I killed the one that came down on top of me, and while I was laying there with that thing bleeding on me, I shot the other two who were attacking Sara. But—" Molly buried her face in her hands and sobbed loudly.

I wrapped my arms around her and lied to her that it was okay. Everything was okay.

It took a long while for Molly to cry herself out. When she did, she stood up straight and looked at me with red eyes. "I shot her. I shot Sara. I guess when I was falling. The bullet hit her in the neck. It went straight through. She was bleeding badly, so badly. I knew she was going to die, but I put my hand over her throat and I tried to stop the bleeding." Molly shrugged as if to ask what else she could have done. "Sara looked at me. She didn't scream or cry. She just tried to breathe. She didn't move. That's when I heard the infected screaming. They were close and coming."

"Whites." I muttered.

Molly nodded. "I checked my revolver. I only had one bullet left. There were four or five coming, maybe more." Molly closed her eyes and put her hand over them as she turned away. In a hoarse whisper she said, "I put the last bullet in Sara's head, and I ran." More sobs followed.

When the sobs came to a stop I said, "It wasn't your fault. What you did for Sara might be the bravest thing I've heard. I don't know if I could have done it."

Molly looked back at me and nodded as her lip quivered. "I feel like a coward. I keep telling myself I should have stayed with her or maybe used the bullet on myself."

I looked at the house. "That's why you weren't beat up when they raped you."

Molly nodded, and after gulping another breath she said, "I thought I deserved what those men were doing to me, for what I let happen to my kids. I let them do—" she cried some more.

"The world is a fucked up place now," I told her after a bit.

Molly looked back at the house and laughed bitterly.

I shook my head and pointed at the house. "You lived through that and all the other stuff. You're strong."

"Aren't you just the Mr. Positive Dr. Phil?"

"I'm just trying to make it through the day," I told her.

Chapter 39

Carrying some kind of tan-colored goggle things in one hand and his M4 in the other, Murphy walked across the driveway to where Molly and I were just finishing up by the Humvee. "What's the plan, Batman?" he said, grinning.

I looked into the Humvee. "We've got about as much stuff in here as we're going to get."

"You got all the fifty cal ammo?" Murphy asked.

I nodded. "Eleven cans. All I could find."

Murphy looked back at the house. "There's a lot of shit in there."

I shrugged. That was plainly true.

"You guys are just going to leave, then?" Molly asked.

"We are loading up the Humvee." I pointed to the stuff piled in the back of our truck. "What exactly are you asking?"

Molly crinkled her brow. "Things are happening pretty fast. I haven't thought about it."

Murphy looked at me, "Before you go all Null Spot, dude, these chicks got everything they need here. Maybe enough food for—I don't know—four or five months, and more guns and ammo than they're likely to need. Shit like this." He held up the goggle things.

I looked at them, but didn't have a guess what they were.

"Night vision goggles," he said.

"No shit." That pleased me greatly. "They don't look like what I've seen on TV."

Murphy shook his head. "There are lots of different kinds."

I reached out, and Murphy handed me the goggles. I started to examine them. "Do they work?"

"Yep."

"Do they take batteries?" I asked.

"Yep."

"And the batteries are still good?"

"These still work."

As I slipped them over my head, I asked, "How many sets of these did you find?"

"Just the one so far," he said.

Molly pointed toward one end of the house. "There are seven more inside."

"Seven?" I asked. "How do you know that?"

Molly looked down at her feet. "They didn't always have me locked up. I earned their trust at least a little bit. The goggles are in the rec room in that pile of stuff behind the pool table."

Shaking his head and shrugging, Murphy said, "I didn't really go through that stuff."

Molly looked at me and went into sales mode. "I saw most of what they brought in. I think I know what they've got."

"Had," I corrected. "It's your stuff now."

"Or our stuff," she suggested.

I looked at Murphy with the silent question on my face. What do we do about the girls?

Ignoring Molly, he said, "Man, you know what we got to do."

"I can help," she said. "We can all help."

"This isn't your fight," I told Molly.

She replied, "Let's team up. We'll all be better off together than alone. You can see that, right?"

Shaking my head, I said, "Not necessarily."

"Are you guys alone?" Molly asked.

"No," I admitted. "It's complicated." I spent a while explaining the situation to Molly, not the history—I glossed over a few quick points—but mostly I told her about our plan to rescue Steph and get out of town. With a nod from Murphy, permission I guess, I told her we were planning to head west, far from all the danger of the Whites in the cities.

When I was done, Molly pointed at a freestanding garage that Murphy and I hadn't checked when we cleared the house of threats. "There's a trailer in that garage. It's got a Porsche in it. I think the guy used it for racing or something and he towed it to the races with the car inside."

"Wait," I asked, "That's why that garage was so big?"

Molly said, "The guy that lived here before the infection hit, he was that guy you killed on the bed—"

"You knew him before?" Murphy asked.

"Yes," Molly answered. "Not well, but he had parties at his house for the neighbors. He's got some old cars and things in there."

"A trailer." Murphy stroked his chin. He looked at me. He looked over at the garage. "Let's go check it out."

I glanced up at the front gate. To Molly, I asked, "How are those other girls doing? Can one or two of them keep an eye on things out here for a bit? I hate not having somebody on watch."

"Considering what they've been through, Zed, they're fine."

"Okay," I said, "I just didn't know—" I groped for the right words.

Molly said, "We're not fragile. If we were, none of us would have made it this long."

Chapter 40

It was as much a showroom as a garage. The guy owned seven cars, all old, all expensive, arrayed for display across a gleaming epoxy-coated floor. The walls were hung with neon signs and old metal car product signs. A row of red toolboxes lined one section of wall, filled with more tools than I'd ever need, likely more than I could identify.

The trailer, parked along one wall just inside one of the garage doors, was fully enclosed. Inside, the front eight feet were set up as a small overnight camper. The back held tool boxes, racks for tires, and a Porsche painted in red, white, and blue racing stripes and numbers. Inside was also mounted a fuel tank for storing a few hundred gallons of custom race fuel for the Porsche.

"If we ditch the Porsche," I said, as though that was a decision we'd have to spend some time thinking about, "there's a ton of room. We could haul off most—if not all—of the food and weapons these guys collected."

Nodding, Murphy said, "And we'll be set when we get to Balmorhea."

"That's what I'm thinking."

Murphy walked around the front of the trailer. "We just need to figure out how to make the trailer hitch work with the one on the back of the Humvee."

Pointing around the room, I said, "I think there are enough tools here that we can make anything work."

Murphy looked at the tool cabinets and nodded.

I looked at Molly. "You talk to the girls and make sure they're on board. If so, we need to get to work." To Murphy I said, "In the three Humvees we'll have room for twelve, but we'll have fourteen people. What do you think?"

"Instead of hooking the trailer up to a Humvee," said Molly, "why not use that crew cab F-350 to haul it, then you've got room for at least five comfortably, and more if you need to squeeze them in."

Shaking my head, I said, "Won't work. The Whites go nuts when they see a running vehicle. They'll break right through those windows and kill everyone inside."

Molly said, "I'll bet there's a welding rig in here. We could cut some metal out of the fence and weld it across the windows or something. That'll protect everyone inside."

"And over the grill," Murphy added. "That'll protect the radiator when you have to run some over. And you will have to run some over."

"That could work," I agreed. "That'll give us enough room for everyone."

Chapter 41

While Murphy spent the afternoon in a shaded spot on the roof keeping an eye on our perimeter, two of the girls—one who'd had some experience welding—went to work with an acetylene torch cutting sections of fence and welding them over the grill and windows on the Ford pickup. Aesthetically, it was hideous. But it was functional. Molly, me, and the other girl spent the afternoon loading the trailer with every weapon, every bit of food, and all the ammunition we could find in the house.

Though the trailer already had tool cabinets built in, we loaded other tools we thought might be of use. After that, we siphoned the diesel out of the tanks of cars in the collection across the front yard and in the cul-de-sac. In doing so, we topped off the tanks of all three Humvees and the pickup. With no need for the high-octane gasoline stored in the trailer for racing the Porsche, we dumped it and put the rest of our diesel there.

It was after midnight when Molly and I climbed the ladder at the back of the house to get onto the roof. Murphy, by that time, had a lawn chair set up on the roof, though he wasn't sitting in it. He was looking through his night vision goggles and scanning along the fence line. As we approached, he asked, "We ready?"

"Yeah," I answered.

He flipped up his goggles and asked, "What's the plan?"

I pointed out at the Humvee with the fifty-caliber machine gun mounted on the roof. "We head out in the dark. I'll drive that one. Murphy, you'll be up on the roof with the fifty. Molly will be right behind us with the trailer. We'll put one of the girls—"

"Marissa," Molly cut in, reminding me of her name.

"Yeah, Marissa," I said. "Each of the other two girls will follow in the last two Humvees. We'll take it slow and stay tight."

Nodding, Murphy said, "Yeah, that should work."

"We shouldn't get too many Whites out after us," I said. "If we do, we'll run down what we can. If we get in trouble, we'll speed up or shred 'em with the fifty."

"We've got plenty of ammo for it," Murphy confirmed.

"And you'll never guess what we found," I said, grinning.

"What?"

"A grenade launcher."

"What?" Murphy asked. "Like an RPG or something?"

Shaking my head I said, "Like some kind of thing with a magazine on the side. It looks kind of like the machine gun but with a barrel this big." I held my hand up and made a big circle with my fingers.

"Probably an MK19."

"So it is a grenade launcher?" I asked.

Murphy grinned. "It's like a big grenade machine gun. I think one of the Humvees has a mount for an MK19."

Smiling, I looked at Molly. She smiled wickedly in return. She was probably thinking of slaughtering the infected. I was thinking of slaughtering Jay and his thugs.

"When are we heading out, then?" Murphy asked.

"We're ready to go now," I answered. "We can go back to the boathouse tonight, get everyone fed, then spend tomorrow afternoon getting ready. Tomorrow night we should be able to get the girls from Jay."

Nodding, Murphy said, "Then we bail out of town?"

"That's the plan."

Chapter 42

My experience in the post-apocalyptic world put me in a state of mind such that I was always surprised when things went as planned. And so I was surprised when our little convoy drove an hour without incident to a residential street that ran along the side of a hill, above the cove where our friends were hiding in the boathouse.

Without seeing a single White after we parked, we offloaded some food and enough weapons for our task. The rest of the night and the next day we spent planning, preparing, and of course, getting some sleep. At least that's what Murphy and I needed most. The others in the boathouse, having spent their time being worried, bored, and hungry, had plenty of time to rest while waiting for us to return.

I'd tried to convince the others that I could rescue the girls all on my own. All I needed was a pair of night vision goggles, my machete, and a dark night. My plan was to swim out to the island, silent and invisible. I'd sneak around until I found Jay sleeping in his hut, dispatch him with a few brutal machete hacks, and maybe whack a few more of his fucktards. I'd then find Steph, Amy, and Megan, pilfer a boat, and get out of Dodge.

To me, it was that simple. But nobody liked my cowboy plan. They thought I might murder one too many innocents as I crept ninja-style around the island.

Dalhover and Gretchen had other ideas. They thought they could intimidate Jay with our newly gained superior firepower. They'd blow up or sink a few boats and threaten to sink the rest. Jay would read the writing on the wall and give over his hostages. The thing they just didn't understand nor accept when I argued the point was that Jay was crazy.

Gretchen had dealt with him, recognized his oddities, but couldn't accept that he'd act more irrationally than he already had.

As for me, I'd seen enough crazy in the eyes of irrational people to know it when I saw it in Jay. So, while Dalhover was finding a way to secure the fifty-caliber machine gun on the bow deck of the cabin cruiser, Murphy had put the MK19 grenade launcher on its tripod on the pontoon boat. I'd insisted, to the point of leaving the group, that I was swimming out to the island. They'd all finally agreed to let me go on with what they saw as my heroic stupidity. I was the backup plan in case Jay went nuts.

The hard part in all of it was going to come when choosing who to kill. I knew there were good people on that island, frightened and following Jay's lead just because he exuded those two most important of leadership characteristics: passion and certainty. Too bad people readily accepted that combination as a valid replacement for competence. History is littered with the fallen empires of kings, dictators, and fools who were passionate, certain, and wrong.

By the time night fell that next day, we were ready. What's more, we couldn't have asked for a better night—well, maybe not much better. Only a sliver of a moon shed light on the lake, but only when it could find a gap in the clouds. The near blackness of the night significantly enhanced the advantage of our night vision.

I looked down at a newly acquired watch on my wrist and looked out the Humvee's window to get my bearings. Using night vision goggles, Rachel drove the Humvee slowly enough to be careful, and quickly enough that no White could follow our sound through the darkness. We'd crossed over the dam and driven up Ranch Road 620 until we made a left on Bullick Hollow Road and were roughly following the shore of the lake on a narrow, winding asphalt road through a dense forest.

Molly, who sat in the passenger side of the front, was also wearing night vision goggles. In her hands she held one of the M4s with a suppressor on the barrel. Rachel's rifle lay between the seats. My machete, three pistols, extra magazines, hand grenades, a flare gun, a life preserver, and a pair of swim fins lay in the back seat with me. The life preserver would keep me afloat with all the extra equipment I'd be carrying. The fins would get me across the quarter mile of lake between the island and where I planned to enter the water.

Molly said, "I don't know where we are."

"That's okay," Rachel answered. "I know this area. We just follow the road and turn left at the T-intersection. Then we're looking for a street I don't know the name of, but I'll know when we get there. That'll take us down to the water, as close to the island as we're likely to get."

"And you guys will keep the Humvee parked back away from the shore, right?" I asked. "If you drive across somebody's yard trying to get the Humvee down to the water's edge, Jay's thugs on the island might hear you."

"We'll stay up at the road," said Rachel. "At least until the shooting starts. Once that happens, nobody will notice the sound of a Humvee coming down to the shore over here. Everybody will be looking at the boats on the other side of the island."

A White wandered into the road in the darkness in front of us. Rachel didn't speed up, she didn't slow down. She didn't swerve. She just ran it over without comment.

Not much was said after that. We drove on for another thirty slow minutes until Rachel made a left turn into a neighborhood of widely-spaced houses with plenty of natural tree growth in between. On our right side, I saw the surface of the lake between the houses. As we proceeded down the street, I spotted the silhouette of Monk's Island out in the water.

I said, "This is the place."

"We'll go down just a bit further," said Rachel. "The shore curves out a little up here. It'll be a shorter swim for you."

"Cool." I watched the island as we passed each gap. "You guys be sure and stay in the vehicle, okay?"

"Yes, Dad." It was Molly.

I huffed. "Whatever."

"It's just up here," said Rachel as she slowed the Humvee.

Two more houses passed, and she pulled into a driveway and killed the engine. On the front porch of the house next door, five or six Whites stood up and looked into the darkness. They'd heard the sound of the engine but couldn't see anything.

I tapped Rachel on the shoulder. I said, "Over there."

Rachel patted her rifle. "We can take care of them if we have to."

"Okay." I looked out the other side of the Humvee. "You see anything out there, Molly?"

"Nothing close enough to worry about," she answered.

I took a deep breath and looked at my watch. "We've made good time getting over here. I've still got an hour before the party starts."

"Are you going to wait before you head out?" Rachel asked.

"Nope," I answered. "It'll be better if I get going. You know, just in case."

"Just in case is what worries me," she said.

"Me too. I haven't had to run for my life in over twenty-four hours." I grinned and swung my door open. I got out, looked around again, and gathered up my equipment. It took only a few moments before I gave the girls a nod and headed down past a house with a machete in one hand, a pistol in the other, a life preserver hanging around my neck, a backpack full of goodies, and a pair of fins tucked into the back of my waistband.

Chapter 43

I found myself standing by some oaks near the edge of the water, looking at a dock that extended thirty feet out into the lake. No boats were tied to it. Anything of use had apparently been scavenged by the people of Monk's Island. The dock was just a row of bare planks with three Whites squatting near the end, staring out into the lake.

Off to my right, the shore curved into a cove. A few floating marina docks had come loose in the flooding and drifted. To my left, each of the neighbors had a boathouse or dock, each with Whites sleeping or looking around into the darkness. The closest of the structures was a boathouse with at least a dozen Whites on the roof, some sitting, some standing and looking in the direction of noises they couldn't see. Most of them were looking in my direction. But I was wearing night vision goggles, they weren't.

None of the Whites I saw were naked, though their clothes were tattered and soiled. I wondered if these, like the ones that had come after us in the cove where we stole the big speedboat, were swimmers. I'd need to be careful even as I got into the water. Too much noise might draw them to me.

The island lay four or five hundred feet off shore. The backside of the old Spanish mission faced me. From where the water lapped on the limestone shore, it would be a steep climb on my hands and knees up to the mission's back wall. Halfway along the length of the back wall, it jumped to a height of twenty feet or so. That section was actually the back wall of the mission's chapel building. On a front corner of the chapel a bell tower stood another twenty feet above the chapel's flat roof. The bell had long since been salvaged for its brass, leaving the tower with only a single purpose, that of an observation post from where everything on this part of the lake could be seen—except for the blind spots behind the back wall.

The islanders had bet their security on being able to see any threats far out in the water, and that bet depended on sufficient light.

Of the two islanders currently tasked with that security up in the old bell tower, I saw one leaning over against a support pillar. He wasn't moving, and I guessed that guard was sleeping. The other guard leaned on another support pillar and stared out at the blackness in the other direction. Both had hunting rifles of some sort, definitely not of a military style.

My chances of getting to the back wall unseen were more than excellent as long as I didn't arouse the curiosity of too many Whites while I was getting into the lake.

I examined the shore for a spot to make my landing, and decided I'd observed as much as I was going to be able to observe given the distance. It was time to proceed. I took off my boots, tied the laces around my belt, and waded into the lake, careful not to splash. When I was up to mid-thigh, I sat down in the water and awkwardly put my fins on. Awkward is the only way to get that done, especially when dealing with a body's natural buoyancy. I then put my life preserver in the water and lay on top of it. I kicked my way as quietly as possible toward Monk's Island.

I looked around at the world of greenish sparkles through my night vision goggles. I looked across the lake. I looked at the trees on the far banks and spotted Whites here and there. It was a wonderfully surreal moment that made it easy, for a bit, to forget about all the craziness.

When I looked up at the tower growing more ominous as I approached, the two guards up there had changed position. They were both standing alert, looking—it appeared—in my direction. One held the rifle to his shoulder, pointed at me. But no shot came. No bullets splashed the water around me.

The more I swam, the more I worried about the guards, but nothing happened, and I started to wonder if the night vision goggles were playing tricks with what I thought I saw. Could it be the guards were looking in the other direction and my brain was taking insufficient visual information and imagining the rest?

When I swam into the blind spot behind the chapel I was no longer able to see the tower. Blind spots work in both directions. But with the tower and its curious guards out of sight, I felt confident that my stealthy approach to the island had worked.

I arrived at the shore, but it turned out not to be a shore at all—just a very steep rock wall from somewhere down deep in the water to ten or fifteen feet over my head. I grabbed hold of a protruding stone and steadied myself in the water as I looked back and forth. From back on the shore, it hadn't appeared steep.

I checked the time. That hour I had when I'd gotten out of the Humvee had all but evaporated. There was no time to swim around to the side of the island searching for an easier point of egress. Climbing was my only choice. I reached down and pulled off my fins, letting them sink to the bottom of the lake. I put a leg forward and found a toehold. I grabbed some more rock in my other hand and slid off the life preserver, putting all my weight on bits of stone I held onto.

Tentatively, I started to climb. It took only a few moments to get myself nearly out of the water when it occurred to me that I should have kept the life preserver. If I slipped off and fell back into the water without it, the weight of the revolvers, the machete, the full magazines, and the hand grenades might drown me. Oh well, I was out of choices on that. My only path was up.

When I was nearing the top, a gravelly noise off to my right startled me and froze me in place.

I listened.

I waited.

Nothing.

I looked back and forth along the cliff and tried to see the wall above, but since it was set back from the edge of the cliff by several feet, I couldn't see anything above me except the top edge of the wall.

I started my climb again.

Nearing the top, I thought I heard another gravelly noise. I stopped and listened again. But the noise didn't repeat.

Once at the top, I felt thankful. Prematurely.

To my right, maybe ten feet away, stood a guard cast in green hues—one of the guys who had been with Rachel when Murphy and I rescued her. His name was Karl. He had a hand on the wall, one on a revolver, and he was staring into the darkness—staring at the sound of my breathing.

He couldn't see me, but he knew I was here.

A quick glance to my left doubled my problems. Karl's malcontent buddy, Bill, was doing the same thing not six feet away.

Chapter 44

Choices?

Jump into the water, confirming my presence for Bill and Karl while putting myself at risk of drowning. What would my next step be after that? My life jacket and fins were gone. I'd have to shed all of my equipment to make the swim back to shore. Risky, but doable.

Or, I could creep back down the wall far enough that the guards wouldn't hear or see me in the near pitch-black night. But a cloud might move out of the way and let a little of the sparse moonlight through, enough for one of them to see me clinging precariously to the wall below them. Then I'd be back to option A, only with a much higher risk of being shot.

Or, I could try to scramble up onto the ledge. It was covered in loose gravel and sand with nothing there to grip. It would be a slow and noisy endeavor, one that would lead to certain discovery. If I got lucky enough to avoid a bullet or a knife during that attempt, I'd likely end up back on option A.

All of my choices sucked, but I still had an advantage—with my night vision goggles I could see in the dark. And I had a silent weapon that I wouldn't mind using on Bill or Karl's ungrateful skulls.

So, I got a solid grip on a piece of rock, and with my left hand I slowly drew my machete while I listened to the crunch of cautious foot steps from my left and watched Karl on the right. The sound of tearing paper on my left caught my attention. When I looked at Bill, my intended first victim, his rifle was dangling from a strap on his shoulder and his hands were busy with what at first glance I thought was a stick of dynamite. But as the incongruity of that sank in, I realized it was a flare. Bill ignited it, flashing my vision to white through the goggles, blinding me.

But, as I'd done on so many occasions, I skipped right through the panic step and chose risky, swift action.

Karl, surprised and still a dozen feet to my right, said something.

Startled, Bill grunted, and I heard the flare hit the ground.

Bullets would come before I was able to see again. I raised my machete and I leapt laterally across the face of the wall, swinging at the place Bill had been before my vision flashed white. Blade hit bone and stuck, a familiar sensation. For a fraction of a second, all my weight was hanging from my grip on the machete handle. I felt the blade wrench through a shinbone, and I heard Bill scream. Gunshots blasted through the air. I bounced against the wall, knocking the night vision goggles off my head. And in the red blaze of the flare, I fell as Bill fell over the side of the cliff above me.

I splashed into the water with the machete in my hand and a lungful of air. Bill splashed in just to my right. I rolled in the water and grabbed at what I could get a hand on, the near severed leg.

Under the weight of my equipment, we were sinking fast. My eardrums started to hurt, and I blew a bit of air through my nose to equalize the pressure. Bill was struggling above me. He'd hit the water while screaming. Screaming was just noisy exhalation when you stopped to think about it. Bill's lungs were empty when he hit the water, and with me gripping his wounded leg, causing him even more pain, I heard his muffled scream continue under water until it cut short abruptly. Panic and habit overrode his logical processes, and he'd come to the end of his air and breathed in for another wail only to get a lung full of lake water.

I let go of the dangling leg. My work with Bill was done. He'd successfully completed his first attempt at drowning all on his own.

Professor Zed gives you an A, Bill.

I relaxed and looked up at a red glow above the water's surface — the flare. I heard a few pops of rifle fire and saw bubbled trails of bullets drilling three or four feet into the water above me.

I wasn't in need of air — well, not desperate need. I figured I'd been under less than thirty seconds. I took a moment to sheath my machete while I rolled over and started swimming into the blackness along the wall, feeling my way as I dragged my hand along the limestone cliff.

Karl, I guessed, would keep an eye on the spot where I'd gone into the water, a spot illuminated by the flare Bill dropped on the ledge, and a spot I intended to be well away from when I came up for air. I swam in Karl's direction, then guessed that I passed beneath him. Pressure on my ears told me that I was getting deeper, not something I wanted. I was already well deep enough to avoid bullets. I kicked a few more times and came to the point where I was running short on air myself.

I reached out for the wall and started an underwater climb upwards. Patient and slow at first, I moved faster and faster as my lungs cried out to breathe. The blackness above glowed into a brightening red. I saw the underside of the wavy surface, and my head broke through. I inhaled.

Looking up, and with my night vision goggles somewhere on the bottom of the lake, I couldn't see Karl on the ledge above. The red glow of the flare was far to my left. A few men shouted angrily from somewhere. All along the lakeshore, five-hundred feet behind me across the water,

Whites howled. The flare and gunfire had piqued their interest.

I pulled a deep breath, let the weight of my equipment pull me under, and swam along the wall in the direction I'd already been going. Getting as much distance from my last known position would only work in my favor. When I came up for the second breath, I felt almost safe, at least from Karl, who I assumed was still up on the ledge looking in the other direction for me.

An explosion rumbled on the other side of the island.

I was out of time.

Chapter 45

Feet ran by on the ledge at the top of the cliff. Karl. Far to my left, the flare still spewed red fire and smoke. A fifty-caliber machine gun was peeling off volleys on the far side of the island followed by another explosion from the grenade launcher. Dalhover and Murphy were busy and probably both grinning like twelve-year-old boys with their first BB guns.

Knowing I had to hurry, and having lost my fear of drowning under the weight of my weapons, I abandoned any thought of caution and started up the slanting cliff face as fast as I could move. I reached the top in what felt like seconds. The adrenaline was pumping, and I was surfing on a wave of confident invincibility.

In the glow of the flare I was able to see up and down the length of the wall. I was alone. Out on the other side of the island, the shooting came to a stop. At least the shooting from the grenade launcher and the fifty-caliber had. A few other small arms popped off shots.

Our plan had been to fire the MK19 and the fifty-caliber machine gun from boats out in the darkness, and then to reposition before any bullets came back their way. Of course, as it was explained to me, the range on both weapons was beyond the effective range of nearly every rifle on the island; moving was more a precaution than a necessity. The goal of the whole exercise was to sink a few of the houseboats in dramatic fashion in hopes of intimidating Jay with our firepower.

From the cloaking safety of the darkness, Gretchen would then use a bullhorn to dictate the terms to Jay. The terms were simple. Free Steph, Amy, Megan, and any other islanders that might be disillusioned with Jay's leadership style, give them as many boats as they needed, and let them go. The alternative, Murphy and Dalhover would systematically sink every boat anchored near the island. After, they would lay siege to the island, basically by floating offshore with their weapons ready in case anyone decided to make a swim for shore. Oh, and by the way, she'd tell him about the night vision goggles. Jay had no cards to play. He'd give up the girls. He'd give up anyone who wanted to leave.

At least, that's how it was all going to work out according to the consensus among the boathouse gang. Unfortunately, reasonable people often have difficulty anticipating irrationality from unreasonable people.

I heard the sound of Gretchen's voice, amplified by the bullhorn and carrying across the water. I couldn't make out what she was saying, but I already knew the content, so it didn't matter.

With Gretchen's voice booming, all eyes on the island would be looking into the darkness on the other side, and nobody was likely to be looking my way, depending on how disciplined Jay's thugs were. Of course, Karl would be inside the wall by now, telling anyone who would listen about Bill and…and what? What would he tell them? A White attacked? A commando attacked? He didn't know.

He might come back with reinforcements if they suspected they were being attacked from the rear while Gretchen held their attention on the other side.

I scanned up and down the length of the wall. It was rough in spots and looked—

What was that sound?

I looked out toward the lakeshore. All I saw was black. But I heard the splash of a few hundred hands clapping the water.

The Whites were swimming toward the island.

The gunfire, the flare, the fire from a houseboat burning on the other side of the island was drawing them in. That was a kink in the plan that nobody had anticipated.

I decided that the best place to make my entrance into Jay's compound was through a window on the back of the chapel, roughly ten feet up. The wall below the window was in rough shape with plenty of places to hold while climbing up. So, I ran down to the chapel wall and went to work as the sound of splashing in the water drew closer.

I slipped a few times when stones gave way and came loose, but I didn't fall. I got a hand to the edge of the window, got another hand up, and pulled myself up to the opening.

A few candles burned inside the chapel. I saw the places where residents had made their beds on the floor, stacks of supplies, but no people. The old oaken double doors on the front of the chapel were swung open. The light from blazing houseboats poured in, dappled by the shadows of people moving around in the courtyard.

A rifle cracked from somewhere relatively close by.

Up in the bell tower.

But what could he be shooting at? Gretchen, of course, but why shoot randomly into the darkness?

Another shot followed. It didn't seem like a random shot at all. I guessed aimed patience. And that immediately led me to a guess as to why Bill and Karl were waiting for me at the wall. I'd been spotted. One of the guards had a night vision scope on his rifle. And now he was using that scope to shoot at my unsuspecting friends out in the boats.

Null Spot the Destroyer was going to have to pay Mr. Sharpshooter a visit.

I pulled myself through the window and tumbled, landing roughly on the floor. I rolled back up to my feet and ran across the small chapel to an open doorway at the base of the bell tower. Inside, a spiral staircase made of steel had been installed so visitors to the island could climb and see the lake from the high vantage of the tower.

Another gunshot sounded from above.

I pulled my pack off my back and knelt on the floor. I reached in, took out a pistol, and tucked it into my belt. I fished around for the hand grenades, four in all, and put them in my pockets—two in the baggy pockets on the front of my pants, two each on the large thigh pockets. Those would beat up my legs if I had to run, but if I found myself in the position of having to run, those grenades would likely already be in the air toward my pursuers.

The rifle upstairs fired again.

Still being barefoot turned out to be an advantage for silence. I stepped onto the spiral staircase, started up, machete in my right hand, grenade in my left.

On the way up, I thought about whether a threat with the pistol from behind the snipers upstairs would be enough to quell their resistance, but my second thought won out. Some fucker was up there shooting at my friends, some fucker who knew Gretchen's voice, who had survived on the island with her and Paul through all those weeks since the plague hit Austin. But despite all that, the guys had no qualms about betraying her to the point of killing her.

So fuck those dudes.

I pulled the pin from a hand grenade and slipped the pin into my pocket. I didn't want to drop it and possibly alert the snipers with the tinkling of the metal pin bouncing on the spiral staircase.

I hurried up the stairs. As I neared the top, there almost no light coming in from the burning houseboats in front of the island. I reached up and touched the bell tower floor above my head. Steel. A very nice modern upgrade. Leaving the old oaken floor up there for tourists to fall through would have been a bad idea. So, the park service, when they installed the stairs, had also installed the steel floor. I just hoped it was thick enough to protect me.

The rifle fired again.

Okay, buddy. Yours is coming.

I reached up through the stairway hole, put the grenade on the floor, and then gave it a hard push across the metal floor. It clinked on the metal above my head as I took off down the stairs.

My bet was on the table, my dice were rolling. If one of those guys up there figured out quickly enough that a live grenade was on the floor and had the presence of mind to kick it back down into the stairwell, I'd likely die.

I was almost halfway down the stairs, running and nearly falling as I went, when an explosion boomed through the stairwell and knocked me off my balance. The air was immediately full of dust. My ears rang. I coughed, but I was alive.

Chapter 46

Expecting something to fall from above, I stumbled down the spiral stairs and reached the bottom. I tripped on something and rolled through the door into the chapel with a villainous grin. I didn't have a count on the number of Jerry's hardcore thugs, but now there were three less of them alive than when I'd arrived at the island.

I scrambled to my left, stepping through what I was coming to think of as post-apocalyptic floor crap. Survivors tended to leave their useful belongings in whatever bag they carried, or they left it scattered near whatever passed for their bed. They were the usual sorts of things — blankets, jackets, and foods packaged in a time before the world went to shit. The other class of post-apocalyptic floor crap was those things that ended up on the floor of a ransacked house, things of no use in a survival situation, or things too heavy to carry. Scavengers didn't tend to tidy up after themselves when they were searching houses for something to fill a belly that had been empty for days.

Anxious hollering from outside made it clear to me that curious armed men would very soon be coming to investigate what was going on inside the old church. I tucked myself into a shadowy corner piled with a bunch of floor crap and drew a pistol. I had no confidence that I could hit anything that wasn't already in machete range, but if I found myself outnumbered by Jay's thugs, noisy gunshots and a hail of bullets would put enough fright into my attackers to ruin their aim.

I heard Gretchen's amplified voice echo through the open door, telling Jay to come to a decision or another houseboat was going to sink in flames.

Jay hollered something angry in return. Then his voice changed. He was ordering his people around, though I couldn't make out what he was saying, at least not enough of his words to make any sense of it. Two explosions, one rapidly following the other, cut him off. Flashes through the open front doors cast the chapel interior into sharp shadows.

No one came in, though. Jay must have guessed the bell tower had been taken out by the grenade launcher.

Good for me.

I ran back into the bell tower and wound my way up the spiral staircase, not pausing at all when I stepped up through the metal floor at the top level. I didn't think either one of the men who'd been up there could have survived the grenade explosion. It turned out to be a good guess. I only saw one mangled body, so the other must have been blown out. Just as well—the forty-foot fall would have killed him even if the explosion hadn't.

I stood behind a roof support column and peeked out over the compound. Two houseboats, one anchored next to the second, fifty yards offshore, were both aflame. For the moment, the gunfire had ceased, the explosions had stopped. The splash of swimming infected seemed to be coming from all directions, though I could see nothing out in the darkness. Then I heard the howls—close by. Some Whites had made it to the bottom of the cliff and were scaling it just as I had. Soon, they were going to come over the wall and into the compound, and that was going to be bad for everyone.

Jay's voice yelled back across the water. "Here are my demands."

I looked down at the courtyard.

Shit.

Jay understood he was in a losing position and had apparently decided that no price was too high to avoid defeat.

A row of islanders was on their knees, facing the water. Jay stood at one end of the row with his pistol pointed at the back of little Megan's head. Next to her knelt Amy. Next to her, Steph's hair glowed red in the firelight. Three of Jay's thugs stood behind the row, looking out into the darkness. Karl was a fourth, talking to one of them and gesturing toward the back of the compound, telling his companion about me, no doubt. The companion wasn't interested though.

Jay yelled, "I'll trade you these three twats for that fifty, that grenade launcher, and all your ammunition. And if you don't scoot those boats up in the light where I can see you and do it in the next sixty seconds, I'm going to start shooting. And this little twat goes first." He looked down at his watch.

"Don't, Jay," Gretchen called back through the bullhorn. She said some more things. She thought talking might help. I knew words were a waste. Jay was as ruthlessly smart as he was crazy.

But I was too.

I turned and went flying down the spiral stairs as fast as I could go. At the bottom, I leapt through the door and into the chapel. Outside, Gretchen was still talking. I crossed the floor toward the back wall of the chapel and spotted exactly what I hoped to find there—fissures in the old wall where stones had fallen away. I took a grenade and jammed it into the first fissure that looked like it was large enough to wedge the device inside. No luck. I tried another. Too small.

A gun outside fired a single shot.

Gretchen's amplified voice turned frantic.

My rage boiled; I knew what Jay had just done. I found a fissure in the stone where the grenade fit. I jammed it in and pulled the pin.

Dammit.

The hole was too small and held the spoon down as if it were still in my hand. It'd never explode that way.

I quickly found another hole, large enough. I lay the grenade inside, and I ran to the other end of the chapel, diving through the door at the base of the bell tower.

The grenade exploded. Rock flew all through the chapel. Whites howled. A dozen voices out front were yelling at once. I peeked around the door hoping, hoping.

Gritty, thick dust blew through the chapel on a breeze that seemed to come from where the back wall had been. There was a hole, a massive hole, larger than the double doors at the front of the chapel. Through the hole, all I saw was black.

C'mon, Whites.

I still heard the howls. They were still out there.

I drew my pistol, ready to coax them in with the noise of a few gunshots. But I didn't need to. They started to pour through the hole in the wall, running toward the light they saw through the open double door, running toward the people outside.

Nothing happened for a long, frozen moment. Everyone was still trying to process the sound of the explosion and the screams of the oncoming Whites. They were all a tad slow in realizing just how fucked they were. Then the gunfire started. The screaming followed. Someone shrieked, and I ran out of the bell tower enclosure and joined a line of Whites running out of the chapel.

Chapter 47

Seven or eight Whites lay dead or wounded just outside the chapel doors. Others were on their knees around the dead, satisfying their hunger. More Whites were pouring through the chaos and running at the gunmen who were defending themselves as they retreated toward the boats anchored offshore. With their gunfire, they were unwittingly drawing the attention of most of the Whites in the compound. The price of ignorance is high.

I scanned quickly around for Steph's blazing red hair. I looked for Jay.

The islanders who had been on their knees were up and running; many of them were in the lake, racing clumsily through the deepening water toward one of the boats anchored offshore. A White tackled a man in knee deep water. Another White jumped on.

And there was Jay with a handful of Steph's hair, dragging her toward a boat behind the cover fire of his thugs. A man was already at the helm working on starting the boat. Jay waded toward the stern, and in water just up to his thigh, he raised his pistol and shot the man in the back. He threw himself over the transom without letting go of Steph's hair. He apparently valued her as a bargaining chip, and he wasn't about to let her go.

Just as well, that made my job easier. My two objectives were in the same place.

Jay's thugs were backing into the water close to the boat Jay had just commandeered.

People were swimming. Not a single normal person was left on dry land. The Whites were pursuing them into the water. I ran across the courtyard, intent on making a flanking move at Jay's men, and then thought better of it. I still had two grenades. I stopped, pulled a pin, and heaved one over the heads of the Whites who were attacking the last of Jay's thugs.

My aim wasn't perfect, but close is good enough with a hand grenade. It bounced on shore just a few paces' distance in front of the gunmen. I saw one's eyes go wide as I jumped to lay belly flat on the ground. The grenade exploded, and I sprang back to my feet.

All three gunmen were down, along with a dozen Whites who'd been closing in on them. I looked up in time to see Jay still flinching from the explosion. He shoved Steph into the seat beside his at the helm, and I saw the water at the stern boil as the propeller started to spin.

I ran at top speed and hit the water with a huge splash, raising my knees high to keep from tripping. But Jay's ski boat was already starting to move as the engine revved loudly.

I wasn't going to make it.

Jay was going to get away with Steph as his hostage.

I wailed a curse.

A stream of tracers cut a path into the stern of Jay's boat. Fiberglass disintegrated, and sparks flew where bullets ripped into the engine. The boat stopped dead and immediately started to draw water and sink at the stern. Jay lost his balance and fell.

I put my faith in Dalhover to cease fire before I arrived at the back of the boat, and I didn't slow.

Explosions sounded behind me up in the compound. Murphy was working on the Whites pouring through the chapel, trying to improve the odds of the relatively innocent islanders making their escape into the lake.

The fifty-caliber machine gun stopped shredding the stern of Jay's boat just before I grabbed on. My weapon in hand was the machete, exactly the weapon Jay deserved to have used on him.

Inside the boat, Jay lay on his back, feet forward and head toward me. Steph had a hand on the windshield and the other on a seat, trying to keep her feet below her as the boat slowly angled its bow up out of the water. She was looking at the gun in Jay's hand, pointed directly at her.

I was only halfway into the boat as I realized that Jay might shoot her at any second.

"Asshole," I yelled.

Jay glanced up and saw me. His face turned to surprise, then fear, as he saw my raised machete.

I was up over the transom by then, tall enough to put some muscle behind my swing.

But Jay was quick and was bringing his pistol to bear as my blade came down. The gun fired, my machete split his skull. I felt the bullet tear a wound on my left side as I fell. The gun fired wildly twice more as Jay's body twitched his dying response to a machete lodged deep in his big, squirmy snail brain.

Steph shouted or screamed. I'm not sure which.

I climbed into the boat as it listed to port. I wrenched my blade out of Jay's skull as I spun around to look for threats that might be coming from shore. Suddenly, standing became difficult. Balance was lost. I was trying to face the shore, but I only saw a black sky speckled with a billion stars. I was looking up, and I was confused as I lost consciousness.

Bobby Adair

Chapter 48

Drizzly, cold wind howled through the aluminum framework that held the canopy up over the pontoon boat. I found myself looking at the black metal legs of the grenade launcher from exactly where someone might sit on the deck of the pontoon boat to operate it. I heard the voices of people in contentious discussion. I felt the deck rock a little too vigorously on swells driven by the wind.

The boat's motor wasn't running. We were anchored or drifting. I lifted my throbbing head and looked around from where I lay on the deck. Two other people lay under blankets on the deck near me. One had a big, bloody bandage on his face. A woman I didn't know sat at the stern, staring emptily at the shore. Beside her, a man I also didn't know leaned on her and slept. To my left, Steph sat fallen over on a padded bench, eyes closed, sleeping, apparently unharmed.

I felt relief.

I lay back on the deck and started putting together my memories from the night before.

Bang.

In all the pandemonium and the noisy violence of modern warfare, the sound of one gunshot stuck crystallized as clearly as a ringing Christmas bell over a frozen field. It was that one gunshot that killed Megan. It enraged and depressed me that a man would murder a child just to further his perverse ambitions. My anger seethed behind closed eyes, and I found solace only in recalling the satisfying crunch of my blade smashing through Jay's cranium and slicing into his gray matter. I hoped when he saw my blade coming down at his forehead he had time in that tick of a second to feel the horror of his impending, gruesome death.

Please God, at least that.

Jay deserved so much worse.

"You awake?" Steph asked.

I looked over at her green eyes, vivid in the gray morning light. She was still laying sideways on the bench, a few strands of red hair stuck across her face, some of it blowing in the wind. Without thinking about it, I said, "You're beautiful."

She smiled, embarrassed. "How do you feel?"

I hadn't thought about it. "Cold."

"You banged your head pretty hard when you fell in the boat."

Thinking back to the moment after I cleaved Jay's skull, I said, "I lost my balance." Remembering Jay's pistol firing at me, I put a hand to my left side. It felt a little odd, just under the ribs. A bandage covered a wound on the left side of my abdomen.

"He shot you," she said.

"I guess I'm not going to die." I smiled as though I was making a funny joke.

"A few inches to the right and it would have hit the bottom of your lung." Steph sat up. "You probably would have died."

Feeling around on the bandage, I said, "A half inch to the left and the bullet would have missed all together."

Steph rolled her eyes but didn't smile. "The bullet went through your oblique muscle just below the ribs under your left arm. You were lucky. The Lucky Null Spot." Steph smirked almost imperceptibly.

I ignored the wisecrack. "I'll be all right then?" I felt the wound under the bandage. It was just about where my elbow would touch the side of my abdomen when my arm was at my side.

"I cleaned your wound when you were out and sewed you up. If you don't get infected, you'll probably be okay. And you bonked your head pretty hard when you fell."

I put a hand to my head and felt another bandage on the back. I propped myself up on my elbow and felt a hammer inside my skull. "Whoa." I laid back down.

"Murphy and Dalhover are on shore looking for antibiotics and whatever else they can find."

"Dalhover shouldn't be on shore," I said. "The Whites will see him."

"He thought you were worth it." Steph smiled. "Besides, we drove the boats way up the lake last night after everything happened. Murphy said there aren't many Whites around."

"It always seems that way," I said. "Then they are."

"You're not the only one who knows that, Zed. Let other people be responsible for themselves."

I looked at her and my expression must have given away my thoughts.

She said, "Thank you for coming to get me."

"Jay was crazy. I had to do something."

Steph nodded but didn't comment on Jay. "I know I'm wasting my breath when I say this, but you need a couple weeks of rest to let that bullet wound heal."

"And my head?" I asked.

"I think history has shown what a hard head you have." Steph shrugged. "You'll probably be just fine."

I made a slow, determined effort to sit up. I leaned on the grenade launcher, facing Steph. "Did Rachel and Molly make it?"

"We picked them up near where they dropped you into the lake."

I looked away from her when I asked my next question out of the smallest of hopes. "What about Megan?"

Steph shook her head and from the sadness suddenly on her face, it was clear that Megan didn't make it.

"Jay?" I asked.

She nodded and her face took on a harder edge. It was as I suspected. Jay shot Megan.

"How's Amy taking it?"

"She's on one of the other boats. She's not talking about it."

I asked, "How many made it off the island?"

"Eleven, counting me."

"Eleven." I slumped. There were probably nineteen people on their knees when I'd blown the wall to let the infected in. Had that choice cost the lives of eight people I'd been trying to save?

Steph got down off her bench, kneeled in front of me, and engulfed me in a hug. "You did what you could to help them. Most of us got away."

"And Jay's men?" I asked, feeling a frog in my throat for the dead and second-guessing my choices.

"Dead, as far as anybody knows."

I wrapped my arms around Steph. "At least there's that."

Chapter 49

I slept through most of the day. Had it not been for haunting thoughts of dying faces and guilt, it would have felt good to do nothing.

As it was, all I had was the peace of having no urgent expectations of me. When I woke from an afternoon nap, Murphy and Steph were sitting next to one another; Murphy had my backpack in his hands, stuffing things into it. Steph was reading the label on a plastic prescription bottle. She looked up. "You sleep a lot after you've been injured."

Murphy laughed; not his big laugh, not the one he had before that day when we'd watched Mandi die. "Zed doesn't know how to slow down until he's exhausted."

Murphy was right about that.

Steph popped the cap off the pill bottle and handed me a couple of small white tablets. She reached out with a plastic water bottle and said, "Take these."

"Antibiotics?" I asked.

She nodded. "Murphy's also got some pills for the pain —"

I stretched my left arm up over my head and felt my wound protest. "I don't need the pain pills."

"Don't move your arm," Steph scolded. "It'll take longer to heal."

Murphy took the pill bottles from Steph and put them in my bag. I noticed my machete and an M4 with a suppressor attached to the barrel were leaning on the bench next to him. He caught my look and said, "These are yours."

Shaking my head emphatically, I said, "You know I can't —"

"These are yours," Murphy insisted. He leaned over and in a soft voice said, "Trouble in paradise."

I sighed. "Already?"

In a calm, adult voice, Steph said, "People are afraid. Last night rattled them. Their friends died. They're confused."

Understandable. I looked back at Murphy for the straight scoop.

He said, "Amy says—" He thought about how to say what it was he wanted to convey. "Man, I like Amy, but she wants nothing to do with us." He pointed a long finger at my chest. "You and me."

"What?" I didn't want to believe it.

Murphy leaned back. "She wants nothing to do with you, especially. She says you're a train wreck. Everywhere you go, everything goes to shit."

My mouth fell open as I shook my head to disagree.

Steph said, "Don't listen to that."

"It's true," Murphy argued.

"I'm not contradicting you," Steph told him.

I wanted to say something in my defense, but what could I say? Both of Amy's companions, Megan and Brittany, were dead. Was that my fault? Everybody from the hospital was dead except Dalhover. Russell and Mandi were dead. I looked away from Murphy and Steph.

Could it all be my fault?

"She says you're a trouble magnet," Murphy finished.

"That's enough, Murphy." Steph was in Captain Leonard mode.

Murphy shrugged, "She does like you, Zed. That's what she told everyone. She just says it's not healthy to be around you."

Well, fuck these people.

I stood up as Steph protested. I reached my right arm out for my bag. Murphy handed it to me. As I took it, I felt a little lightheaded, but I held my balance, determined and pissed.

Murphy said, "Keep the M4. I loaded you up with some ammo, some grenades, and another set of night vision goggles. I don't know how all this is going to shake out, but we're not gonna be empty-handed again." Murphy nodded for emphasis.

"Murphy," Steph said, "it's not like that."

Murphy held his forearm up next to Steph's, making the contrast of his white skin next to her naturally pale skin obvious. "I'm not gonna get brown again. I'll always be white. Zed will too."

Steph leaned forward and looked up at me. "There's a lot of animosity between the group that stayed on the island and the ones that left with Gretchen. Amy and the others want to go back to the island."

"It's not safe there," I said.

"Nowhere is safe, Zed."

Looking at Steph, thinking about it, I couldn't disagree.

She said, "If we leave them a few sets of the night vision goggles—"

"Those batteries won't last," argued Murphy.

"That's their problem," Steph told Murphy. "They can go find a solar charger or something." She looked back at me. "And if we leave them a couple of M4's with suppressors, they'll be able to defend themselves on the island without attracting more Whites from the shores."

My feelings were whirling around in confusion and growing angrier. We'd gone out of our way not to hurt those people on the island—well, except for Jay's thugs. Some of the islanders died as a result. Well, maybe a lot of them died, but Jay would have killed them anyway. Or, the question I had to ask myself was, had we abandoned Steph and the others, would the islanders have lived happily ever after?

"Sit down, Zed." Steph took my hand and tugged. "You're getting worked up over this."

I didn't sit. I turned and looked at the survivors, sitting, standing, talking, deciding, spread over five boats all anchored in the cove. I glared at whoever would look in my direction. I said, "Fuck these people. We've got three Humvees and a trailer full of supplies. We've got diesel fuel, ammunition, food, even blankets and pillows. My vote is we take whoever wants to go, get in our Humvees and get out of Dodge. The rest of 'em can do whatever they want. We don't have room for everybody anyway."

"Word." Murphy fist bumped me.

Chapter 50

Twelve of us left the cove in the two boats we had used to attack Jay and his thugs on the island. Of the islanders, only Steph and one guy came along. The rest...well who cares about them? I was pissed. They could all go back to the island and fuck themselves. They hated both me and Murphy. They made that clear when they'd sided with Jay against Gretchen on that first night. Even on their knees with Jay's gun to the backs of their heads, they still thought my White skin was a greater danger. Double fuck them.

Murphy was right. Other people's fears would haunt us forever.

The islanders took their three boats with a few M4's with suppressors—Goddamned valuable equipment—and two sets of night vision goggles. With a few thousand rounds of ammunition and a little patience, they wouldn't have any trouble clearing their island of the infected. They just had to sit offshore and shoot the Whites. If the infected swam after them in numbers too great to handle, they only had to drive their boats up the lake a bit and come back when things settled down. Once they had their island back, there were rifles and handguns left there by Jay's dead thugs. Provisions they'd had would likely be ransacked, but the canned goods they'd collected would still be there. None of the Whites we'd come across had yet been able to figure out what to do with canned products.

So without guilt for their future, I watched the islanders head back toward their home. Our group turned our boats into our cove late in the afternoon. Two of our three Humvees and the F-350 with the enclosed trailer still attached were parked just as we'd left them on a street a hundred yards up a hill from the water. They were ready to go.

We docked our boats at the floating boathouse where we'd been holed up for the past few days. We didn't see nor hear a single White on shore as we got everyone moved inside. Once there, Dalhover spoke up. "It'll be dark in a couple of hours. That's when we'll head out. By the time the sun comes up tomorrow, we'll be far enough west of here that most of our troubles will be behind us. We might even be in Balmorhea." He looked over to Gretchen and then to Steph. Both nodded. I guessed the pecking order still wasn't clear. I didn't care. They had plenty of time to talk about it on the trip west.

Dalhover continued, "We've got room to seat seventeen. There are thirteen of us. Figure out your seating arrangements, and let Gretchen know. We need primary drivers and backup drivers for each vehicle. Anybody with experience pulling a big trailer gets the F-350. I'll be in the Humvee with the fifty, Murphy will be in the one with the grenade launcher. We need backup operators for those as well." Dalhover looked around for questions.

Gretchen stood up. "Murphy, Rachel, and Molly will take a boat across the lake to get the Humvee we left over there last night. As soon as they get back here, if we don't have any Whites around, we need to top off the fuel tank as quickly as possible, get loaded into our vehicles, and go. We'll take it slow on the roads since we'll be using the night vision goggles to drive. We'll stay in a tight line with two Humvees in front, the trailer third, and a Humvee in back."

Dalhover said, "The main thing is we need to get that Humvee gassed up and go as quickly as possible. We'll be vulnerable at that point, climbing the hill up the lake to the Humvees with no protection."

The islander guy whose name I didn't catch said, "But we've got weapons."

Dalhover told him harshly, "Don't shoot unless you have to. Unless you absolutely have to. What you never had the chance to learn on the island is that shooting at the infected never ends well."

"Nevertheless," Gretchen interjected, "there are plenty of weapons and ammunition in the trailer. We'll all be armed before we head up the hill tonight. Sergeant Dalhover and two other volunteers will head up there early, and mount the machine gun and the grenade launcher. They'll bring back enough weapons so we'll each have a rifle, a sidearm, and a bladed weapon of some sort."

"The main thing," Dalhover said, "is that we do everything quick and quiet. If the infected don't know we're out there, they won't mess with us. If we lollygag and start making noise, things will go bad. If they go bad, run to get into a Humvee as fast as you can. But only if you can make it safely. If you can't, get back to the boat and get away from the shore. We'll work out the rally points at places along the shore up the lake. If we get separated, don't panic. We'll meet up at the rally points. We'll get everybody loaded, and then we'll head west together. Everybody good?"

People nodded. Nobody had any questions.

Chapter 51

I was convalescing again while others busied themselves. They scoured the boathouse for anything that might be of value: screwdrivers, rope, empty gas cans, anything. The trailer still had room, so why not pack it with anything that might have any potential use at all?

Twilight was fading to full dark. The fifty-caliber machine gun and the grenade launcher had been mounted. Everyone had his or her weapons. Lookouts were standing on top of the boathouse, wearing night vision goggles. Two were up at the Humvees, with one standing behind the machine gun, using the height as a vantage point to see up and down the road. But not a single White had been seen or heard while preparations were underway.

I was lying on an empty worktable using a life preserver for a pillow. I'd told Steph at least a dozen times that I felt fine sitting up. Sitting in a folding chair beside my table, she insisted that I remain on my back. It was hard not to bow to her insistence. Somewhere over the hour or so that I'd been laying there talking with her, her hands came to be cradling one of mine, a situation neither of us was going to comment on but neither of us was going to change either. It made me feel optimistic about our impending ride off into the sunset.

We talked a bit about nothing. We talked about what life might be like for the next few years out in the middle of nowhere. We talked about when we might one day come back to Austin. We speculated about the state of the rest of the world and what life would be like in a world where humans had a second chance to try to get it right. And that was the thing about that conversation that struck me as the strangest of all. It was an optimistic conversation built on a foundation of assumptions that enough of we humans would live to rebuild.

Gretchen burst in through the boathouse door and stole everyone's silent attention. She pointed to our parked Humvees up the hill. "They're here."

We whispered our cheers. Murphy, Molly, and Rachel had made it back safely.

Gretchen said, "Let's go."

Steph helped me to sit up as the others filed out the door and onto the deck on the backside of the boathouse. Feet stepped lightly on the roof. Knees and elbows bumped the siding as the lookouts climbed down.

Steph, doting over me, slowed us both as we walked toward the door. We should have hurried, but the attention of a pretty girl was never something I could shirk off. We were the last two out. Someone started up the engine on the pontoon boat with a muted rumble. It gurgled exhaust into the lake water.

The others were standing on the deck, excited. Our first real chance at peaceful sleep, at safety, lay out in west Texas, and if luck was with us, we'd be there before the sun went down tomorrow. Steph and I joined the others on the boat, taking a seat on one of the benches.

Out of habit, I adjusted my M4 in its sling, ready to shoot from the hip as Murphy had shown me days before. My machete was in its sheath across my back. My pistol was in a holster on my left. I opened my bag and reached in for extra magazines. I wasn't wearing a MOLLE vest—a shortcoming I'd need to correct—but I did have pockets that could hold four magazines. Along with the one in my rifle, that meant I'd have one hundred and fifty bullets all ready to fly if I needed them.

Steph put a hand on my wrist and shook her head. She said, "Don't worry about those. You've done your part. Just get yourself into the Humvee. That's all you need to do."

My hands lingered on the magazines. "But—"

"No buts, Zed. Just get yourself into the Humvee. Let the others do their part." She smiled.

I let go of the magazines. "Yes, boss." I smiled and zipped up my bag.

Bobby Adair

Chapter 52

With the pontoon boat's shallow draft, we ran it aground pretty close to shore, with a grind of limestone on its double aluminum pontoons. The passengers each jumped off the flat deck at the bow and waded across a dozen feet of shallow water. Once they were out of the water, they walked quickly or jogged up the hill toward the Humvees.

"Don't run," Steph told me as I started to follow. "You'll open your wound."

Just as well, I thought. The effort of getting out of the boat and through the water was more taxing than expected. With Steph on one side of me and Gretchen unexpectedly on the other, we started up the slope. At the top of the hill, Dalhover was standing up through the top of a Humvee behind the fifty-caliber machine gun, looking around. Murphy, Rachel, and Molly were out of their Humvee which they'd left idling loudly behind them. Molly had experience driving the big pickup truck with the trailer, and she was heading that way. Murphy would ride out to Balmorhea in the Humvee with the grenade launcher and Rachel was riding with him, so they were standing together.

With just seventy-five yards of rocky slope to cover, I had the thought that we were going to start our trip without incident, that maybe the Whites on this side of the lake had wandered off to other parts of west Austin, that maybe our luck had finally turned. But in truth, keeping your guard up one hundred percent of the time is hard work. I was tired. We were all tired. We hadn't seen nor heard a White all day. That allowed us to indulge complacency, and complacency as we'd learned so, so many times, lay at the doorstep to disaster.

I heard one howl at first, barely recognizable over the sound of the Humvee's diesel engine rattling as it idled. I thought for half a second that it was something strange in the engine noise, but before I even finished that thought, that single White's howl was joined by a dozen, a hundred, maybe a thousand others. Somewhere off to our left and up the hill, a horde lurked in the trees.

I shouted, "Steph, Gretchen, run." I pushed Steph from behind to urge her to move.

Gretchen took a few quick steps and turned to look at me with anxious eyes.

"Go," I yelled at her. "Go."

Gretchen's face turned to worry, but she spun and rushed up the hill as fast as her old legs would carry her.

Steph put a hand under my arm to pull me along.

"You go too, Steph. I'll catch you there."

"C'mon. We're going together."

"No." I was breathing heavily with the exertion. That bullet had taken a lot more out of me than seemed possible. "I'll be fine. I'm White too. They won't fuck with me. Go."

Steph ignored me and pulled harder. We were halfway up the hill. It looked like we were going to make it. But that changed.

A flood of naked Whites poured out of the trees.

"Shit." It was immediately obvious that we weren't going to make it to the Humvees.

Anxious but not yet panicked, Steph yelled, "We have to run, Zed."

I tried to run, but I instead lumbered on molasses-slow feet.

All the others were in their Humvees already. The engines rapidly fired up one by one. Dalhover's fifty-caliber machine gun thundered, and Whites fell all across the hill.

Steph figured out at that moment that we weren't going to make it up the hill. She pulled me to a stop and yelled, "Back to the boat."

Whites were among the Humvees up on the road. An endless wave of them poured out of the trees. Grenades exploded, and other small weapons fired. I turned with Steph and we started to run, but there was already a smattering of Whites behind us.

Dammit!

I stopped, raised my M4 to my hip and sprayed a full magazine of bullets across our path, then ran after Steph as fast as I could. I tripped over my sagging toes and tumbled across the rough ground. Steph's pistol fired.

"Run for the boat," I hollered at her. But she didn't. She was trying again to help me to my feet.

"Run," I commanded.

Screams filled the air, punctuated by gunfire. Whites were everywhere, but the boat was just ahead.

A blur of white flashed across my vision and before I realized it, Steph was being tackled. I let go of my empty M4, pulled out my machete and hacked at the White's back, cutting through its spine. Blood gushed from the wound as Steph struggled out from underneath it.

But more Whites were around us. I hacked at another and drew my pistol. Whites were close enough that I could make every round count. And as much as I preached at others never to fire a gun at the Whites, Steph and I were past the point of caution. I was buying seconds of life with my bullets. I fired, and Whites fell around me.

Steph was getting to her feet with her rifle up. She let go with automatic fire in front of us, clearing a path to get us another dozen feet closer to the boat. I ran into the gap, swinging my machete with all the frail might I could muster.

Her pistol fired at the Whites around us as she came behind. When my foot splashed into ankle deep water, I thought we'd made it. The naked horde was afraid of water. With every step now we'd get closer to safety. I turned as I emptied the last of the bullets from my pistol, but Steph got tackled again. Without the slightest thought of anything but killing the beast on her, I stepped away from the water, hacking and screaming.

Another white jumped on Steph, and then another. I cut at them. I roared. I cut at the ones close by as she struggled to get up. I beat at whites with the butt of my pistol and I hacked, but there were so many. There were so, so many. They were all over Steph by then. She was struggling and screaming, screaming not from anger, but pain. They were ripping at her. I reached in for her hand and tried to pull her toward the water as I chopped at the monsters on her.

Just get to the water.

Just get to the water.

But all I saw were grasping Whites and blood. I pulled, and she held my hand, knowing instinctually it was mine, knowing —

Her hand went slack.

And in that one heartbeat, as I hoped for her to re-grip my hand, I knew she was dead.

I swung my machete and let rage run away with me. I was feet from the water, a dozen feet from the safety of the boat, but I didn't know anymore in which direction it lay, and I didn't care. I was surrounded by Whites who couldn't get through the mass of their brothers to reach Steph's warm body, and they focused on me, wounded, bleeding, and marked for death by my choice to shoot my gun.

But I didn't care. I just wanted to spend the last of my living moments mauling them with my blade and watching their faces turn to fear as their blood spewed from their wounds.

A grenade exploded nearby, followed by a wave of White howls. A second later, another grenade exploded, knocking me and all the Whites down around me. When I looked up, a little dazed, I saw Murphy. He ran at me through the smoke, grabbed me by my backpack, and without slowing, pulled me into the water, splashing through to the pontoon boat.

At the boat, he turned and fired at the Whites brave enough to wade in after us. "Get in the goddamned boat," he yelled.

Unable to think for myself, I did as I was told and crawled in, rolling onto the deck and gasping for air from the effort.

Murphy's gun continued to fire, then his feet were pounding across the deck, and the boat's engine was revving loudly. More firing. The boat lurched off the lakebed, and we were afloat, moving away from shore. I was still lying on the deck trying to breathe, wishing I had the energy to roll off the flat deck and wade back to shore.

Bobby Adair

Chapter 53

We'd been drifting out in the lake well offshore from Pace Bend Park for several hours. The motor was off, and the pontoon boat bobbed on the waves while Murphy stood at the helm, night vision goggles on, watching.

Not a word was said between us.

I sat on the flat deck, holding onto a canopy support post, dangling my feet in the water, listening to the slosh of waves, and staring into the darkness. My gunshot wound had ripped open in the fight. It bled and didn't seem to have any interest in slowing down.

I didn't care. I felt the blood soak into my pants. I felt it trickle down over my knee and down my shin to mix with the cold lake water.

My life was never meant to have a happy ending, of that I was certain. Looking back, it was a surprise to me that the bits of happiness that tumbled serendipitously down even managed to stick to me long enough to ever make me smile. And though the intellectual parts of my brain told me that I should remember Steph's smile, the smell of her hair, and the angelic way she looked wearing Sarah Mansfield's jeans and t-shirt that day in her living room when she was caring for me after another losing round with a White, I couldn't. I was drowning in numbness, and when I came up for air, all I felt was hurt.

Murphy said, "I see 'em."

I looked up into the darkness. In the night, I could barely make out the squat, white cliffs standing over the lake's edge.

"One, two, three," Murphy counted. "The truck and the trailer. They all made it."

I didn't care.

He said, "I don't see any Whites anywhere." He started the engine and headed the boat across the lines of waves, splashing me each time our starboard pontoon hit a crest. "You'll be fine," he told me. "We'll all get to Balmorhea, and we'll all be fine."

Weakly, I said, "I'm not going."

"What?"

Louder, I said, "I'm not going."

"Don't be stupid."

We splashed through the short waves for another ten minutes or so, then Murphy cut the engine and we drifted up to the tip of the long peninsula on which Pace Bend Park lay. As we got close, I saw Dalhover, Rachel, Gretchen, and a few others coming down a wooden stairway built on the side of the cliff.

Murphy came up to the front of the boat. The port side pontoon bounced against a wooden swim platform at the bottom of the stairs. He jumped out and tied us off on the railing.

Feet were clomping down the stairs. Murphy came back onto the boat to help me up.

I said, "I was born to live in a world of Whites. I just never knew it."

"You're low on blood. You're talking gibberish."

I knew I wasn't. Murphy didn't want to hear what I was saying. "I'm staying here, Murphy."

"You'll die if you don't get help. We need to go."

"Help?" I asked. "Help from who? Steph is dead. Nobody has any medical training."

Murphy looked up at the stairs and back down at me.

"Murphy, I know you think I'm half stupid from loss of blood—"

Murphy looked down at my shirt and shorts, drenched with my blood. His face was solid with worry. He started to reach under me to pick me up. I pushed him away with more strength than I thought I still had.

"We're never going to fit in with them," I said, half pointing to the people on the stairs. "Never. Maybe you can make a go of it. I can't. I'm staying here."

Rachel was suddenly down in front of me, pleading with me to go, but I could only half pay attention. I needed most of my mental energy just to keep myself upright. Dalhover said something. Gretchen's voice turned urgent.

I was staying. Austin, Texas was my home. It was the place where I was born. It was where I had struggled to live. I was going to die in Austin, not out in some bumfuck West Texas desert where I'd be hated by everyone lucky enough to have immunity in their blood and pigment in their skin.

Somewhere in a blur of voices, I leaned over against the support post. I could no longer keep myself upright without it. I gripped it with all my might. I wasn't getting off the boat.

Chapter 54

Between the blood loss from the initial gunshot wound, along with all that bled away after reopening my wound while I was killing Whites after Steph died, I was too weak to be of much use for anything. Murphy carried me to a house near the shore. He poured too much good vodka on my wound and not enough into my mouth. He sewed me up as best he could and put me into a bed upstairs. I slept fitfully on and off for a few days. I guess it was a few days. It could have been a week. I remember it turning light, then dark again several times. Murphy fed me. He brought me water to drink. And neither of us spoke.

One morning arrived and I woke. Light came into the room at an angle and cast a yellow glow around the shadows. I sat up in bed. I felt a little dizzy, but I was lucid. To my right, Murphy was sitting in a cushy chair, his M4 across his lap. He looked tired, but he was awake. He looked at me with no trace of a smile. All he had were hard eyes and a clenched jaw.

I looked at him for a long time as I put the sequence of my memory's events in order. I said, "Thank you, Murphy."

He nodded.

"You okay?" I asked.

"I am."

I nodded. He looked fine, physically.

"You okay?" he asked me.

I rotated my left arm around my shoulder and felt it stretch at the stiff wound under my rib cage. I breathed deeply. "I'll need a couple of days, I think. But I'm okay."

"You hungry?" he asked me.

"Yeah, I am."

"Can you walk?"

I nodded, though I had no idea.

"I can bring you something."

I shook my head and threw my legs over the side of the bed. "I need to get up." I slid my feet down to the floor, careful to keep my hands on the bed. The effort was significant, and I had to pause to catch my breath.

"It's the blood loss," said Murphy. "What little you have left isn't enough to do much at all. Do you remember passing out in the boat?"

I nodded.

"You were probably pretty close to kickin' it. You're lucky I got you here and sewed you up."

"Thanks."

"It might take a couple of weeks before you can get back to anything like normal activity levels."

"Normal?" I smiled.

"You know what I mean."

"How do you know all this stuff?" I asked.

"You lost a lot of blood that first night. Steph told me most of it after she fixed you up."

I felt a stab of something in my heart. It was sharp and jagged. It tore, but fell away to bleak gray. I didn't want to think about Steph. Every memory of her was wrapped in a layer of bloody, brokenhearted death. I had to wash those memories in gray. I had to forget.

With one hand on the bed, keeping my balance, I stood. Or that's to say, I tried to stand. When I toppled over, Murphy jumped up to catch me. What started out as an effort to move my feet, to get away from a pain in my heart, turned into the humility of hanging from Murphy's arms.

"If you need to do this," Murphy said, "I'll help you."

I nodded. "I need to." Feeling vulnerable and completely indebted to Murphy for his help, for being a friend that would do anything for me, I felt tears in my eyes and sniffled them back. I took a step. Murphy carried my weight forward. I took another step.

It was a slow, tiring process, but we made it from the upstairs bedroom down to the kitchen. Murphy put me in a kitchen chair near windows that looked out over the lake. I leaned on the table and thought about what an effort it was just to stay upright.

"I was planning on oatmeal," said Murphy. "They got some brown sugar and pecans. No butter though."

I shrugged and stared out at the glistening water. Behind me, I heard the clicking of an igniter on the stove, and then the sound of a jet of flame. Water poured into a pot and Murphy scooped a few cups of rolled oats into the water. The pan clinked as Murphy sat it on the stove.

What?

I turned to look at Murphy standing in front of the stove. "There's gas?"

Murphy nodded. "There's one of those big propane tanks or whatever outside. I guess it ain't empty."

"A hot meal." I laid my head on the table. It had been so long since I'd eaten anything hot. "A hot meal."

"I know." Murphy said it with a pinch of his old enthusiasm, and I smiled as I looked at the lake.

While Murphy was cooking, I asked, "The others?"

"It's just us here."

"They went to Balmorhea?" I asked.

Murphy nodded.

"Even Rachel?"

"She's better off out there than here."

"You cool with that?"

"She doesn't need me to hold her hand."

When the oatmeal was ready, Murphy brought me a bowl and I slowly ate. It was fantastic. Murphy ate his much more quickly than me, but courteously waited in silence while I finished.

"Do you want more?" he asked.

I shook my head. "Thanks. I'm full."

Murphy smiled weakly. "You're gonna be okay."

"Thanks for taking care of me."

"It's nice outside this morning. Do you want to go out on the porch for a while?"

I looked up at the distance from the table to the back door, then from the door to the nearest deck chairs outside. I wanted more than anything to be out there feeling the warmth of the sun on my face. But I smiled and sniffled as another tear filled my eye. I shook my head. There was no way I could make it all the way out there, not even with Murphy's help.

Murphy smiled. He stood up and said, "Put your arm over my shoulder. C'mon." He lifted me in his arms. "Good thing there's plenty of food here. We need to fatten you up before you blow away."

Murphy carried me outside and put me in a chair, the one in the sun that I was hoping to get placed in. But I wasn't going to ask. It was hard enough being carried around like a child, without making special requests.

"You good?" he asked.

I leaned my head on the chair's back and let the sun shine on my face. "Yeah."

Murphy took a chair on the other side of a small table. "You want any water or anything?"

I shook my head. "I just want to sit here."

Some mockingbirds were making a racket in a tree nearby. Wind blew the branches, and the oak leaves, brittle but still green, sounded like Styrofoam packing peanuts rattling in a shipping box. But it was a familiar sound, a comforting sound. It was the sound of Texas in the autumn.

Somewhere out there in the world, a sound was different though—faint, guttural, thumping.

The sound grew.

I sat up straight and looked out over the lake. Murphy was already sitting up, looking.

"I hear it too," he said.

We continued to scan the sky. As the sound grew louder in the distance we both knew what it was. It was distinct.

Murphy pointed far to the southeast.

I looked.

"That's a Black Hawk helicopter," he said.

"Army?" I asked.

Murphy nodded and sat back to watch it cross the sky in the far distance. No other helicopters joined it.

After a while, Murphy asked, "What do you think it means?"

I looked at the dark-colored dot making its noisy passage in the crisp blue sky and thought about it. Eventually, I laid my arm on the end table and pushed it up beside Murphy's. He looked down at my arm. I said, "You're white. I'm white. We'll always be white. Whatever that helicopter means, it doesn't mean shit to people like us."

The End

Final Words

Before forcing you to read a bunch of blah blah crap that you might not find interesting, I'll tell you right up front:

There WILL be some more Slow Burn books

This is obviously a reversal for me. I'd planned to end the series at six, well as you read, with everyone who is left alive riding off into the sunset to live happily (or not) ever after. But, just as many of you have, I've gotten very attached to both Zed and Murphy through the course of six books. Admittedly, Zed is hard for me to write. Because of Zed's past he has difficulties dealing with people in an emotionally healthy fashion. To write him believably, I have to put myself as best I can, in his mindset. I have to believe I'm in the situations that he's in. I have to imagine myself as him. I don't know if other writers do the same when they write but that's what works for me.

Imagining myself in Zed's shoes takes an emotional toll that's sometimes hard to pay. Frankly, that's one of the reasons I wanted to draw the series to a close. I didn't know how long I could keep writing him and still hold onto my own emotional stability — okay, that sounds melodramatic, but hey, I'm a writer.

On the other hand, Murphy is fun to write. He's gregarious. He's funny. He doesn't get too hung up in the bullshit of life even if life is full of zombies. He makes the post-apocalyptic world kind of fun.

My other concern for the characters and the story is that I didn't want to take the simple idea of seeking a safe place to live and wear it out. I didn't want to write a zombie version of Gilligan's Island where the whole series is predicated on the fact that the castaways want to get off the island but never do.

In ending book 6 in the way I did, I left some of the survivors going to find safety, which seemed like a good way to bring the story to an end. Zed and Murphy, plausibly, and in character, choose to stay behind in Austin. For them, the quest for the pot of gold at the end of the rainbow — sanctuary — is over. Instead, they're going to get into some trouble in a post-apocalyptic Austin and the books that follow those adventures will be stand-alone, 1-book novels. Maybe they'll even track down Mark and finally kill him. And who doesn't want to see that happen?

I'm not going to make any promises about when the next Slow Burn book will come out. I may write one or two next year. For the moment though, I need some time away from Zed and Murphy so I can torment other characters in my imagination.

Thank you so much for reading the series. All of the feedback you've given me through Amazon, Facebook, and the other social media sites has meant a lot to me and helped me keep writing even on those long, long nights after working a full day in the cubicle. I really do appreciate it.

– Bobby

Where to find me...

If you'd like to join the email list or any of your favorite social media sites to keep tabs on the progress or get alerted when the release date nears, click one below. We also have goofy contests and a lot of fun.

My website

http://bobbyadair.com/subscribe/

Facebook

https://www.facebook.com/BobbyAdairAuthor

Pinterest

http://www.pinterest.com/bobbyadairbooks/

Twitter

https://twitter.com/BobbyAdairBooks

Reviews

I received an email this afternoon that said that every time a reader leaves a book review, a crippled monkey gets a free banana. I couldn't believe it. After all the books I've read through the years, had I only been leaving book reviews, I could have been feeding those tiny, frail, hairy, little critters.

But I didn't leave reviews and I've had to live with the burdensome guilt of causing the starvation of those cute, little, cymbal-banging, Shriner-hat-wearing apes.

So I beseech you, free yourself of the coming guilt. Help a monkey. Leave a review.

Thanks for reading! – Bobby

Other Books by Bobby Adair

Thrillers

Ebola K, book 1

Post-Apocalyptic Fiction

The Last Survivors

Horror & Zombie

Slow Burn: Zero Day, book 1
Slow Burn: Infected, book 2
Slow Burn: Destroyer, book 3
Slow Burn: Dead Fire, book 4
Slow Burn: Torrent, book 5

Satire

Flying Soup

37656090R00170

Made in the USA
Middletown, DE
01 March 2019